A

PIGGLY WIGGLY
CHRISTMAS

ALSO BY ROBERT DALBY

A Piggly Wiggly Wedding
Kissing Babies at the Piggly Wiggly
Waltzing at the Piggly Wiggly

A
PIGGLY WIGGLY
CHRISTMAS

Robert Dalby

G. P. PUTNAM'S SONS
New York

G. P. PUTNAM'S SONS
PUBLISHERS SINCE 1838
Published by the Penguin Group

Penguin Group (USA) Inc., 375 Hudson Street, New York, New York 10014, USA ·
Penguin Group (Canada), 90 Eglinton Avenue East, Suite 700, Toronto, Ontario
M4P 2Y3, Canada (a division of Pearson Penguin Canada Inc.) · Penguin Books Ltd,
80 Strand, London WC2R 0RL, England · Penguin Ireland, 25 St Stephen's Green,
Dublin 2, Ireland (a division of Penguin Books Ltd) · Penguin Group (Australia),
250 Camberwell Road, Camberwell, Victoria 3124, Australia (a division
of Pearson Australia Group Pty Ltd) · Penguin Books India Pvt Ltd, 11 Community
Centre, Panchsheel Park, New Delhi–110 017, India · Penguin Group (NZ),
67 Apollo Drive, Rosedale, North Shore 0632, New Zealand (a division of Pearson
New Zealand Ltd) · Penguin Books (South Africa) (Pty) Ltd, 24 Sturdee Avenue,
Rosebank, Johannesburg 2196, South Africa

Penguin Books Ltd, Registered Offices: 80 Strand, London WC2R 0RL, England

Library of Congress Cataloging-in-Publication Data

Dalby, Rob.
A piggly wiggly Christmas / Robert Dalby.
p.   cm.
ISBN 978-0-399-15677-9
1. City and town life—Mississippi—Fiction.   2. Christmas stories.   I. Title.
PS3554.A4148P53   2010   2010025940
813'.54—dc22

Printed in the United States of America
1   3   5   7   9   10   8   6   4   2

BOOK DESIGN BY AMANDA DEWEY

This is a work of fiction. Names, characters, places, and incidents either are the product
of the author's imagination or are used fictitiously, and any resemblance to actual persons,
living or dead, businesses, companies, events, or locales is entirely coincidental.

While the author has made every effort to provide accurate telephone numbers and
Internet addresses at the time of publication, neither the publisher nor the author assumes
any responsibility for errors, or for changes that occur after publication. Further, the
publisher does not have any control over and does not assume any responsibility for
author or third-party websites or their content.

In loving memory of my father,
who made possible my ongoing journey as a writer

A
PIGGLY WIGGLY
CHRISTMAS

· One ·

That Santa Fe Feeling

Gaylie Girl Dunbar wanted her Santa Fe honeymoon to go on forever. But, alas, it flew by within the short space of a week. It wasn't just the romance that made it an especially memorable day and night in the cozy vacation home she had inherited from her first husband, Peter Lyons. It was the reaction of her new husband that put her in mind of a schoolboy on his first field trip. The affectionately nicknamed Mr. Choppy Dunbar was overflowing with earnest questions, wherever they went, whatever they saw, and it endeared him to her more than ever.

"Is that buildin' over there real adobe or that faux-dobe stuff you told me about?" he asked her that first sun-splashed, clear blue afternoon when they had strolled the busy Plaza hand in hand.

"I can't say for certain," she had answered. "It all started after the Palace of the Governors was restored, but you'd have to live here year-round to tell the difference."

Mr. and Mrs. Hale Dunbar Jr. of Second Creek, Mississippi, had left no rose-colored stone unturned in their exploration of "The City Different," taking in everything from the Georgia O'Keeffe Museum to all the quirky galleries along Canyon Road; from the Cathedral Basilica of Saint Francis of Assisi to the breathtaking sight of the yellow-tinged aspens ranged above the city in the Sangre de Cristo Mountains.

"It really is a totally different world out here," Mr. Choppy said on their last evening walk together. "Back home, we're so darn flat. A part of me never wants to leave all this rugged scenery. Maybe we could somehow take it with us."

Gaylie Girl agreed with the sentiment but struggled against expressing it out loud. After all, they had another life waiting for them in Second Creek. He had his mayoral duties, and now she was his First Lady. Her prevailing thought as their honeymoon wound down, however, was that she wanted above all to preserve that "Santa Fe feeling" upon returning to the Mississippi Delta. It was a feeling borne of control and confidence, knowing Santa Fe the way she did and having embraced it so enthusiastically in her first marriage. She needed to be in that kind of comfort zone now that she was going to be living permanently in the Deep South.

"The first thing I'm going to do when we get home is to make a list of civic projects I'd like to support," she said to Mr. Choppy, as he was driving their rental to the Santa Fe airport. "I want to make my mark."

He turned and gave her a knowing smile. "And you'll no doubt get the Nitwitts behind whatever strikes your fancy."

She raised her eyebrows slyly. "Naturally. Nothing gets done in Second Creek without the Nitwitts. Especially now that I'm a full-fledged member."

Indeed, many people gave that enterprising group of wealthy women of a certain age their fair share of credit for helping elect Mr. Choppy over the thoroughly corrupt incumbent, Mr. Floyce Hammontree, back in February. Gaylie Girl felt sure that she could win them all over to any pet project she proposed.

"Do you have any specific ideas yet?" Mr. Choppy asked.

"I was thinking mainly about Christmas. This is September, so we have a few months to dream up something built around that."

Mr. Choppy looked intrigued. "Such as?"

"Well, Christmas caroling first came to mind. The Square is so picturesque, I was thinking that maybe some sort of choir activity involving lots of the local churches might be something to explore."

Mr. Choppy tilted his head first one way and then the other as he considered her vision. "I don't think Second Creek has ever done anything like that. But you're right— The Square kinda lends itself to the idea, now that I think about it. Hey, we already use it every June for the Miss Delta Floozie Contest, and everyone flocks to that to see the ladies in their feather boas and costume jewelry. Why not this?"

"So you approve?"

"It sounds real doable to me."

"Then I'm calling a meeting of the Nitwitts, and we'll put on our thinking caps."

Gaylie Girl bore down and continued working out the details in her head as they flew home high above the mountainous grandeur of New Mexico sprawling beneath.

❄

Second Creek in mid- to late September was always a time of transition for the town's celebrated weather patterns. Rarely violent, as was the case in the winter and spring, they were usually an appealing combination of summer and autumn. Days remained long and might be spiked with heat, but the nights no longer breathed fire. Here and there, ceiling fans were turned to a lower speed and light blankets were thrown on beds in anticipation of the chill certain to come. That much the town had in common with most other areas of the country.

For many Second Creekers, however, there was something more. It was a matter of fine-tuning their dispositions, maintaining a healthy respect for the meteorological mysteries they could never take for granted. Not considering all the destruction and consequent rebuilding they had endured over the years. Or peculiar manifestations like the mass disappearance and sudden return of so many fireflies that had occurred over the recent summer months.

It had been nearly three weeks since the Nitwitts had assembled for an honest-to-goodness meeting, and Gaylie Girl thought she was never going to be able to get to the business at hand. All the girls wanted to hear about was her honeymoon with Mr. Choppy. She didn't much blame them, though. What widowed woman in her sixties and beyond wouldn't want to hear about such romantic details? Especially from an attractive and trendsetting newly married woman in her seventies.

Among the Nitwitts gathered at Gaylie Girl's freshly renovated Victorian fixer-upper on North Bayou Avenue for a light luncheon shortly after her return, current president Renza Belford was perhaps the most persistent of the lot. "You've told us oodles and oodles about the buildings you all toured. I can't believe the honeymoon was mainly about architecture. I mean, I've never heard so much carrying-on about doorways in my life. I'm more interested in what went on behind them, dear."

Novie Mims, still the group's world traveler and purveyor of impossibly dull slide shows, momentarily delayed the inevitable. "Oh, but a doorway in Santa Fe is not your average entrance. I was absolutely enchanted on my visit out there. Such attention to detail—the vigas and canales and all the flat roofs. Just mesmerizing—almost otherworldly."

Myrtis Troy, the fashionable owner of the town's most elegant bed-and-breakfast, Evening Shadows, quickly added her testimony. "Everyone should tour Santa Fe once in their lives. It's cultured and laid-back at the same time."

Despite the interruptions, Gaylie Girl surveyed the expectant faces of her friends and saw that they were all still pretty much on Renza's side. "Well," she began, after taking a sip of the sweet tea she had served to the group, "I'm sure I've mentioned before that Hale is no slouch in the affection department. But I have to say that the Santa Fe mountain air had a very salubrious effect on his ardor.

We carried on the way we did in that Romeo and Juliet suite at the Peabody Hotel when we were courting on the sly up in Memphis last year. It was, shall we say, a classic honeymoon with all the delicious trimmings."

Renza toyed with her tomato aspic for a few seconds. Then she emphatically set her fork down on the edge of her plate and sighed dramatically. "I'm not quite sure I know what *salubrious* means, Gaylie Girl, but I'm envious anyway."

"Same here," Denver Lee McQueen chimed in. "I do miss romance with my dear departed Eustice. It's prob'ly the main reason I've had so much trouble with my weight and developed this infernal diabetes. I read magazine articles all the time about food bein' a substitute for a good session of you-know-what."

Laurie Hampton, who enjoyed president emeritus status among the group and always took the high road in any conversation, put in her two cents' worth. "I'm thrilled it all went so well for you, Gaylie Girl. And I'm eager to hear all about your new civic project idea."

Gaylie Girl had to restrain herself from jumping up and going over to give Laurie a heartfelt hug. Leave it to the inveterate diplomat of the group to give her a much-needed opening. And she lost no time in explaining her concept of Christmas Caroling in The Square.

The newest Nitwitt member, Euterpe Simon, piano teacher extraordinaire to each of the others, waxed eloquent at once. "I think it's an inspiring idea, Gaylie Girl. And I have a suggestion for you. So many of the buildings around The

Square have those charming lacework balconies. Why not have the choir members stationed on the balconies while the citizens mill about below? It will create a delightful seasonal effect. You know—angels we have heard on high—and also looking down upon the flock for good measure."

"Oh, I think that's an absolutely marvelous addition to my concept," Gaylie Girl replied, winking smartly at Euterpe. "You've fine-tuned it beautifully. What do the rest of you girls think?"

There were many affirmative murmurs as well as a general nodding of heads around the table, and Gaylie Girl knew that the next official Nitwitt project was well on its way to fruition. After they had finished their lunch of aspic and chicken gumbo, they would take a vote and divvy up the duties, and that would be that.

It was, in fact, after the official unanimous vote had been taken, and tasks assigned and then recorded by secretary Novie, that the subject of their ailing member and founder, Wittsie Chadwick, emerged. Now safely ensconced in a memory care unit at Delta Sunset Village in nearby Greenwood for her rapidly progressing Alzheimer's, Wittsie was never very far from the minds of her good friends. They all still continued to visit her throughout the week, each one dutifully showing up for lunch on a different day to keep the connections alive as best they could in the face of her irreversibly declining faculties.

"Is there a way we could get her over here to see this when the time comes?" Gaylie Girl posed. But she did not wait for a response. "I know that Dr. Milburne wouldn't let her come to my wedding week before last. Said it would be too disorienting for her, as I recall, and I'm sure we can all understand that."

The group went silent, looking stumped at first, but then Laurie, always the successful schemer among them, straightened up in her chair. "Let's talk to the doctor and see if he'll agree to an excursion this one time. I think his concern about your wedding was the sheer number of people she would have to contend with, not to mention the noise and confusion of the reception afterward. But listening to choir music is in a different category altogether. Maybe he'd agree to allow us to shepherd her about, considering the spirit of the season."

"Heavens, Laurie!" Renza interjected. "I've said it a thousand times, but it's still worth repeating. You always find just the right words for every occasion. I just wish I had your gift."

Gaylie Girl nodded with relish. "Yes. I think that's our next move." Then, sensing that Renza might be getting a tad bit restless having control momentarily wrested from her, Gaylie Girl wisely deferred. "But what does our president think—officially, I mean?"

Renza's face was a mixture of surprise and delight as she adjusted the fox furs that always adorned her shoulders. "Oh . . . well, yes, I see no harm in approaching the doctor about this. As I said, Laurie's suggestion is spot-on. We do want to do everything we can for our dear Wittsie. By the way, girls, my visit with her yesterday was less than satisfactory, to say the least. She was having one of her blanker days. She just sat there and squinted at the food for the longest time as if it were an eye chart instead of something to eat. I was very distressed by it all."

"Well, of course, she's not going to get any better," Denver Lee added. "Not that I should talk with the way I'm managing my diabetes. What I really need is one of those round-the-clock sitters to slap my hand when I sneak things out of the fridge. Or someone to go with me to the grocery store and wag a finger at me when I grab something off the shelf that I shouldn't have in the first place. But, yes, I'm afraid we're all in for some sad times with our dear Wittsie."

Gaylie Girl surveyed all the long faces around the table and decided to lighten the mood. "Let's get started next week on our visits to the churches, shall we? Novie, read back all our assignments again, if you will."

Novie zeroed in on her scrawl and said: "I've written down here that Denver Lee, Renza, and Myrtis will be in charge of publicity—contacting *The Citizen* and radio stations and out-of-town churches and such. And I have a circled sentence here that says we shouldn't hesitate to call on Powell Hampton to help us with any copy for the ads just the way he did with all those radio spots—"

"Don't hesitate to do that," Laurie interrupted. "You all know the crackerjack job my Powell will do for us. He guided us through Mr. Choppy's election campaign beautifully."

Novie resumed after an enthusiastic nod. "And then it says here that Euterpe will work with the choir directors on their schedules and selections. And finally, myself, Laurie, and Gaylie Girl are to keep the actual appointments with all the local ministers, rectors, priests, and pastors. My, we have everything here in Second Creek but rabbis, don't we? But I know we have several Jewish families. Just not enough for a synagogue. I think the Adlers and the Beekmans go up to Memphis for temple every Friday—"

Laurie interrupted her with a pleasant smile. "Novie, you're wandering in the desert, dear."

"Oh, sorry. Let's see now—we've agreed to call on the Catholics, Episcopalians, Methodists, Presbyterians, Baptists, and, oh, yes, the Church of Christ." She paused and let out a little giggle. "I wonder what you call people who go to the Church of Christ? Are they Church of Christians?"

Renza quickly interrupted the polite titters that ensued. "Now, a while back you mentioned including a couple of black churches. Were you serious about that, Gaylie Girl?"

"Oh, I think we must invite the black churches," Gaylie Girl explained. "I see our event as not only ecumenical but also in the spirit of racial harmony. 'Tis the season, after all."

Renza's cantankerous nature began bubbling up as usual. "I suppose you realize that these black choirs don't sing the same way the white choirs do. It's a completely different sound, and they always carry on so."

Gaylie Girl was about to offer a soothing and tactful retort when Myrtis took the floor forcefully. "Oh, for God's sake, Renza, they aren't going to be out there doing rock and roll and R & B numbers. This will be a respectful program of Christmas music. And so what if they add their unique flavor to it? My Raymond exposed me to all sorts of popular tunes over the years with his record shop, and I have to say, I enjoyed all the different sounds and am certainly the better for it."

"Yes, we know all about you sitting out on your back porch spinning creaky Frankie Valli and Motown forty-fives," Renza replied. "You have to be the world's oldest bobby-soxer in panty hose."

Gaylie Girl cleared her throat and plastered a generous smile across her face. "Be that as it may, we need to get started on this pretty soon. Coordinating all those choirs will take some doing. We need to exert every bit of our charm as Nitwitts in getting everybody aboard."

"I know we all voted for this without blinking an eye, but do you think we'll actually be able to pull this off?" Renza posed. "People can be so touchy when it comes to religious matters. You'd be surprised what they think should be off-limits."

Gaylie Girl gave her a thoughtful stare and continued smiling. "Look at it this way. The Nitwitts took a stab at backing a political candidate and helped elect my Hale to the Mayor's office with those wonderful radio spots. It seems to me that rounding up a few choirs to do some Christmas caroling should be something we can handle as well."

There were a few raised eyebrows among the group, but Gaylie Girl dismissed the gestures as nothing more than cautionary and certainly not an indication of anything unconquerable.

❄

Mr. Choppy came home late from the Mayor's office that evening. After washing up, he plopped himself down at the beautifully set dining-room table and eyed his supper of pork tenderloin, cheese grits, and biscuits that Gaylie Girl had lovingly prepared. The crash course Mr. Choppy had given her over the past few months in whipping up his favorite Southern cuisine had paid off handsomely. He had even made her a gift of his mother's weighty bound volume of family recipes to study in her spare time. *Gladys Dunbar's Goodies*, it had been titled long ago. It was way past time to dust it off and put it to good use again. Nonetheless, he pushed his plate away ever so slightly and exhaled forcefully.

"Not hungry tonight?" Gaylie Girl said, the worry clearly creeping into her face. "Or did something happen at work?"

He seemed reluctant to answer at first, twitching his lip from side to side, but finally relented. "It's just that it looks like you're gonna have to take over as my secretary a little sooner than we thought, and I didn't know how you would react. The last thing I'd want would be for you to be overwhelmed."

Gaylie Girl quickly reviewed the status of her husband's ever cheerful but pregnant young secretary, Cherish Hempstead. Having suffered a couple miscarriages earlier in her marriage, she had been advised by her obstetrician to take maternity leave sooner rather than later, and the informal agreement was that Gaylie Girl would fill in until her return. The most recent understanding was that Cherish would withdraw from her duties around Thanksgiving.

"How soon is sooner?" Gaylie Girl asked, not particularly disturbed by the news.

He answered in a hushed, awkward tone. "End of the month, she says. Doctor's orders. She says certain things aren't going as well as expected with the pregnancy, although it's really nothin' serious. Just the mornin' sickness goin' on a tad bit longer and stronger than usual. They don't want to take any chances, and I can't say I blame 'em. I have noticed that Cherish has been excusin' herself to go to the ladies' room a lot lately."

Gaylie Girl's maternal instincts rose to the forefront, her memories of the trouble she had had carrying her own Petey and Amanda crowding in. The doctors had eventually resorted to C-sections both times because of her prolonged labor all those long decades ago. "I'm completely sympathetic. No reason for Cherish to take risks. Besides, I can multitask as well as the next person. I know I can handle the caroling project and all those secretarial duties at the same time."

Mr. Choppy immediately appeared more sanguine and picked up his fork. "I didn't want to make any assumptions, though. The office is always fulla people askin' for favors, and then there are the ones with the most unbelievable, ticky-tack complaints in the world, as well as the councilmen and all their territorial business. It's not like dealin' with the Nitwitts."

"I'm not so sure about that," Gaylie Girl replied, keeping her amusement in check. "Favors, ticky-tack complaints, territorial business. Sounds an awful lot like the girls to me."

"You know what I mean."

Gaylie Girl laughed brightly. "Of course I do. So you want me to start the first of October?"

"Thereabouts, I think."

"Call it a done deal."

"You're a trooper, Gaylie Girl."

"Ha! I'm a Nitwitt. One of the newer ones, granted. But I'm getting the hang of it rather quickly."

They began eating their dinner in earnest, occasionally pausing to give each other the sort of vaguely wicked smiles that had filled their honeymoon days and nights. Over Mr. Choppy's favorite dessert of black walnut ice cream sprinkled with cocoa powder, Gaylie Girl decided to tell him all about her Santa Fe feeling and how it had been the impetus for her current Nitwitt Christmas project.

"The first time I laid eyes on Santa Fe, Peter had just bought our vacation house and he asked me to decorate it from stem to stern. So I immersed myself in that, and it took several trips out from Chicago to do it right. I scoured all the Santa Fe shops and galleries for that Southwest touch. But each time we visited, I became more and more at home. So many people seemed to have come to live and work with their special agendas. It was so different from Lake Forest and my life with Peter up there. That was so regimented. Santa Fe had a flexibility to it, allowing people to come and bend it this way and that. But they never broke it. It seemed to mold them as much as they molded the city. I know for a fact that Peter and I were so much better together in Santa Fe than we ever were in Chicago." Then Gaylie Girl brought herself up short. "Oh, Hale, I hope you don't mind my going on about Peter like this. I was just trying to make a point."

Mr. Choppy put down his spoon and cupped his right hand under his chin, nodding thoughtfully at the recognition that flooded his brain. "I don't mind one bit. Some a' that sounds an awful lot like my life here in Second Creek, especially the part about people comin' here with their agendas. I was halfway thinkin' that your Santa Fe feelin' might be akin to our Second Creek solutions."

"That's the way I see it, too. Oh, the architecture is different, and one place is the Old Southwest and the other is the Old Deep South, but they're both special places determined to do things their own way and not lose their identities."

Mr. Choppy finished off his ice cream and then helped his wife clear the table. Over the sink, he said: "Oh, I meant to tell you—I talked over the Caroling in The Square idea with all the councilmen, and I don't think you and the churches'll have any trouble gettin' a special event permit from the city. And you haven't said anything, but my guess is that things went well with your Nitwitts this afternoon."

She rinsed out the ice cream bowls and put them in the dishwasher before answering with an undeniable friskiness in her tone. "And you knew that because?"

"Because if any of the ladies had raised a stink, I would have heard about it long before the ice cream came out. Am I right?"

Gaylie Girl's laughter was masked somewhat by the dishwasher starting up. "You know you are. They all went along, and now we've divvied up all the duties to within an inch of our lives. Imagine—the Nitwitts soliciting heavenly music."

Mr. Choppy paused for a moment and then shrugged his shoulders. "How hard can it be to get people together to sing Christmas carols? Not much controversy in that, to my way of thinkin'."

· *Two* ·

In Search of Angels

The Nitwitt trio of Gaylie Girl, Novie, and Laurie set out on their mission to the various Second Creek churches the very next week. Unexpectedly, however, Novie called up the other two and insisted that she was going to be their driver and escort. "Par excellence. I have a fun surprise in store for the both of you," she explained, offering no details when Gaylie Girl pressed further at her end.

"It's perfectly fine with me, then," Gaylie Girl answered. "Both you and Laurie know the town a whole lot better than I do. I have no idea where several of these churches are. So, drive on, my good woman!"

Early Monday afternoon, Gaylie Girl was sitting quietly on the rose-colored Belter sofa in her freshly decorated drawing room. She was also finishing up a cup of herbal tea while scouring the latest issue of *Southern Living* for recipes when she was startled by the extremely loud honking of a horn. Of course, she knew that it would be Novie picking her up, but she was hardly prepared for what she encountered when she walked out onto the porch and closed the front door behind her. There, parked before her at the end of the boxwood-edged brick walkway that divided her diminutive front yard, was an enormous white-paneled van with a window or two thrown in for good measure. The kind, in fact, that some churches used to transport their indisposed members to and from services, pancake breakfasts, and potluck suppers. Or, more notoriously, akin to the model favored by drug dealers making their clandestine deliveries in the middle of the night.

"Great heavenly ham and a plate of applesauce, Novie!" Gaylie Girl exclaimed, reaching out gingerly to touch the side of the van as Novie rolled down the window. "Where in the world did you get this monstrosity?"

Plump little Novie then shut off the engine, climbed down out of the captain's chair, and waddled her way around the ostentatious vehicle, unable to suppress a giggle. "Isn't this sheer lunacy? My Caddy is in the shop, and they were supposed to get me a loaner, but this is all the rental car place had. They said it once sat fifteen passengers."

"What do you mean—once sat?" Gaylie Girl said, frowning. "Is there something wrong with it now? Is it the 'incredible shrinking van,' by any chance?"

Novie opened the front passenger door and gestured dramatically at the empty space that revealed itself inside the vehicle. "No, nothing like that. They just took all the seats out except for the captain's chair and the back row and made it into a cargo van. You and Laurie will have to sit back there while I drive. But at least you can keep each other company."

Gaylie Girl folded her arms, half in frustration, half in amusement. "For heaven's sake, Novie, why didn't you tell me about it? We could have gone in my car. Why in the world do you want to put up with this clunky old thing?"

Novie drew herself up defiantly, thrusting out her chin. "I wanted to keep it a surprise. Besides, I like the challenge of it. I fully intend to get my money's worth. The Caddy won't be ready for three more days. It'll be fun. I've always wanted to drive one of these."

Gaylie Girl blinked in disbelief. "You have? I could live a hundred more years and not get the urge. Can you even see over the steering wheel?"

"Of course I can. I'm not that short. Have you no sense of adventure? You know *I* have. Now, come on, let's open the sliding door and get you back there. We've still got to pick up Laurie, and I don't want to be late for our appointment with Reverend Somerby."

Dutifully, Gaylie Girl stepped up, lowered her head, and carefully made her way to the back row, where she took her seat all by her lonesome. From this distance, Novie had all the accessibility of an airport shuttle bus driver. It soon came to Gaylie Girl that the two of them were likely going to have to shout or at least raise their voices to conduct a conversation.

Novie looked back briefly and smiled before fastening her seat belt. Then she turned the key, and whatever it was she was saying to Gaylie Girl at the time was utterly drowned out by the sound of the humming engine.

"What?!" Gaylie Girl shouted back, cupping her ears.

Novie quickly picked up on the difficulty and upped her voice a decibel or two. "I said, 'Fasten your seat belts! We're flyin' high!'"

Gaylie Girl quickly surveyed the area around her and shrugged as she shouted back. "There's no seat belt back here!"

"Oh, well, hang on!" Novie returned, giggling like a giddy schoolgirl.

Gaylie Girl braced herself as Novie pulled away from the curb and the adventure began in earnest. Laurie seemed even more perplexed when the van pulled up in front of her little raised cottage a few blocks away but soon fell to and joined Gaylie Girl on the backseat, where the two of them immediately began conversing in whispers.

"Did you see this coming?" Gaylie Girl began. "It feels like one of those old *Candid Camera* stunts. Do you think Fannie Flagg will be waiting for us when we get to the church?"

"Or the ghost of Allen Funt?" a snickering Laurie whispered back, rolling her eyes at the same time. "What do you suppose has gotten into Novie?"

"Probably travel withdrawal symptoms. She told me the other day she hadn't been on one of her travel junkets in well over six months. I guess she just needs that touch of excitement in her life, even if it's just a trip around town in a rental van only Godzilla could love."

Just then, the van hit a pothole, causing Gaylie Girl and Laurie to fall against each other like a couple of toppling bowling pins. Up front, there was only the sound of Novie's incessant giggling, followed by a loud "Oops-a-daisy!"

"Did you have a little snort before you headed out this morning?!" Laurie shouted.

"Nothing of the sort. I'm firmly in control!" Novie shouted back.

After a few more unscheduled bumps in the road, the van finally pulled up in front of St. Luke's Episcopal Church, where the Reverend Zane Somerby greeted them in front of the Gothic façade with a look of bewilderment.

"My word, ladies! I thought you were from the nursing home in this thing!" he began, as Gaylie Girl and Laurie stepped out of the vehicle and took deep breaths when their feet hit the ground. Novie soon joined them, looking as if she had just been decorated with Olympic gold.

"That was invigorating, wasn't it, girls?!"

Gaylie Girl smiled but was unable to restrain herself. "If a bit edgy without seat belts."

Reverend Somerby, a rotund, jovial man with a trimmed red beard that often put parishioners in mind of Henry XIII himself, gestured toward the towering redbrick Parish House next door. "Well, ladies, shall we head on in and discuss the pressing business at hand?"

Choirmaster Lawton Bead awaited them in Reverend Somerby's cozy office, which was colorfully accented by a small, stained glass window. He lost no time in reacting to the caroling issue after the perfunctory introductions and offerings of coffee and tea. Gaylie Girl found Mr. Bead's pale, ascetic appearance a bit off-putting, not to mention that he remained standing throughout the entire conversation with the distracting habit of bending over at the waist and popping back up to emphasize certain words. It was almost as if some clever puppeteer had seamlessly attached him to wires in the ceiling.

"I particularly like your idea of choir members occupying the lacework balconies around The Square," Mr. Bead was saying. "*In excelsis Deo*, you know. But there is a complication we need to consider."

Gaylie Girl took the plunge cheerfully. "And what would that be, Mr. Bead?"

"Simply put, our choir members must be positioned all along the same side of The Square. They must all be able to see me directing them from some central point below. They can't just be scattered here and there. I can't be running back and forth all out of breath."

"Yes, I can see your point," Gaylie Girl answered, secretly amused by the frantic imagery. "And since you're the first church we've called upon, you'll have your choice of exactly which side you'd prefer for your fifteen minutes of fame, so to speak."

Mr. Bead spent a few seconds in contemplation. "Ah, yes, you said each choir would get approximately fifteen minutes each before the public? Are you sure that's going to be long enough?"

"Considering what the weather could be like on Christmas Eve, we don't want anyone to have to spend too much time outdoors. A well bundled up fifteen minutes of carols for each choir should be just about right. We certainly can't count on seventy-degree temperatures that time of year. Let's err on the side of comfort, shall we?"

Reverend Somerby straightened up in his desk chair and gestured emphatically in his choirmaster's direction. "Well, which side is it to be, Lawton?"

Mr. Bead's eyes shifted from side to side as he mulled things over. "The north balconies, I think. I prefer the view from there."

"North it is, then," Gaylie Girl replied. "Novie, make a note, please."

Novie went to work, scribbling in her notepad. When she had finished, she looked up and said: "I also have a reminder here to be sure and mention Euterpe's role to Mr. Bead."

Gaylie Girl gently nudged Laurie and deferred. "Why don't you handle this one?"

Laurie cleared her throat and offered one of her typical diplomatic smiles. "Mr. Bead, I'm sure you've heard of Euterpe Simon, our Mistress of the Scales. All of us Nitwitts are making remarkable progress taking piano from her. She really has a wonderful gift."

Mr. Bead appeared unmoved. "Yes, I've driven past her school many times. Didn't it used to be the Piggly Wiggly? I shopped there now and then for odds and ends."

"It did, indeed. Then it was Mr. Choppy Dunbar's campaign headquarters during the mayoral election, and now he's leasing it to Euterpe as a music studio. She's doing quite well, and we couldn't be happier for her."

"And the point of this is?" Mr. Bead offered, a hint of impatience creeping into his voice.

"Just that Euterpe Simon will be coordinating the appearances of all the choirs and keeping an eye on the time. And she has suggested that it might be a good idea to work with all of you choirmasters in making sure the selections don't overlap. We'd like each church's contribution to be unique," Laurie continued. "Euterpe's awfully good with people."

Not a muscle twitched in Mr. Bead's long, narrow face. "You mean someone else will determine our musical program?"

"No, of course not, Mr. Bead. You'll determine that for the most part. We just thought it might be more effective not to have all the choirs singing 'Joy to the World,' for instance. The audience might get a bit weary. After all, there are so many delightful carols to choose from."

"But if people show up at different times during the event, how will they know what the previous choirs have sung? Wouldn't they have to remain for the entire two hours for a point of comparison?"

It was at this point that Reverend Somerby stepped in to defuse the growing tension. "Lawton, I met Mrs. Simon at a recent social gathering and she's perfectly charming. I'm sure you'll enjoy working with her on this project. And I'm equally sure she'll value your opinion, as talented as you are."

"Oh, yes," Gaylie Girl added quickly. "Euterpe is the ultimate listener. She makes you feel like you've known her for ages the instant she walks into a room. Even if you are likely to do a double take when you see that pet poodle of hers at her shoulder like a sleeping baby."

"Well, that's quite a recommendation from the lot of you," Mr. Bead said, his demeanor softening somewhat. "I suppose we can work things out amicably."

Gaylie Girl turned to Novie, gently wagging her index finger. "We'll set up a meeting for the two of them soon, won't we?"

Novie nodded and made another note. "It's as good as done."

"I do have one other suggestion," Mr. Bead continued, his tone at its most solemn once again. "We need to take into consideration the hour of the caroling. You've suggested early evening, but I believe early afternoon would be better. That way it won't interfere with our regular Christmas Eve services or anyone else's. People can attend both, and I know we wouldn't want them to have to choose on a holy day of obligation."

Reverend Somerby spoke up with authority, stroking his beard all the while. "Excellent point, Lawton. I wholeheartedly agree."

"One to three o'clock Christmas Eve afternoon instead of six to eight in the evening, then?" Gaylie Girl inquired. "Only the Ten Commandments are written in stone."

The unexpected bit of humor actually brought a smile to Mr. Bead's lips. "I have to admit that's rather clever."

With that, the revised hours quickly met with everyone's approval, and the Nitwitts brought the first foray of their angelic mission to a successful close.

❄

The Second Creek United Methodist Church was an easy two blocks away, so Novie was unable to get up to a speed fast enough to wreak any havoc upon her two passengers in the back of the van. Easier still was the personality of

Choirmaster Press Phillips—a welcome contrast to the high-maintenance Lawton Bead. A short, plump man with an incessant smile on his ruddy face, Mr. Phillips immediately embraced the Nitwitts' unique proposal after they had all settled around his office.

"What a delightful quest—to be in search of angelic voices for the citizens of Second Creek! Of course, this will take a little extra planning for my group," he explained as he picked up another butter cookie from the plate he had passed around to his guests. "We have two members who are deathly afraid of looking down from heights, even something as innocuous as the second-story balconies around The Square. I know this because I chaperoned a church bus trip to the Smokies a couple of summers ago, and we did a good deal of hiking and climbing. That turned out to be anathema to the Biddle sisters, Larissa and Camilla, who have devoted their entire lives to the sweet music of the church. Such heavenly sounds, such an inner beauty. True angels, the both of them. Unfortunately, they have a not-so-beautiful inner ear problem and just can't look down from any sort of height at all." He paused to indulge a curious little snort as he finished off his cookie.

"I personally have long suspected it's an earwax buildup problem that they could relieve over the counter, but they insist otherwise. At any rate, I couldn't ask them to take up a position anywhere on those balconies. But I'll gladly have them below in The Square as I conduct the others. They'll relish the spotlight. I can picture it now—one on either side of me, lifting up those voices worthy of coloraturas at the Met."

"Yes, of course," Gaylie Girl said, absentmindedly fingering the cookie she had taken out of politeness with no intention of eating. "We wouldn't want to leave anyone out of the proceedings. Christmas is hardly the time for that."

"Never fear. A touch of vertigo never kept a good Methodist from a potluck supper or choir practice."

"Excellent. And what side of The Square would your choir prefer?"

After brief consideration, Mr. Phillips lit up. "North, I believe. In honor of the North Pole. Just a whimsical touch for all the children we have dedicated this year and whom we hope will come to listen to us with their parents."

Novie made yet another note and said: "That's two votes for north and counting."

❄

In rapid succession, the affable choirmasters of the Second Creek Church of Christ, First Presbyterian, First Baptist, and St. Thomas Aquinas Roman Catholic Church were all persuaded to participate in Second Creek's first Caroling in The Square on Christmas Eve. All except the Baptists, who opted for the west balconies, chose to stage their appearance on the north side of The Square. Fortunately, Gaylie Girl and Laurie were none the worse for wear in the back of the van after they both ganged up on Novie and told her she would have to slow down or they would go on foot the rest of the way.

Novie had briefly protested as she glanced at the speedometer. "Why, I'm doing the limit—no more!"

Gaylie Girl in particular was having none of it. "It's not

your speed so much as all the potholes downtown. You've managed to hit every one of them without fail. Hale insists he's going to do something about it even if we have to have a special election to repave every street around The Square. It seems Mr. Floyce preferred to concentrate on paving the rural roads to assure the outlying vote. But until Hale takes care of business—please slow down. Laurie and I don't wear black and blue very well!"

And Novie had acquiesced as they set out on what they surmised might be the more difficult part of their mission: soliciting the participation of a few of the community's black churches. Feeling somewhat out of their element, they did not know what to expect but had vowed to be as evenhanded as possible in the matter.

"I got as much information as I could out of Hale when he gave me a pep talk last night," Gaylie Girl explained to Laurie as they rode along Lower Winchester Road toward Hanging Grapes A.M.E. Church for their appointment with Brother Willyus V. Thompson. "Hale actually visited with Brother Thompson during his campaign even though Hanging Grapes was always firmly in the Floyce Hammontree camp. The scuttlebutt was that all sorts of favors were being done for the church under the table by Mr. Floyce. So it could be that Brother Thompson will still be a bit peeved at losing his influence with the Mayor's office and might not be too pleased to see me coming. But perhaps he'll let bygones be bygones and rise above it all in the spirit of Christmas."

Laurie looked perplexed and shrugged. "That really would be holding a grudge in my book."

"Nevertheless, a grudge never stood in the way of a Nitwitt, right?"

"Right."

But the clever confidence that Gaylie Girl and Laurie had carried with them into the newly expanded Hanging Grapes Hall of Fellowship ten minutes later soon faded when Brother Thompson met their proposal with a profound shaking of his head.

"I see you ladies have no sense of history," he began, avoiding their eyes as he spoke with obvious reserve, his shiny bald pate lifted skyward.

The Nitwitts were all seated directly across from him at one of the enormous dining tables used for church socials, so it was particularly disturbing to Gaylie Girl that he continued to avert his gaze as if she and her companions weren't even in the room.

"I don't understand what you mean, Brother Thompson," Gaylie Girl said, forcing a smile to the forefront. "Would you be good enough to explain what a sense of history has to do with our Caroling in The Square proposal? Other than the fact that I've been assured it's never been done before. We offer this to your choir as a chance to make local history."

Brother Thompson continued with a demeanor that was nothing if not well above the fray. "I'm speakin' of our state's not-so-glorious past, Miz Dunbar. I and many members of my congregation can remember a time when us black folk were forced to sit in the balconies of all the movin' picture theaters. And if we wanted to attend the weddings of the white folks many of us worked for, we had to sit way up in the balcony. We weren't good enough to sit on the ground floor. I'm afraid balconies leave a very bad taste in our mouths."

A feeling of panic exploded somewhere behind Gaylie Girl's sternum, and she realized that she needed immediate help. After all, she had only recently come to the Deep South to live and was not prepared to address its historic burdens on the spur of the moment. She quickly searched the faces of her companions and came to rest on Laurie's reassuring gaze. "Perhaps Mrs. Hampton here could discuss this with you more effectively, Brother Thompson."

Laurie stepped in with her usual diplomacy, her tone both even and friendly. "Mrs. Dunbar is not from Mississippi, Brother Thompson. She's lived almost her entire life in Chicago, but I'm sure she's sympathetic with your perspective, as we all are. No one could possibly deny the past difficulties that black people have endured here in the South. But it was our intention as a social club to make sure that black churches were included in this event from the get-go. I can assure you that using the balconies has nothing to do with the discriminatory policies of the past. Instead, we thought of the balconies as an almost angelic prop. Second Creek is unique in having such beautiful and historic structures available for our caroling concept, and we come to you today only in search of angels."

Brother Thompson finally came down to eye level and said: "I believe what you say, Miz Hampton, but I cain't speak for everybody in my choir. Some a' them still got bad memories of the stores and restaurants in The Square and all that. I can run it past my choirmaster and my people and see what they want to do, but I cain't promise you anything right now."

Gaylie Girl resumed the exchange at that point. "Well, that's all we ask, Brother Thompson. We want your participation in this event and hope you will see it as an opportunity to promote your church in a positive and charming way. Surely there can be no harm in that."

"Like I say, I'll run it past my choir. I just cain't promise. I'll get you an answer tomorrow, though, one way or another."

On the way back into town, Gaylie Girl was having trouble letting go of what appeared to be their first setback, reviewing the entire conversation with Brother Thompson in her head. "I can't see that we did anything to warrant his negative reaction, do you, girls?"

Novie answered first from the driver's seat, revving up her voice a notch to be heard. "Don't even think of blaming yourself, Gaylie Girl. He's the one with the problem!"

"I agree," Laurie continued. "I was obviously wrong about the grudge thing. Looks like he still resents Mr. Choppy's victory over Mr. Floyce."

Gaylie Girl's sigh was tinged with defiance. "I can tell you that Hale has no intention of buying off the people of Second Creek the way Mr. Floyce did. He campaigned and won on an ethical approach to the office, and he intends to stick to it."

"That's why we all voted for him," Laurie added. "It's way more than a stretch that anyone, black or white, would take offense at singing Christmas carols from a balcony because of the Jim Crow laws of the past. That's probably the weakest excuse for saying no that I've ever heard. I think it's playing the civil rights card in a way that's an insult to the civil rights movement. From what you've told me, Brother Thompson just didn't want to come right out and tell you the real reason. Fact is, he knows good and well that our Mr. Choppy cooked the goose that laid the golden egg."

"Well, let's not dwell on it any longer. Because all is not lost," Gaylie Girl said with a renewed energy. "Hale told me last night that we were quite likely to have success with the Reverend Quintus Payne of the Marblestone Alley Church of Holiness, who supported him enthusiastically in the election. I can't imagine that Reverend Payne won't want to have his choir raising their voices to heaven on Christmas Eve."

"Then let's head on out, Novie!" Laurie proclaimed. "But please, dear, no pedal to the metal!"

❄

The reception the Nitwitts encountered at the quaint Marblestone Alley Church of Holiness across town could not have been more cordial. Reverend Quintus Payne greeted the three ladies at the door of Holiness Hall with all the gentlemanly ardor his lanky frame could muster. Once inside the white-clapboard and green-shuttered building, they were escorted to a dining room full of tempting aromas and what looked like a welcoming committee.

"Ladies," Reverend Payne began, "I'd like you to meet our choirmistress, Mrs. Vergie Woods, our organist, Miss Saleesha Patton, and my assistant pastor, Reverend Thaddeus Jefferson."

It took a minute or two for the completion of all the handshakes and perfunctory smiles that normally accompany introductions, but soon everyone was sitting around one of the tables discussing the details of Caroling in The Square. It was Mrs. Woods, a voluptuous vision in purple from head to toe, who quickly offered the most dramatic response.

"I think y'all must've read my mind. Why, over the summer I believe I went to Reverend Payne here and told him I'd been prayin' we could come up with some sorta Christmas event in The Square to get people downtown and in the spirit of the season, didn't I, Reverend?"

"You did for a fact, Vergie. That's why I wanted all y'all to hear out Miz Dunbar and the rest of these ladies today, since it seems like your prayers've been answered. But you know, that's not unusual for Second Creek. I think many of us who live here are in tune with each other, no matter what our different backgrounds are."

Gaylie Girl matched Mrs. Woods's enthusiasm with her own. "My husband has told me before about your Second Creek solutions, and he also said we'd likely find an audience here for our project. I'm also supposed to remind you again how much he appreciated having the support of so many of your church members in the recent election."

"Mayor Dunbar's a good man," Reverend Payne added, puffing himself up. "For true, I did endorse him from the pulpit, which I rarely do. But I see I wasn't mistaken in my judgment. He's already done some good things in the short time he's been in office. We needed new blood to run this town, and we got it now. As for this caroling event, Miz Dunbar, Miz Woods will cooperate with y'all in any way you need. We intend to have the Marblestone Alley Church of Holiness well represented on Christmas Eve."

"You and our secretary must huddle before we leave, Mrs. Woods," Gaylie Girl said, gesturing toward Novie. "But meanwhile, I just have to ask someone or I'll explode from curiosity. What is that heavenly aroma that's been filling this room from the moment we walked in?"

Reverend Payne chuckled richly and pointed in the direction of the kitchen. "That's my wife, Yolie, back there makin' her famous bread pudding for a bake sale we're havin' tonight. Matter a' fact, I think I can arrange to get you a little taste, and if you like it, you can take some back to the Mayor with our compliments."

Gaylie Girl demurred without thinking. "Oh, you must let me pay you. I'd like to contribute to the bake sale."

"Nonsense. My Yolie always makes plenty extra. Let's get y'all on back there for some samplin' and see what you think."

Yolie Payne, who was as tall and gracious as her husband, lost no time in making them all feel at home as soon as they entered her culinary territory. "I just finished up a batch, ladies. This is the best time to sneak you a little taste while it's still warm from the oven."

Despite their faint protestations, all three Nitwitts ended up carting home generous complimentary servings of the most delicious bread pudding they'd ever put in their mouths. It was not too heavy, as bread pudding can sometimes be. Instead, it was custardy with a hint of eggnog flavor, a dusting of nutmeg, and chock-full of plump raisins. Then the gregarious Yolie Payne had generously drizzled it with a sinfully rich, buttery rum sauce of her own invention. Gaylie Girl couldn't wait to spring it on her Hale as a surprise dessert that evening. It would be the exclamation point on a mission well accomplished to all of the churches they had set out to impress—with one notable exception.

As he had promised, Brother Willyus V. Thompson called Gaylie Girl the next day and officially notified her that Hanging Grapes A.M.E. Church would not be participating in the Christmas Eve caroling event. "We voted to sit this one out," he told her. "But we appreciate you askin' us."

Gaylie Girl was not disappointed in the least, having made a good faith effort to win him over. As she hung up the phone, she even said it out loud with great optimism in her voice: "Mark my words: The Nitwitts will have you singing on those balconies next year, Brother Thompson."

Three

Gaylie Girl Friday

There was no question in Gaylie Girl's mind that Cherish Hempstead had started to show. Somewhere in the middle of her second trimester, Mayor Hale Dunbar's trusty little secretary was making no attempt to disguise the little bump in her belly and had stoutly refused to switch over to maternity clothes.

"I'm so proud to be pregnant again. Why shouldn't I show off? And I just know we're goin' to see this one through. I'm determined not to have another miscarriage," Cherish kept telling Gaylie Girl over and over during their "training time" together one week before temporarily relinquishing all her secretarial duties.

"You certainly have that telltale glow, Cherish. I'm sure everything will work out for you and Henry this time. You just go home, eat plenty of good food, and rest to your heart's content," Gaylie Girl had insisted as the two of them worked through the location of important files, a crash course on using the computer, screening phone calls, and other mayoral office protocol.

"And I'm just as sure you're gonna do fine helpin' your husband out until I come back," Cherish returned, flashing her customary sunny smile. "Just remember—I'm only a phone call away if somethin' comes up that puzzles you. No need to go it alone, Mrs. Dunbar."

Finally, the first of October arrived with a modest chill in the air, and the torch was passed. Gaylie Girl was on her own—bound and determined to make both herself and her Hale proud. Why, there was nothing she felt she couldn't handle from the get-go!

Which is precisely when Lady Roth, Second Creek's only faux-accented, faux-royal, indefatigable law unto herself, marched into the office all in a huff—bright and early that very first morning. Why was that always the way of things?

"What on earth are you doing here?" Lady Roth began, hovering imperiously over the reception desk with her turban-wrapped head thrown back. "You are Mrs. Gaylie Girl Dunbar, aren't you? What have you and Mr. Choppy done with that adorable Cherish girl? I've come to rely upon her discretion and efficiency, and that's remarkable among today's youth!"

Gaylie Girl couldn't quite believe what was happening. Cherish had made quite a to-do of giving her an entire page of instructions on how to deal with Lady Roth when the occasion inevitably arose, and now here was the old girl herself in the flesh with her God-only-knew-what agenda of the moment.

"Good morning to you, Lady Roth," Gaylie Girl answered, determined not to betray both her surprise and her uneasiness. "Our delightful Mrs. Hempstead has taken maternity leave, doctor's orders, and I'm filling in for her until she's able to return."

Lady Roth plopped herself down on a nearby comfortable armchair and proceeded to bark orders. "Announce me to the Mayor at once! I have other errands to run this morning and I don't want to be put off my schedule!"

Gaylie Girl's brain raced, trying to remember bits and pieces of the time-honored advice Cherish had written down for her, but was ultimately unable to retrieve anything specific. Instead, she settled for the polite and perfunctory. "What do you need to see the Mayor about this morning, Lady Roth? I believe he's on the phone with someone right this second."

"As it turns out, I need to see the both of you. So tell him to hang up. He can call whoever it is right back!"

Fortunately for Gaylie Girl, her Hale did happen to hang up that very instant, as the light on the phone line in use conveniently blinked off. She immediately buzzed him and announced Lady Roth's presence.

"I'll be right on out," Mr. Choppy replied through the intercom and losing no time in appearing. He then executed an amusing little bow as his visitor rose from her chair. "Ah, Lady Roth! And to what do I owe the pleasure today?" He gestured toward his office, allowing her to enter first. "Gaylie Girl, will you come in and take notes, please?"

Dutifully, Gaylie Girl followed, and it was after they'd all taken their seats inside that some of Cherish's instructions came flooding back in upon her. *"Always treat Lady Roth like the royalty she claims to be. We all know better, but play along come Hell or high water,"* Cherish had written. Followed by: *"Mr. Dunbar and I have found out the hard way that it's best to humor her, no matter what. You'll never get her out of the office, otherwise."*

"Now then, Lady Roth," Mr. Choppy continued from behind his desk, "tell us what's on your mind. We're always here at your disposal."

Unexpectedly, Lady Roth turned toward Gaylie Girl as she pontificated. "It's providential that I find you here this morning, Mrs. Dunbar. I had intended to discuss my concerns with your husband and have him pass them along to you, but this will meet the case even more satisfactorily. Now, it came to my attention earlier this week that you and your friends have gotten all the churches around Second Creek to agree to a caroling event in The Square this upcoming Christmas Eve. I must say that I wholeheartedly approve."

Gaylie Girl managed a measured reply, even though she was completely taken aback by Lady Roth's opening gambit. "Why, yes, we did just that. Well, we didn't convince all of the churches, you understand, but many of them. I'm delighted to hear that the word is getting around so quickly. I must remember to tell Denver Lee, Myrtis, and Renza that their publicity efforts are already beginning to pay off handsomely."

"Never mind all that. Don't dwell on something I already know," Lady Roth added, waving her off as if she were swatting at a fly. "What is of the utmost importance to me now is that I have had a most egregious falling-out with our bloody choirmaster at St. Luke's. That pasty-faced, finicky Lawton Bead is intolerable. Stalking about the Parish House like the Ghost of Christmas Past the way he does. At any rate, once I found out about the caroling, I went to Mr. Bead and gave him my demands. It turns out he will not allow me to be a soloist in our program of Christmas music, and I absolutely insist on being featured. I'll have you know that I took voice lessons during my period of theatrical aspirations as a young girl. I was quite accomplished even though I did not achieve my ultimate ambition of becoming world-famous actress and singer, Vocifera P. Forest."

Gaylie Girl did her dead-level best to keep the frown and desperation from her face while wisely deferring to her husband. "Hale, dear, won't you give Lady Roth your input and expert opinion on this?"

Mr. Choppy responded quickly and firmly. "Well, Lady Roth, I do appreciate your viewpoint as always, but I wonder what either myself or my wife can do to persuade Mr. Bead. Do you think he would listen to either of us?"

"I'm here to tell you that you simply must prevail. At least one of you must, and I really don't care which. That utterly odious man seems to forget that I make substantial contributions to the church. He has such an exaggerated opinion of himself and his authority."

It took all the restraint Gaylie Girl could muster to suppress the obvious response about the pot calling the kettle black, but she acquitted herself beautifully. "I suppose I could have our Euterpe Simon meet with Mr. Bead and see if she can work something out on your behalf. She's quite good at that sort of thing, you know."

Lady Roth frowned before a spark of recognition overtook her. "Are you referring to that piano teacher with the poodle that's come to town and put out her shingle at the old Piggly Wiggly building?"

"The very same. Among other things, Euterpe's in charge of coordinating the caroling selections with all the choirmasters. I suppose that this would fall within her bailiwick."

"Very well, then. I leave this up to you to handle since you seem to know her so well. But I will not accept anything less than a solo from one of the balconies on Christmas Eve," Lady Roth concluded, rising up from her chair as crisply as her age and arthritis would allow. "That is all."

Once she was gone, Mayor and Mrs. Hale Dunbar Jr. immediately huddled at his desk. "What are we going to do about Lady Roth's ultimatum?" Gaylie Girl said. "I already feel guilty pushing this off on poor Euterpe."

Mr. Choppy appeared momentarily stumped before a little gasp brought a smug grin to his face. "Didn't you have Laurie Hampton with you when you went around to tell all the choirmasters about Caroling in The Square? There's your answer. Put her on the case. She'll come up with somethin' brilliant. I know all the Nitwitts swear by her, and I still have the fondest memories of all that waltzin' at the Piggly Wiggly that she came up with to try and help me keep my store open."

Gaylie Girl remained slightly uncomfortable nonetheless. "Whether I saddle Euterpe or Laurie with this, it's going to take a bit of maneuvering. But I think you're probably onto something there. If anyone can keep Lady Roth from ruining this for everybody, it's Laurie."

Mr. Choppy sank back in his chair and smiled the way people do when they are about to say something complimentary. "I'm gonna have to give you an A plus, sweetheart."

Gaylie Girl was caught off guard, managing only to tilt her head like a curious puppy.

"What I mean is—you held up pretty well just now. Not many secretaries have to put up with the likes of Lady Roth first time out. I think you're gonna do just fine as my Gaylie Girl Friday. Hey, the worst may be over already!"

"You really think so? I have to confess that I was a lot more nervous than I let on."

"I'd never have guessed. Cherish was really good at that 'even keel' business, too. I don't think the office of Mayor Hale Dunbar is gonna miss a lick."

❄

It didn't take long for a couple of the Nitwitts to call up and check on Gaylie Girl's maiden voyage as a working girl. First to grill her later that morning was Renza, who seemed much more concerned with the latest Nitwitt gossip than truly finding out how things were going for Gaylie Girl at the Mayor's office.

"I think Denver Lee is up to something," she told Gaylie Girl, after inquiring perfunctorily about the initial go-round of secretarial duties. "She keeps hinting that we ought to have our next Nitwitts' meeting to discuss the progress of the caroling project at her house instead of mine. Well, I'm still president of the Nitwitts, so I see no reason to drag everyone over to Denver Lee's. Besides, that house of hers is beyond bizarre. I get the heebie-jeebies every time I'm over there."

Gaylie Girl could hardly disagree. She had visited the house that Eustice McQueen had built for his Denver Lee only once since moving down and had been completely unable to figure out what the man was trying for. Oh, it was conventional enough on the outside with its two-story brick façade and evenly spaced shuttered windows. Inside, however, every room was cluttered with his failed inventions, none of which had offered much eye appeal to begin with and all of which had aged badly by now. As a result, the overall effect was of an unkempt museum of the arcane, if not downright deranged. The center of the living room, for example, was occupied by something that resembled either an enormous broken-down unicycle or perhaps a futuristic spinning wheel. It was truly impossible to tell which, but all the seating was grouped around it, making conversation a distracting proposition.

The long central hallway featured a lot of metallic bits and pieces dangling from the ceiling on wires, the lot of which Denver Lee had explained away as the intricate parts of a large mechanical nutcracker that had worked just once and then exploded rather violently in front of the only corporate executives who had ever expressed any interest in purchasing the patent. It seemed to remain a point of pride with Denver Lee, however, that no one had been injured as a result of that explosion. Her Euss, she insisted, had lovingly preserved what was left of the mess, being unable to let go of yet another of his contraptions that would have taxed Rube Goldberg's imagination.

"I can appreciate what you're saying about that house," Gaylie Girl began. Then she suddenly decided to emulate Laurie in trying for the role of peacemaker. "But I think Denver Lee's been having a very difficult time controlling her diabetes lately. Maybe humoring her and letting her host one of the meetings wouldn't hurt." Gaylie Girl knew better than to leave it at that, however. "You're still the president, though, no matter what. It's up to you."

Renza fell silent for a while, apparently placated by Gaylie Girl's careful maneuvering. "I'll think about it. I still believe Denver Lee has some sort of ulterior motive. She always does, you know."

"I'll go along with whatever you decide," Gaylie Girl continued. "Oh, by the way, all of you must be doing something right with the publicity. Lady Roth was in here earlier demanding this and that as a result of her interest in our project."

"Why, we haven't done a thing yet, other than talk to Powell Hampton over the phone. We're supposed to meet with him around the first of November to plan the actual ad campaign. Of course, I'm not really surprised that Lady Roth already knows everything there is to know. She has her flies on every wall in town."

As there seemed to be nothing Gaylie Girl could think of to top that, she begged off, claiming piles of work in front of her. In fact, she spent the next fifteen minutes filing a stack of important documents in their proper folders as Cherish had taught her to do with utmost efficiency. Then she announced Councilman Morgan Player, who strolled in for a meeting smelling of smoke from one of the many cigarette breaks he took throughout the day in The Square below.

Euterpe Simon was the next to phone up, and, oh, what a welcome respite from Renza's sharp, suspicious tongue! "Just think of your day the way you think of your piano exercises," Euterpe offered in that musical voice of hers. "One note at a time, one task at a time. And before you know it, everything will be flowing beautifully—whether a playful little tune or your office routine. You'll be a winner at this just as you are every time you sit down at the piano, my dear."

"You're always so full of encouragement!" Gaylie Girl exclaimed. "But, really, I'm managing just fine at the moment. It's a snap so far." Then she remembered Lady Roth's obstreperous solo demands as well as the quarrel with Lawton Bead, and her mood immediately darkened. It hardly seemed fair to saddle such a lovely, thoughtful person as Euterpe with this pressing quandary, and she made up her mind then and there to wait and broach the subject first with Laurie Hampton, as her husband had advised. "Thanks for calling, Euterpe," she continued. "There's no metronome in front of me on my desk, but I'm definitely into a comfortable rhythm already."

By the time lunch had come and gone, Gaylie Girl was convinced that no one, not even Renza Belford at her most curmudgeonly, could possibly disturb that rhythm. But then came the unexpected long-distance call from her son Petey in Lake Forest, and her composure was manifestly shaken.

"You'll never guess, Mom," Petey began, sounding like a mischievous little boy at the other end. "Meta and I are getting married, and you're the first to know. Don't you feel special? Anyway, they say the third time's the charm—so I'm bound and determined to make this one work!"

Gaylie Girl was speechless at first, though she had her suspicions that something like this might be in the offing. Petey had met and fallen hard for Meta Belford, Renza's tall, artistic daughter, during the pre-wedding, whirlwind weekend the Nitwitts had staged to win him over—along with his sister, Amanda—to the cornucopia of eccentricity that was Second Creek. They had succeeded, of course—perhaps a little too well. Given Petey's track record of two divorces before the age of forty, however, Gaylie Girl wasn't quite as sanguine as her son about this newest alliance.

More important, she didn't relish the prospect of suddenly being related by marriage to the Nitwitts' current president and most outspoken member. All she could envision was one annoying phone call after another from Renza, who no doubt would be taking her daughter's side against Petey on every marital issue known to husband and wife. Whatever else occurred as a result of the impending union, that much would be a given.

"Well, sweetie, you and Meta have been thick as thieves up there in Lake Forest all this time, haven't you?" Gaylie Girl said, doing her best to disguise her misgivings. "My warmest congratulations are certainly in order. Have the two of you set the date yet?"

"Maybe sometime around early spring, we're thinking. No real rush, though," Petey replied. "Meta and I had such fun at your wedding to Hale that we want the Nitwitts to throw us the same sort of shindig. Think you can get together with the ladies and conjure up something like that for us? That reception tent out at Evening Shadows was beyond spectacular, especially with all those fireflies flitting around the way they did there at the end. It was like a magic show."

Gaylie Girl's smile was effortless as she recalled the mysterious display. "And the magic continued even after that, Petey. Those fireflies followed us in the honeymoon getaway car all the way up to the Memphis airport. God's escort, I like to think of it. But to answer your question, I'm sure Myrtis Troy would be more than happy to offer her Evening Shadows again, especially with that kind of lead time." She paused briefly, continuing to search for small talk. "So, Meta enjoyed her visit to Lake Forest and Lyons Manor, I take it?"

"That she did. But we've made another couple of momentous decisions. She's going to pull up stakes from St. Augustine and open a new Meta, Unlimited, Art Gallery on The Square down there in Second Creek. I know she'll just fit right in. Meanwhile, I'll be moving down myself to keep an eye on my newest corporate investment. I've decided I want to adopt a hands-on approach—maybe even get to know some of my key employees real well. Dad always told me that that was what kept Lyons Insole on the up-and-up all those years. Of course, I'll want you to help me pick out one of those beautiful historic Second Creek mansions, and I'll let Meta decorate it to her heart's content. She can hang her artwork all over the place—even over the johns in the bathrooms if she likes. Bet you thought I would never desert the old manse up here in Lake Forest, huh?"

Indeed, Gaylie Girl would never have dreamed of such a turn of events. She had considered his recent purchase of Second Creek's largest employer, Pond-Raised Catfish, to be strictly a matter of the business acumen he had inherited from his late father. She was certain he would hire a competent plant manager to run the place for him and settle for being one of those successful but absentee owners of a profitable industry.

"What's the real estate market like down there right now?" Petey continued even before Gaylie Girl could react to his many revelations.

"Oh, I'll have to ask Renza Belford's brother-in-law Paul about that. He was the one that got us such a great deal on our new place. As you know, Hale and I finished the renovation in record time and moved in right after the honeymoon. Everything couldn't look spiffier, and I've spotted more than a few fixer-uppers around town that could use some tender loving care."

"Excellent! Meta and I really want to become Second Creekers and do the whole thing up right just like you're doing with Hale!" He let out a peculiar little snicker that went on a bit longer than it needed to.

"What's so funny, son?"

"Meta's across the room on her cell phone right now

giving her mother the news. I can see the face she's making from where I'm standing."

Gaylie Girl winced ever so slightly. Oh, the inevitability of Renza! Possibly forever. "I hope it's a happy face."

"You'd have to see it to really appreciate it. At any rate, you'll probably be hearing from Mrs. Belford when everybody hangs up."

"Oh, yes. As sure as the sun rises faithfully in the east every morning, I will."

Petey indulged a hearty laugh at his mother's expense. "By the way, you call up Sis and let her know, okay?"

"I'll be sure and do that now. And we'll talk again soon. Meanwhile, I've got to get back to work. There's a meeting with Hale and the councilmen coming up in about five minutes, and I've got to get myself ready for it since I'm the one taking all the notes now."

"I know you'll do a super job with all that secretary stuff," Petey added, though it sounded to Gaylie Girl for all the world like a hurried afterthought. "I bet Hale's the best boss in the world to work with. He sure is a great stepfather."

"No complaints so far. I imagine we'll tally up the final results around the dinner table when we both get home."

❄

There was indeed no shortage of things to discuss when the Mayor and his new secretary sat down to their evening meal. The list was so long and involved that neither was paying much attention to their food, and the sautéed chicken breasts, buttered succotash, and rice and gravy that Gaylie

Girl had thrown together were lukewarm by the time they both fell to.

"What did Amanda have to say about the engagement when you phoned her up?" Mr. Choppy was saying after Gaylie Girl had brought him up to speed on Petey's exciting news.

"Surprisingly, she was in favor of it. I think she likes Meta quite a lot. Says she believes Petey's finally got it right."

"Let's all think positively, then."

Gaylie Girl shot him a skeptical glance with the suggestion of a smile there at the end. "I will, as all good mothers do where their children are concerned. But there's still going to be Renza to deal with. In fact, I've already received an earful."

Mr. Choppy took a sip of his beer and shook his head sympathetically. "Ah, yes, the feisty Miz Renza. And what did your favorite Nitwitt have to say for herself today?"

"Oh, she pretended to be happy about it all when she first came on the line, but I could sense she was just getting wound up for one doozy of a curveball. And she delivered, I have to admit. She finally got around to the subject of Petey's divorces. 'They're just out there hanging, aren't they? And not like ornaments on a Christmas tree,' she said in that syrupy judgmental tone of hers. I just took a deep breath and let that slide."

"Wise move."

"Of course, she wasn't finished. She kept talking about the two of them moving down here together without the benefit of marriage right away. I pointed out that Petey was over forty, and Meta had a big toehold on her thirties. They hardly needed adult supervision and would certainly resent ours. Finally, I changed the subject to our Caroling in The Square project, but I probably would have been better off sticking to Renza's fretting about our children getting married."

"Why? What happened?"

Gaylie Girl pushed her rice and gravy around with her fork for a second or two and then managed a plaintive little sigh. "She's on Denver Lee's case like you wouldn't believe. It seems Denver Lee wants to host our next Nitwitts' meeting and has been calling everyone up telling them about a big surprise she's got that will make our Caroling in The Square project even more appealing. Although I'm not crazy about Denver Lee's house, I'm perfectly willing to show up there and listen to whatever she has to say. But Renza is completely territorial as usual and dead set against it. *Relentless* is her middle name."

Then Gaylie Girl sat back in her chair and quietly put down her fork. "But enough about all my Nitwitt business. I'm sure we'll work it out. What's the Mayor's official verdict on his new secretary? How did she perform as his Gaylie Girl Friday on her first day?"

Mr. Choppy matched her playful gaze, smiled, and cleared his throat as if he were about to read a proclamation. "The Mayor is officially impressed. Cherish Hempstead would be impressed, too. You did just great, sweetheart. Right after you left the room, all the councilmen commented on how well you kept up and read everything back perfectly.

Not to mention, you got all my messages straight, and I'm sure you filed everything properly."

"So you'd call me a keeper?"

Mr. Choppy leaned toward her as they gave each other a peck on the lips. "From the first time I laid eyes on you in the Piggly Wiggly fifty-something years ago."

Four

Blame It on the Bossa Nova

espite Renza's ongoing protestations, the next official meeting of the Nitwitts was definitely going to take place on a late October Saturday afternoon at the house that Eustice McQueen had built long decades ago for his ever-faithful wife. All the others were simply too curious to ignore Denver Lee's insistent promise of a first-rate surprise to boost the success of their Caroling in The Square event on Christmas Eve. In fact, everyone except Renza had been wagering among themselves behind the scenes as to what that surprise might turn out to be. The Nitwitt that came closest to the truth, however distant that guess might be, would walk away with the kitty.

Gaylie Girl had offered the notion that it might some-how be connected to one of Euss McQueen's inventions, hidden away in some closet all these years and now to be revealed in all its glory or probable lack thereof; Laurie had put her money on Denver Lee's never-realized ambition to be a trained singer dating all the way back to her college days at Ole Miss; always the party planner, Myrtis leaned toward some sort of special reception that Denver Lee might spearhead either before or after the caroling; Novie fell back on her obsession with travel and suggested that Denver Lee would propose a nice trip for the choir that did the best job—upon which the Nitwitts would vote, of course; while Euterpe's entry wafted in straight out of left field. She claimed to have dreamed what Denver Lee was actually up to when images of people engaged in some sort of exotic dance step came to her in her sleep.

"It was my interpretation that Denver Lee was conducting an orchestra. I could see the baton swinging from side to side, but all these people couldn't seem to stop this fevered dancing," Euterpe had elaborated with each of the other bettors in turn over the phone. "So I'll just take a wild stab and say she's going to go with a marathon Christmas dance in The Square after the caroling is over. I've been right to trust my dreams so many times in the past."

It had fallen to secretary Novie to record and date each of the guesses and note the amount of each bet to keep the competition on the straight and narrow. So it was she who took the liberty of revealing all the club shenanigans to Denver Lee in a polite phone call the evening before their meeting.

"We Nitwitts are a creative bunch, I have to admit," Denver Lee responded, utterly delighted by the news of the contest. "But you'll get no hint from me as to who might be on the right track. That is, if anyone is at all." Then, a sour note: "Is Renza coming? She's made me well aware of her opinion in the matter."

"She didn't much like being overruled by the rest of us," Novie admitted. "But she's likely as not to appear anyway. She's still entitled to preside over all of our meetings no matter where they're held. I rather think she'll get over herself and show."

"Well, I'd hate to see her miss a treat, Novie. This may be remembered as my finest hour."

❄

Gaylie Girl was surprised to find that she was the last to enter the foyer of Denver Lee's house right at two o'clock Saturday afternoon. It was totally out of character for every Nitwitt to be on time for one of their meetings. Usually, someone would develop car trouble and have to be picked up at the last minute, or thought they could get away with running to the grocery store for a few staples and then invariably bump into an old friend they hadn't seen "for ages." For this meeting, however, every Nitwitt—including a reluctant President Renza—was already enjoying her customary libation or nibbling at something decorative and savory on a cracker as Gaylie Girl greeted and joined them with gusto.

"Welcome to our First Lady!" Denver Lee exclaimed, warmly embracing Gaylie Girl when the others had finally relinquished her. "The gang's all here. Now run and go fix yourself a little happy and hurry on back. I can't wait to tell all of you what this is about."

"After you've allowed me to open the meeting, I presume," a kibitzing Renza interjected none too amicably.

It was only after returning from fetching herself a Bloody Mary in the kitchen that Gaylie Girl noticed how much open space there was surrounding the group. That enormous whatchamacallit Euss McQueen had saddled Denver Lee with since long before he had left the planet was no longer in evidence, leaving plenty of room for all the Nitwitts to maneuver socially.

"I hope you don't mind my asking, but what happened to that wheelie-looking thing in the center of the room?" Gaylie Girl said after downing one of the olives that was floating between her ice cubes.

Denver Lee quickly lowered her voice as if passing along a well-kept secret. "I had my handyman lug it upstairs to the attic, where it will now gather dust judiciously forever and ever. No more paying the maid to clean it every week while suffering through all her strange looks."

"Well, good for you," Gaylie Girl added. "And by the way, what the hell *was* that?"

Denver Lee enjoyed a prolonged laugh, her generous girth shaking with delight.

"I'll tell you what I've been telling the others over the years. I have no idea what it was. I don't even think Euss knew what it was. My suspicion has always been that it was just something that got the better of him, and he couldn't let go of it. Maybe it was a crazy reflection of all the whirligigs and doodads he had running around inside his head. But that's in the past—over and done with." Denver Lee turned and gestured dramatically toward a far corner of the room.

"Over there is the wheelie-looking thing's most practical and melodious replacement and the reason for this meeting." She spotted a spoon on a nearby hors d'oeuvres tray, chimed her drink several times, and raised her voice. "Ladies! Fellow Nitwitts!" She waited briefly until all the chatter had died down. "If you will all direct your attention to my new organ in the corner of the room. I know some of you have been asking me about it from the moment you walked in, but I wanted to wait until everyone was here to unveil my surprise."

Renza and proper protocol were not to be ignored, of course. "Then may I now open our meeting?"

"By all means," Denver Lee replied, remaining unruffled throughout Renza's rote declaration of club business officially under way.

Everyone quickly gathered around the organ, murmuring pleasantries while sipping their drinks, and Gaylie Girl was particularly complimentary. "It certainly does something for the room. I know what a difference my grand piano makes now that it's at home in our drawing room on North Bayou Avenue. Since I didn't know how to play it before, it did nothing but sit there and soak up furniture polish all those years up in Lake Forest."

"This one's a beauty, isn't it? A Hammond with a Leslie speaker," Denver Lee continued. "That may or may not mean something to any of you, but this is a state-of-the-art instrument. I can do the most fabulous things with it, and I can't wait to show you all."

Renza resumed her contentious line of questioning. "So we've come here this afternoon for an organ recital? This is your surprise? Horse apples! Now really, Denver Lee, what does this have to do with Caroling in The Square? We still have serious matters to decide."

"If you'll just let me finish explaining, everything will become clear. You see, my piano lessons have been going so well, I decided to take things to the next level by purchasing this organ. I've always wanted one, and now I can actually play, thanks to the expert instruction Euterpe's been giving all of us."

The town's Mistress of the Scales held tightly on to Pan with both hands as she shifted him from his recumbent spot just below her shoulder. Then she acknowledged Denver Lee's praise with a little bow and whispered to her most precious pet. "There, there. Mommy just wanted to make sure her baby didn't fall."

"I can appreciate this mutual admiration society the two of you have got going as much as the next person," Renza put in, "but I'm still waiting for the payoff. What does this organ of yours have to do with our Christmas Eve event? You're not thinking of dragging it down to The Square to accompany all those choirs, are you? That would be one mighty damn long extension cord. Besides, it was my understanding that all these carols were supposed to be sung a cappella."

Denver Lee ignored Renza's prattle and made a big to-do of taking her seat on the bench. "If that's what all the choirmasters prefer, then so be it. Euterpe says some of them might prefer a bit of background music. So I was going to offer to make up a mix tape accompaniment for any of the choirs that wanted to play it back while they're singing up on the balconies. My stomp box can duplicate tons of delicate, Christmasy sounds—like harps and flutes and even the jingling of bells."

Gaylie Girl immediately verbalized the question that was on everyone's mind. "What on earth is a stomp box?"

"Oh, that's the buzzword for the effects pedal. I manipulate it with my feet, which I will soon demonstrate. I thought I'd play 'It Came Upon the Midnight Clear.' That's always been my absolute favorite, and it's sure to be one the choirs will choose." After turning on the power, Denver Lee began walking everyone through the procedure out loud. "Next, I press the rhythm key in play mode—"

An insistent, exotic beat suddenly exploded from somewhere within the organ, and Denver Lee's language took a salty turn. "Well, dammit to Sam! I pressed the wrong rhythm pattern for playback! Somehow I've turned on the bossa nova—and the fast version at that!"

"No harm done, I'm sure," Gaylie Girl said. "Just change it to angelic sounds or something churchy like that. You implied you had tons to choose from."

Denver Lee fumbled around for a few seconds, but the bossa nova beat would simply not back down. "The key seems to be stuck. Now how in the world did that happen? Let me go have a look at the manual." For the next few minutes, Denver Lee thumbed through the brochure she had retrieved from inside the bench, spent some time poring over one particular page, and then gave a resolute little sigh. "I know what. I'll just shut everything down and start from the beginning. As Gaylie Girl put it—there's no harm done!"

But when Denver Lee tried the sequence again, the

bossa nova beat remained loudly intact. "I guess I'll just have to call up that technician and get him to come down from Memphis to look at it. I haven't had the least bit of trouble with it until now. But I was careful to pay for an extended warranty. There's probably something very simple I'm not doing. Oh, foot! Everything was just perfect when I practiced last night."

Despite her frustrations, Denver Lee tackled the first few bars of "It Came Upon the Midnight Clear" anyway, even if the end result was more like Carnival in Rio than Christmas in Second Creek. Or anywhere else, for that matter. Meanwhile, some of the Nitwitts decided to make the best of it, being the good-time girls full of giggles and snickers and liquor that they were.

"Please keep on playing, Denver Lee," Myrtis begged. "It sounds a bit perverse, but I kinda like it anyway. By the way, would someone care to dance with me? This reminds me of the time back in the day when Raymond brought home 'Blame It on the Bossa Nova' from his record shop. We both loved Eydie Gormé and that big clear voice of hers at the time, and that was one of her biggest hits in the early sixties—if I remember correctly. In fact, I still have the original forty-five in my back porch collection, and I can't resist giving it a spin on the old turntable every now and then."

Denver Lee momentarily stopped her recital to turn and stare Myrtis down, but she couldn't keep a straight face for long. Finally, she gave in to the absurdity of it all and continued with the south-of-the-border rendition of her favorite Christmas carol. In rapid succession, Novie decided to join the fray and fulfilled Myrtis's request for a dance partner;

Laurie and Gaylie Girl decided to try their best bossa nova steps together; and Euterpe lowered Pan to the floor to take the briefest of turns with Renza, who had finally given herself permission to unwind and stop being such a pain in the rear about every little thing. Even with all the added space, however, there was a collision or two, followed by a few impulsive partner switches in hopes of smoother results.

Eventually, they all had their fill of cavorting at about the same time Denver Lee grew tired of producing such unorthodox, surreal sounds. No matter which Christmas carol she summoned from her repertoire—"Away in a Manger," "O Holy Night," "The Little Drummer Boy," or "Greensleeves"—they each had that frenetic bossa nova beat beneath them. It was way past time for the Nitwitts to catch their breath with fresh cocktails and address the more serious club matters at hand.

Gaylie Girl was the first to update progress on Caroling in The Square from her perch on one of the sofas. "I spoke again with Lawton Bead of St. Luke's just yesterday, and he informs me that Lady Roth is still bugging him around the clock about that solo business. We all know how impossible she can be. But Mr. Bead insists that she simply cannot come close to carrying a tune. It would be an unmitigated disaster and even cruel to put the spotlight on her. He's at his wit's end, so I think it's going to be up to us to figure out a way to placate Lady Roth before she makes big trouble for all of us." Gaylie Girl gestured broadly to where Laurie was sitting across the room. "Therefore, I think we should call upon the Nitwitts' most astute, veteran problem-solver for the way out of this maze—the one and only Mrs. Powell Hampton."

Laurie gave her a sideways glance, her smile projecting just the appropriate touch of resignation. "I should know by now that it's always up to me."

"And why not?" Gaylie Girl declared. "You found a way to keep Lady Roth under control during all those waltzing at the Piggly Wiggly antics last summer. And then you were absolutely brilliant the way you convinced her to portray Susan B. Anthony during my husband's election campaign. She would have been a genuine liability otherwise, phoning up people and telling them how they should vote. Or else. That alone could have swayed the election for Mr. Floyce. Let's face it—Lady Roth is best taken in thimble-sized doses."

"Gaylie Girl is right, Laurie," Renza added. "You know good and well that you're the only one who can come up with a solution to this."

Laurie accepted the challenge with a nod of her head and then said: "I'll get Powell to put on his thinking cap, too. Between the two of us, I'm betting that we zero in on something that'll work."

Gaylie Girl gave a sudden gasp. "Oh, speaking of betting, shouldn't we decide which one of us came closest to winning that money we had on the line? It came to me just this second who I think the winner should be."

A wave of bewilderment swept across the room, but Gaylie Girl was determined to enlighten everyone. "Think about it now. We just finished all that frantic dancing, and

Denver Lee's rhythm key or whatever you want to call it got stuck. Isn't it obvious who called this one? Or got close enough."

Then Novie gasped, too. "I'll be damned!"

Renza folded her arms, indulging one of her more potent frowns. "Well, I don't have the degree in sleuthing that you two apparently do. Stop all this theatrical, I-know-whodunit gasping and let me in on it!"

"Don't you see? Euterpe's dream was all around it!" Gaylie Girl exclaimed. "Denver Lee's surprise had to do with music, of course, and there she was conducting an orchestra in the dream. Not to mention all that furious dancing that wouldn't stop. We were pretty much a passel of bossa nova demons there at the end, weren't we?" Gaylie Girl sank back against the sofa with an incredulous expression on her face. "Now how in the world did you manage to conjure all that up, Euterpe? I've positively got goose bumps."

"How shall I put this?" Euterpe began, her tone very measured. "I never know when something is going to be leaked to me through my dreams. Because I firmly believe the universe works just that way. We only have to be open to all the helpful voices that are out there speaking to us. Perhaps they're angels, or perhaps something more momentous."

Gaylie Girl was nodding thoughtfully. "That certainly is a Christmasy sort of message."

Then Novie spoke up in her official capacity. "Ultimate sources aside, is everyone agreed that the kitty concerning Denver Lee's surprise should go to Euterpe?"

Oddly, the only dissenter was Euterpe herself. "To be fair, my prediction was that Denver Lee would have everyone participating in some sort of marathon dance competition in The Square. Instead, she wanted to provide a musical accompaniment to any choir that was interested."

"A mere technicality!" Gaylie Girl exclaimed. "You had elements that were close enough, and let's face it—this isn't rocket science."

Euterpe thought for a while as she gently stroked her Pan. "Very well, then. But I will accept the money on one condition. That you let me donate it right back to our slush fund for our next project."

"That's certainly in the spirit of the upcoming season," Novie said. But she was quick to point her index finger at everyone else in turn. "Although we all came off pretty cheap with our bets. There's barely enough money in the kitty to buy one of us a good dinner at the Victorian Tea Room."

"Just how cheap were we?" Euterpe wanted to know. "I know I threw in ten dollars, and I think that's a decent amount."

Novie drew herself up, but the air she exhaled immediately after had the effect of an indictment. "You'll be pleased to hear that your ten bucks officially made you Mrs. Moneybags among us. If everyone had been at least that generous—and I'm not excusing myself here—we'd be talking about rustling up a banquet somewhere. Unfortunately, our grand total came to only twenty-three dollars and seventy-eight cents."

"You're right," Gaylie Girl added. "That *is* dinner for one at the Tea Room—without an appetizer or dessert, of course."

Euterpe shrugged it off with her customary wit. "To the

slush fund with my fortune, then! Isn't it written somewhere in our bylaws that no Nitwitt shall ever dine publicly without benefit of at least four courses?"

"No. But it's not a bad idea," Novie added, as everyone enjoyed a good laugh and the issue of the kitty was put to bed.

Despite the unexpected mechanical problems with her new instrument, Denver Lee remained upbeat and put the exclamation point on the proceedings. "I just want everyone to know that I still fully intend to offer that accompaniment tape to any of the choirmasters that might be interested. That is, if I can get Xavier Cugat and his orchestra out of my stomp box."

❄

Laurie had just finished summarizing for Powell the gist of what had transpired at Denver Lee's meeting earlier in the day. They were sitting across from each other at the kitchen table, just beginning another of her gourmet dinners, and he couldn't stop snickering between bites.

"I can't get the part about that rhythm glitch out of my mind," Powell told her. "I would have given anything to be there, if for no other reason than to show all of you how to do the bossa nova up right!"

"Yes, I'm sure you could have done just that," Laurie said, feeling as if he were being too cavalier about the entire business. "Once a ballroom dance instructor, always a ballroom dance instructor." She didn't bother to disguise the slight irritation in her voice.

"Come on, now. You Nitwitts always manage to put yourselves in the damnedest situations, and you know it. Hey, the entire club deliberately chose to waltz down the produce aisle with me at the old Piggly Wiggly. And you all took on the Hokey Pokey at Gaylie Girl's Labor Day wedding without batting an eyelash. You have to know by now that the Nitwitts hold a special place in my heart. Especially the one I'm gazing fondly at right this instant."

Laurie swallowed a bite of her stuffed pepper and then gave him a flirtatious glance. "Okay, okay. I'm a sucker for sweet talk. It's just that there's something I haven't told you yet. I was the unanimous choice of the girls to come up with another of my brainstorms to keep Lady Roth out of our hair, and I'm afraid I might be running dry."

"What's the dear ossified thing up to now?"

Laurie took a sip of wine for courage and began explaining Lady Roth's ongoing tiff with Lawton Bead. "Bottom line here is that she sings even worse than she dances, and we all remember what a ham she was hoofing it at the Piggly Wiggly last summer. But this is supposed to be Christmas, not Halloween or the Miss Delta Floozie Contest. Mr. Bead assures us that the second she opens up her mouth, people will run out of The Square as fast as their legs will carry them. And then some."

Powell looked amused at first. Then he sat back in his chair, briefly thinking things over while stretching his long legs under the table. "I can't imagine you running dry of ideas. It would be totally out of character."

Laurie looked sheepish, averting her eyes. "There are only

so many times a thirsty person can go to the well. Besides, I told all the girls you'd be happy to help me come up with something brilliant. You know—two heads, et cetera."

"I think you ladies are going to have to admit your first male member if this keeps up. Seems I'm in on everything eventually, whether I want to be or not. I'm already working with Renza, Denver Lee, and Myrtis on the publicity campaign, as you know, and now this."

He paused to take a healthy swig of his wine. "Oh, I meant to tell you—we've just received a commitment from WHBQ in Memphis to bring a crew down and cover the event on Christmas Eve. Got the e-mail just before you got home. We're going to get that helpful television coverage again, just like we did for all the waltzing at the Piggly Wiggly."

Laurie brought her hands together prayerfully and rested them under her chin. "That's wonderful news. Have you told Gaylie Girl yet? She'll be thrilled to pieces, of course."

"I thought I'd let you do the honors."

"You lovely man—letting me be the bearer of such good tidings. Are you sure you really want to be a Nitwitt, though? I think you may be missing the all-important gossip gene."

He threw back his head and laughed. "Among other things. For now, just let me kibitz brilliantly on the side and lead the occasional Nitwitt around the dance floor."

On that note, they opted for a prolonged session of brainstorming, eating the rest of their food largely in silence. They were almost like a couple of cows chewing their cud. Every once in a while, there were barely audible grunts in place or the customary soft lowing. For all intents and purposes, however, they appeared to be stymied. They could tell just by exchanging frustrated glances that nothing remotely suitable was coming to mind.

"Have we both finally run dry?" Laurie said later over their coffee and crème brûlée.

"Looks that way. I don't see how we can satisfy Lady Roth if we deny her the spotlight she always craves. She's like a veritable barracuda once she goes after something."

Suddenly, the spark that Laurie had needed this time around surfaced, and her eyes were flashing as she dramatically pointed her finger at Powell. "That's it! What you just said! Say it again!"

He put down his coffee cup and looked at her sideways. "Uh, I have no idea what I'm looking for."

"Never mind. I've got it now. You mentioned denying Lady Roth the spotlight. But that's exactly what we shouldn't do. We must let her have yet another fifteen minutes of fame."

He was squinting now. "I'm afraid I don't understand. We inflict that voice on the general public?"

"No, no, no. It was the word *spotlight* that gave me the idea about the same time I remembered the Christmas cards I've ordered for us this year. If we could convince Lady Roth to portray Susan B. Anthony during Mr. Choppy's campaign, I know she'll agree to what I have in mind," Laurie explained further. "But I'd like for you to come along with Gaylie Girl and myself when we make our pitch. After all, we're the three most compelling people she knows."

Powell listened intently as Laurie fed him all the minute details, nodding enthusiastically there at the end. "I don't see why it wouldn't work. It accomplishes everything in one fell swoop."

Laurie could hardly keep still, savoring the smugness that had enveloped her like a long, warm soak in the tub. "Lady Roth is about nothing if not getting as much attention as possible."

"Do you think we should use a special setting? Maybe invite her over here for one of your special dinners to really set the hook?"

Laurie reviewed everything and shook her head emphatically. "No, I think a reservation at the Victorian Tea Room might be the better ploy. I don't want to be distracted by slaving over a hot stove and putting things on the table at the last minute. I know I make cooking look like a breeze, but it's a diligent and time-consuming affair. Plus, you know how I always manage to burn the bread. It's my one failing over the years. I just turn my head for a second, and I've got carbon on my hands. No, let's put the food and wine in Vester Morrow's capable hands, and the three of us will triple-team Lady Roth with our irresistible words."

And with that, Laurie shot up from her chair and headed over to the phone.

"Gaylie Girl is just going to fall out when she hears what we've come up with. Not to mention all that good news about the television coverage. I can't see anything to stop us now. I predict our Caroling in The Square will be a smash success!"

Five

O Broadway Star
of Bethlehem

Vester Morrow was in rare form as he continued to fawn over his most anticipated diners on this chilly November Saturday evening. The moment Laurie and Powell, Gaylie Girl and Lady Roth appeared at the door for their eight o'clock reservation at the Victorian Tea Room, his behavior had shifted into an even higher gear of fastidiousness. He had ushered them across the floor of chatting diners and tucked them away into a cozy, fern-potted corner with an enormous stained glass window for a backdrop. Now he intended to wait on them himself. Not even the most experienced of his waiters would do for this high-profile party of four. But first—a bit of seamless prying with no one the worse for wear.

"It isn't every night I have the privilege of hosting the

Mayor's wife, the town's most elegant dancing couple, and, of course, the nonpareil Lady Roth at the same table," the tuxedoed Vester was saying, swaying this way and that and gesturing broadly all the while. "And is our fabulous Mayor Dunbar so busy watching over our fair Second Creek that he couldn't join you?"

"How perceptive of you, Vester!" Gaylie Girl exclaimed. "He did bring some important work home with him, as it happens. He's working on a bond issue—The Pet Pothole Project, as he likes to call it. If he's able to get Second Creekers to pass it, we'll get a much-needed overlay of all the downtown streets. But he definitely asked to be remembered to you and your divine cuisine meanwhile."

"Ah, each to his own purpose in time. Mayor Dunbar to mind the potholes, and Vester Morrow to mind the pot roast. Perhaps we'll see him another evening, then. I know with that enormous sweet tooth of his, he won't be able to stay away from us very long. He's never been able to resist our warm walnut-pecan pie à la mode."

"Oh, don't you dare let me forget," Gaylie Girl added, touching a finger to her temple smartly and then patting her perfect coiffure. "I'm to bring home a healthy slice in a to-go box. Minus the à la mode, of course. But don't you worry. He'll still get that big sugar high as he burns the midnight oil."

"Duly noted. Our naked pie should do the trick quite nicely," Vester said, his pencil immediately poised for cocktail orders.

A minute or so later, he was reviewing the instructions for the bartender out loud. "Now, let's see—a Manhattan straight up for Mrs. Dunbar and don't forget the cherry, a glass each of our own delicious Delta muscadine wine for Mr. and Mrs. Hampton, and for you, Lady Roth, a dirty Gibson with not one, not two, but three pearl onions. Do I have everything straight?"

Lady Roth immediately delivered a monologue in her barking mode even as everyone else was nodding pleasantly. "Just be sure you don't skimp on those onions! Oh, and I forgot to tell you to put them on one of those little plastic swords that you find in all those fussy umbrella drinks. I don't like my garbage resting on the bottom like so much Mississippi mud. The way I've devised for drinking a Gibson is a very important ritual to me, and I simply must have the convenience of that little skewer. I start out with an onion just before I take my first sip, then have a second halfway through, and finally—en garde—the one that's soaked to the gills after my very last drop."

Vester appeared to be writing an essay on his ordering pad and mumbled out loud while casting surreptitious glances at Lady Roth.... *The ... one ... that's ... soaked ... to ... the ... gills ... after ... the ... very ... last ... drop.* Then he straightened his tall frame and crisply bowed his head. "I'll run this order right over to the bartender and get your very special evening here at the Tea Room under way posthaste."

Lady Roth continued her running commentary the instant Vester was out of earshot. "You would think he knew why we were all here the way he was carrying on so. Not that he doesn't usually flit around the premises that same way. I get exhausted just watching him. But did he somehow hear through the grapevine that my role in the upcoming

Caroling in The Square on Christmas Eve is finally to be revealed to me tonight?"

Laurie stepped up with the perfect retort. "When we called up for the reservation, Lady Roth, we told Vester that we expected the best of everything the Tea Room has to offer. Nothing less would do on this momentous occasion. But we didn't reveal anything more than that."

Lady Roth appeared supremely pleased but did not maintain that demeanor very long. "I will admit that I like your approach, dear. This keeping-me-in-suspense business has its charms, I suppose. I enjoy parlor games as much as the next person. But by the time I've gobbled up that third cocktail onion, I expect to have every little detail of my Christmas carol assignment under my belt."

While Laurie and Powell exchanged hasty glances, it was Gaylie Girl who seized the moment, keeping the mood upbeat. "That will happen shortly, and we're certain you'll be pleased with the very special role we've created for you."

❅

It was a few minutes past the third cocktail onion, and Lady Roth was still trying to digest everything she'd just been told. Since Laurie was the one who'd been appointed the official messenger, it was she who was now handling Lady Roth's reaction with kid gloves.

"I just remembered how pleased you were to portray Susan B. Anthony during the recent mayoral election," Laurie was saying. "No one could have done it better—your historically accurate costume and demeanor were dead-on. It was a role played to perfection and with passion to boot. As a result, I truly think you got the women of Second Creek excited about taking part in the process. Think of this new assignment in the same vein. I'm sure you'll be an inspiration to everyone."

"That's all well and good," Lady Roth answered, staring down into the bottom of her empty Gibson glass as if she had just received a "bad news" telegram. "But the fact remains that I shall not be singing during this caroling event. That is what you just said to me, isn't it?"

"Yes, I did say that. But in this case, I believe silence is golden. What could be more dramatic than you portraying the Star of Bethlehem on the widow's walk atop the courthouse? As a practical matter, you'd be too high up for your voice to be heard, but everyone in and all around The Square below will see you. We'll have a special spotlight rigged up for you on one of the balconies across the way. You're certain to be the center of attention throughout the entire event."

There was a hopeful pause from Lady Roth during which her wrinkled features softened somewhat. "But what sort of costume shall I design? How on earth do you make someone resemble the Star of Bethlehem? Susan B. Anthony was nothing in comparison to this. I simply went to the library and Lovita Grubbs helped me look her up."

Laurie had rehearsed every possible response with her Powell standing in as Lady Roth and had her reply at the ready. "After some consideration, our idea to suggest to you was a long, flowing dress made of a heavy white fabric of some kind. Floor-length with lots of folds and perhaps gold sequins for accents. You'll want to keep warm up there if the weather isn't cooperating. And then we envisioned some sort of brilliant gold headgear in the shape of a star. Lightweight, of course. We don't want you losing your balance and tumbling over the railing up there. We want you portraying a star, not a comet."

"Are you implying I am unsteady on my feet? I know I have a touch of arthritis, but I get around quite handily, I'll have you know. I've never taken a pratfall in my entire life."

Gaylie Girl cheerfully chimed in. "That was the last thing on our minds, we can assure you. Think of what everyone will be saying about you, Lady Roth. What dedication to the spirit of the season to portray such a glorious symbol atop the greatest of Second Creek's buildings! You'll be towering over everything—keeping watch over your flock just as the shepherds once did on that eventful night long ago!"

An even longer pause suggested that Lady Roth might finally be buying into the scheme. But, no, another objection. "Suppose it's not just cold? Suppose we're having one of our unpredictable Second Creek storms?"

This time it was Powell who spoke up with a conspiratorial expression on his face. "In that case, all bets are off anyway. We'd have to cancel the event, God forbid. But for anything short of that, you'll put on your trusty long johns beneath that dress. No one will ever be the wiser. And since when has a veteran Second Creeker like yourself ever allowed the weather to keep her from her appointed rounds?"

There were hopeful smiles all around the table, and Lady Roth quickly responded. "I have to admit this is just the sort of unforgettable moment I've always tried to achieve in my career. But I still wish I would be allowed to sing. Couldn't they rig up a microphone for me up there somehow?"

"Not easily, I don't believe," Powell said. "I briefly looked into it, and Mr. Choppy said he doubted it could be done without taking some risks. You never want to take chances with jury-rigging things."

In fact, neither Powell nor anyone else had looked into the matter. But they had all huddled about anticipating the detours and dead ends of Lady Roth's circuitous thought processes. Their conclusion was that a firmly discouraging position from the outset would be advantageous to bringing her aboard.

"Let me think on it throughout the meal," Lady Roth proclaimed. "A few more questions will no doubt occur to me."

❄

Lady Roth had just downed the last of her stuffed portabella mushroom appetizer, along with the third pearl onion of her second dirty Gibson. She was clearly in her element now, having waved to a few people she had recognized at nearby tables, smiled obsequiously in their general direction, and then given her dining partners hushed summaries of their deepest, darkest secrets.

Did they all know, for instance, that Adelia Marlowe Standard over there underneath the ceiling fan had once been nearly convicted of embezzlement when she had briefly worked for a bank down in Yazoo City before she was married? Why, it was rumored that her wealthy father had paid a pretty penny to get her off scot-free. More's the pity, however, he had been unable to rescue her from bad taste since that hat she was wearing this evening looked like it had been decorated with spoiled supermarket produce. Now, what on earth could she have been thinking?

And were they aware that the overdressed Renette Pauly Pierce in the opposite corner of the room had once tried out at Radio City Music Hall eons ago but was told her legs were far too spindly to look good doing fan kicks? And that the reason she always wore those floor-length dresses even to this very day and on this very evening was to hide her offensive chicken legs from the eyes of the general public? Lady Roth went on and on, eliciting only patient nods and forced smiles from Gaylie Girl, Laurie, and Powell all the while.

When Lady Roth had finally concluded her scathing review of much of the Tea Room's clientele, she decided to embark upon another of her famous tangents. But at least it was relevant to the task at hand. "I couldn't help but wonder how you came up with the idea of juxtaposing the Star of Bethlehem with someone such as myself, Laurie. It's not like you can run across that sort of thing as an adorable piece of fluff in the latest issue of *Better Homes and Gardens*."

Having just finished off Vester's signature salad of arugula, red onion, mandarin orange slices, and slivered almonds with a balsamic vinaigrette dressing, Laurie was fueled for battle in proper gourmet fashion. "You're right about that, of course, but my inspiration was rather mundane as these things go. I just happened to remember the specially designed Christmas cards I had ordered this year from one of those catalogs, and the focus was the Star of Bethlehem. Several of us had been wondering all along how to create a spotlight role for you, and everything just fell into place from that point on."

"You never know how, when, or where one of Laurie's schemes is going to pop up," Powell added, nodding affectionately in his wife's direction. "She can sometimes seem to be all over the map, but she never gets lost."

Then Gaylie Girl joined the triple team. "I truly believe that featuring you as the Star of Bethlehem puts the spotlight on you far more effectively than a mere choir solo would."

Lady Roth carefully adjusted her turban and then leaned in, lowering her voice. "Of course, you all know my most heartfelt ambition was to sing and dance and act on Broadway as Vocifera P. Forest. I wanted the biggest stage possible for my talents, but, alas, it was just never meant to be. So perhaps settling for staging on the widow's walk atop the courthouse shouldn't be all that much of a stretch for me. There have been worse venues in my life. My entire marriage to Heath Vanderlith Roth, for instance. Believe me, you didn't want tickets to that."

"Then does this mean you accept our Christmas Eve vision for you?" Gaylie Girl asked. Her tone was nothing if not hopeful, while both Laurie and Powell looked as if they were waiting for the opening of an envelope at an awards ceremony.

"Let me enjoy the rest of my dinner first. I shall inform all of you of my decision over dessert."

❄

A third Gibson and an expertly prepared entrée of grilled mahimahi with a crawfish cream sauce had Lady Roth letting down her hair, even though she kept her turban rigidly in place.

"I don't know when I've enjoyed food or company more," she was saying. "I do spend an inordinate amount of time alone out at my Cypress Knees. It's difficult to have stimulating conversation with a roomful of family heirlooms, particularly when most of them came from Heath's family. His mother, Julianna, was insufferable. She practically claimed that every stick of furniture they owned came over on the *Mayflower*. Of course, I don't know how she would know something like that unless she was there, helping them unload it all, the old relic!"

Gaylie Girl quickly swallowed a bite of her medium-rare steak and decided to run with the opening. "You must come into The Square more often, Lady Roth. Now that I'm a working girl, I'm always looking for someone to have lunch with downtown. Hale is so frequently tied up with his duties or the councilmen that we rarely get to eat together. But you and I could be girlfriends together over soup and salad somewhere if you'd like. All you have to do is give me a little notice so I can square it with my schedule."

The ploy clearly caught Lady Roth off guard. "That's most gracious of you, Gaylie Girl. I'd have to classify it as being very much in the approaching Christmas spirit. But are you sure you know what you're letting yourself in for?"

"As the First Lady of Second Creek, I can honestly say

that I do. Part of my job description, informal as it may be, is to interact with Second Creekers in meaningful ways. Only then can I really feel a part of the community. That's why I came up with Caroling in The Square on Christmas Eve."

"Well said, of course. But despite what all of you probably think, I do know that I can be a pain in the derrière."

"Why, nothing of the kind!" Gaylie Girl insisted, though her words were strictly a reflex action.

"You're just being tactful." Lady Roth paused for an introspective chuckle and surveyed the table. "The truth is, once I started being deliberately difficult all the time, I discovered my brain wouldn't allow me to back out of the agreement. I read an article in the dentist's office once about synapses and wiring and all that sort of clinical stuff, and it made perfect sense to me. At this late stage in my life, I don't think I'm capable of learning a new language of behavior."

She cackled with an edgy robustness that suggested the Gibsons were taking their toll, even on a full stomach. "Now this is priceless. I wish I had a mirror to hold up to all your faces. You'd think I'd just discovered the meaning of life and passed it along. I must try this again sometime. Lowering my guard, I mean."

Though truly nonplussed, Gaylie Girl somehow found the right words. "You can always be candid with us, Lady Roth. Speaking of which, have you reached a decision yet?"

"Ah, but I haven't had my dessert, and I do think I've left room. Vester is such a naughty boy tempting us with all these calories the way he does. We must summon him to the table at once for the indulgent finale."

❄

Warm walnut-pecan pie seemed to be the most popular choice when Vester took the dessert order a short time later. There was, of course, the piece that Gaylie Girl would be taking home to Mr. Choppy for a treat, but Powell and Lady Roth each opted for a slice of their own then and there.

"I like to say that we stole the recipe for it from Mount Olympus," Vester commented with a playful wink. "Zeus, but it's wickedly good!"

Laurie managed a polite smile. "That it is, but I think I'll settle for a bite of Powell's tonight. Otherwise, just decaf for me with cream and sugar."

It did not take long for Vester to reappear with the dessert course and make his usual tactful exit. Then followed the moment of truth—inelegant and rambling as it turned out to be.

"What the hell!" Lady Roth began. "Or should I say, 'Why the hell not?' Yes, why should I not grab the Star of Bethlehem by the horns and wrestle it to the ground?" She paused long enough to roll her eyes a couple of times. "I realize that my metaphor was probably mixed. But then I always like things well mixed. Which reminds me—they do a first-rate dirty Gibson here, don't they?"

As it was completely unclear to whom Lady Roth was addressing the comment, and the others were occupied with their coffee and pie, Gaylie Girl decided to field the question. "Judging by the Manhattan I sipped and savored, I'd have to agree. But just to clarify—am I hearing that you want to be our Star of Bethlehem?"

"You hear correctly. If I can't shine on Broadway, I can sure as hell shine on top of the courthouse. And I am a widow, so I have every right to walk the widow's walk." Obviously amused with herself, Lady Roth produced more raucous laughter. "And talk the widow's talk, for that matter."

"Right on both counts," Gaylie Girl added. "And we're all absolutely delighted to hear that you'll be gracing our little production come Christmas Eve. Your star will never shine brighter, I'm sure."

❄

It was nearly eleven o'clock, and Mr. Choppy had just finished the last of his warmed-up walnut-pecan pie and pushed back from the kitchen table. Meanwhile, Gaylie Girl had contented herself with watching him indulge while sipping her coffee and bringing him up to date on the evening at the Victorian Tea Room.

"Of course, you and Miz Laurie planned everything perfectly," Mr. Choppy commented at one point. "The way to Lady Roth's heart is definitely through her ego. Winin', dinin', the whole kit and caboodle. I'm not surprised you finally wore her down."

Gaylie Girl could not resist a triumphant little chuckle. "And literally got her to agree to keep her mouth shut on Christmas Eve."

"Hoo, boy! I wonder how many people have ever gotten that kinda result before?"

"You may be looking at the first one." Then she decided to switch subjects. "How's your work on the overlay bond issue coming?"

"Well, I got most of the changes we needed worked out tonight. Then it's back to the councilmen for their approval. The books say we can swing it from a bonded indebtedness point of view, but it's still gonna be up to the voters when we tackle it next spring." He turned and pointed toward the refrigerator. "Oh, sweetheart, could you get me a little swallow a' milk. Nothin' like this kinda sugary pie to coat your windpipe somethin' awful."

He waited for the milk to arrive, downing it quickly and clearing his throat before resuming his train of thought. "Yes, indeed! That does hit the spot! Anyway, if the general public is as upset with all those potholes as you and Miz Laurie were that day Miz Novie drove you all over creation without seat belts, I expect we'll win this thing handily."

Gaylie Girl leaned in on her elbows. "Then it looks like both our projects are well on their way to success. My latest report from Euterpe says all the choirmasters have been cooperating with her on the selections, and we shouldn't have any more complaints from Lawton Bead now that Lady Roth has agreed to refrain from her screeching."

"Oh, I meant to tell you," Mr. Choppy put in. "Henry Hempstead called up while you were out this evenin'. He just wanted to give us an update on things. Two trimesters down and one to go. Cherish is in great spirits and would love to have us drop by anytime. With a little advance notice, of course."

"I'd love to, but I don't know when we'd find the time. Maybe when we get a little closer to Christmas, and we both get some time off from the office. A visit in the spirit of the season might be just what we all need about then."

Mr. Choppy leaned back in pleasant contemplation. "You know, I really do think of Cherish as a daughter more than ever now. Seems both she and Henry have lost their parents, so maybe I fill the void from their point of view, too. Do you think it'd be too pushy of me to suggest myself as the godfather of their child?"

Gaylie Girl reached over and gently patted his hand. "That's a lovely idea, Hale. All she can say is no, and something tells me she won't. First things first, though. Let's just concentrate on getting the baby here safe and sound."

· Six ·

Getting Wired

Meta Belford turned to her fiancé, Petey Lyons, and gave him a lengthy bear hug just inside the doorway of 18 Courthouse Street North—the somewhat antiquated store on The Square they had just purchased for a song. It was typical of commercial buildings put up in the late 1800s throughout the South, featuring two stories of brick, shuttered windows, and a fanciful lacework balcony. Back in the day, the merchants who owned them had kept their stores on the ground floor while living above with their families. The concept was now returning to favor amid a new wave of adaptive restoration, and Second Creek was becoming a prime example.

Meta finally loosened her hold slightly, and Petey managed to suck in a draft of air and exhale dramatically—all in one seamless maneuver.

"You've got quite a grip for a . . . girl!" he exclaimed.

She pulled back a bit more, feigning offense with an impish glee. "You just said 'girl' as if it were a dirty word. It was there in your hesitation. But I am a girl, at heart. An honest-to-goodness, romantic, artistic, daughter-of-a-Nitwitt girl. So don't hold the fact that I work out at the gym against me. Which reminds me, does Second Creek have a gym where I can keep on exercising once we move here?"

Petey flashed a broad, triumphant smile. "Just so happens that the company I bought down here has a very state-of-the-art exercise center for the benefit of employees and their families. So I'd say the future wife of the owner of Pond-Raised Catfish certainly qualifies. You'll be able to get all the reps you need."

She scoured his tall frame and then playfully pointed at his stomach. "We should work out together, you know. I think I detected a hint of those dreaded love handles the last time we did it."

"You detected nothing of the sort." He gently grabbed her and pulled her toward him with a wicked grin. "I'm as fit as they come. Weigh the same as I did in college."

"And I can go you one better, Mr. Peter Armistead Lyons Jr. Since the summer I shot up a tad bit over six feet at the age of fifteen, my weight hasn't varied more than two pounds either way."

He couldn't resist giving her the exact same hug he'd just received. "Looks good on you, *girl*. There now. Did I put the right emphasis on it this time? No hesitation, I trust?"

She responded not with a smile of affirmation but with a kiss. The slow, fervent kind that only comes with being very much in love. "That was my official girlie-girl kiss. That should tell you everything you need to know."

"I'll make a note of it for future making out."

In fact, Meta Constance Belford was a lot to take in all at once. It wasn't just her height that made her stand out in a crowd. Her flowing blond mane seemed to take on a swirling life of its own every time she offered up a saucy tilt of the head. Petey himself had confessed to his mother that he had felt positively intoxicated the first time he had laid eyes on her just a few months back. All Gaylie Girl could answer then was, "She's a tall drink of water, son!"

Meta had been just as smitten with him at first glance. She had even made a point of telling him that first evening back in September that he looked like he might have stepped out of the latest issue of *GQ*, what with his tanned skin, dark hair, and fashionable suggestion of stubble, while all anyone could say behind the scenes once they'd heard about the engagement was that the two of them were going to blow everyone away with the beautiful children they were going to make.

But there were one or two other issues to resolve before that fertile prospect could take place. The first was Renza Belford's insistence that the wedding needed to be scheduled sooner rather than later—her concession to the idle minds she was certain were out there working overtime. Renza was Renza, of course, and would be properly dealt with in due time.

More pressing on this cold December morning was the matter of the newly acquired but long-unoccupied building that would soon become the second incarnation of Meta,

Unlimited, Art Gallery—formerly of St. Augustine, Florida. Vacant way before the rash of closings caused by the coming of the MegaMart a few years earlier, 18 Courthouse Street North was going to need a bit of renovation to make it a suitable showcase for Meta's inventive watercolors and edgy paper sculptures. One preliminary step was having all the wiring checked out, and Petey and Meta continued to wait downstairs patiently with their arms around each other for warmth while the initial inspection was concluding upstairs.

Momentarily, Rusty Jahnke of Jahnke's World of Wiring interrupted the couple's heated display of affection, leaning over from the lacework balcony above and getting their attention with a wave of his hand and a quick shout. "Hey! Uh . . . folks!?" He waited for them to move into view. "I've checked it all out, and I got some bad news for ya. You got you some major code violations, I'm afraid. But that's par for the course in a buildin' as old as this one is. Could be sixty, maybe seventy years since the wirin' was put in! Needs rewirin' real bad. First you got you some—"

"Why don't you come down here and go over everything with us, Mr. Jahnke? I've already got a crick in my neck looking up at you!" Petey interrupted.

The diminutive electrician was down in a flash, whereupon he removed his camouflage-style hunting cap, revealing the thick head of rust-colored hair that had spawned his nickname. Then he took a notepad out of his back pocket and began reading a mile a minute. "It ain't pretty, folks, and I wusht I could say otherwise, but you got you an uncovered junction box and an overwired panel to start with, and then you got a whole mess a' backstabbed wires everywhere and no GFCIs that I could find and—"

"Whoa, there!" Petey exclaimed, pushing out his hand as if he were stopping traffic in the middle of the street. "Slow down. I don't know the first thing about wiring. You might as well be speaking a foreign language. Could you maybe cut to the chase in layman's language here?"

Rusty looked up from his list quickly and wagged his brows. "Sorry, folks. That's a failin' a' mine, I guess. I get so carried away with my job. Wirin's my life, ya know!"

"So we gather," Petey observed, adding a pleasant smile to the equation. "You come highly recommended by Paul Belford. So we're not disappointed in the least that you're enthusiastic about your work. Just two things: what is this rewiring job going to cost us? And will you take the job?"

"Now as to that, the news is good. I can sure as all get-out do the job for ya." Rusty tore a sheet from his pad and handed it over. "And there's your damage. My good faith estimate. But I can assure ya, that's the best price you'll get in Second Creek. Mr. Belford's right to swear by me, since I been workin' with him ever since I started up my bid'ness."

Petey took the sheet and scanned it while Meta looked on eagerly. "Seems reasonable to me. Takes a few thousand to make a few thousand, huh? At least that's what my daddy always said while he was running Lyons Insole."

"Will it take long to do everything?" Meta wanted to know. "I just can't wait to open my gallery. We'll worry about moving in upstairs later. I was hoping maybe we could have a soft opening in time for the new Caroling in The Square event on Christmas Eve. That should bring lots of people downtown to mill around, and some of them are bound to drop by the gallery if we're open. Even if you don't make a sale, you get the word out that you're open for business, and that's everything in the art world."

Rusty cocked his head and squinted as he scratched the nape of his neck. "It wouldn't take all that long if you didn't have so many new outlets to install. But if you're gonna be spotlightin' all that artwork you told me about on these walls, you'll need you plenty more to plug into. You could save you some money by not havin' us put 'em in on the second floor just yet. We charge double for that, ya know."

"Then double it will have to be, Mr. Jahnke," Meta replied without batting an eyelash. "We intend to make our home on the second floor, so we won't accomplish anything by not having that properly wired, too. Might as well do it all at once." She gave Petey a hurried glance. "Right, honey?"

"Makes sense to me."

"I understand what you're both sayin'," Rusty added. "But no matter where we put 'em, we gotta cut lotsa holes in the walls to snake the wires and then you'll want us to patch 'em up, I'm guessin', and—"

Meta interrupted with a patient smile. "Mr. Jahnke, we're convinced you know what you're doing. Just tell us how long the work will take."

"Oh . . . uh, a week or so. Maybe a little less if everything goes right. Are you wantin' it all done by Christmas for sure?"

"If at all possible. I realize the building has a bare-bones look and feel to it now, but we artists don't mind working with that. Sometimes, people expect a funkier, more offbeat ambience when they walk into an art gallery. You know—the rustic, exposed beams, the walls with the worn plaster, that sort of thing. But we absolutely have to have those lights for effect."

Rusty managed a friendly chuckle. "And some heat'd help, too, I imagine. Saw where we're predicted to keep havin' this cold weather all the rest a' this month. I got someone to recommend to ya for your HVAC work, if you want. Ronnie Lutrelle's the best in town, and he could prob'ly get a system installed for ya real quick. I can work with him pretty close on that. Meantime, I'll make a note to bring me a coupla space heaters so my crew don't freeze to death once they get to work. Guess I don't have to tell ya, it's like an icebox in here."

Petey had been making mental notes and gave Meta a reaffirming glance. "I think we're ready to take all your recommendations and get started then. Full speed ahead!"

❄

Rusty Jahnke had no sooner driven off with mission accomplished than Petey and Meta were approached by Novie Mims's son, Marc, and his partner, Michael Peeler, of How's Plants?—the clever botanical boutique located on the other side of The Square. Most Second Creekers found them fascinating to observe from the "opposites attract" angle: Marc was small and delicate with a tangle of dark, curly hair, while Michael was a big sturdy, freckle-faced redhead.

"My mother told us you were in town getting ready to start work on this art gallery," Marc said after the usual round of greetings. "It's very exciting to hear that we'll have some more new blood here on The Square. Especially the kind that will contribute to Second Creek's cultural life. Michael and I have made it our mission not to let that languish, and we both wanted you to know we're behind you one hundred percent. Oh, and congratulations on your engagement." He paused briefly, looking slightly embarrassed.

"I didn't mean to make that sound like an afterthought. It seems to be the talk of the town. We pretty much figured out you two were going to become a permanent item by the way you hit it off during that extravaganza at the Victorian Tea Room over the summer." Then he quickly turned toward Michael. "'Betcha anything they're a match!' I said to you, didn't I?"

"You did, and they were. Just like the two of us."

Meta seemed particularly charmed by their banter. "There's no doubt about that. And as for your support of my gallery, I would expect nothing less from a son of a Nitwitt."

Everyone laughed as Marc continued. "All roads do seem to lead back to that dear group of ladies, don't they? I even get the feeling that everyone in Second Creek is somehow related to one of the Nitwitts."

"That would include me now, as a matter of fact," Petey added. "My mother's a full-fledged member, too."

"Ah, yes!" Michael chimed in, his broad face beaming. "The very glamorous and energetic Mayor's wife. We have nothing but good things to say about the new administration and all of their original ideas. We also can't wait for Caroling in The Square on Christmas Eve."

"Absolutely!" Meta exclaimed. "We're hoping to get the gallery up and running in time for that, though it could be a tight squeeze."

Michael managed an exaggerated little shiver and said: "That would be fantastic if you can swing it. Meanwhile, may I suggest that we not continue this conversation any further without benefit of a little warmth. It's a bit raw today. Besides, we've had our 'out to lunch—back soon' sign in the window long enough. We don't want our customers beating down the door for our bushes and ferns. So, why don't we head across to our place and take the chill off with a cup of coffee or two?"

A few minutes later, they were all contentedly sipping away around a long table flanked by huge potted ficus plants with special sale price tags hanging from them. Sufficiently warmed now, Meta resumed her earlier train of thought in earnest. "My mother tells me she's been working on the publicity campaign with Miz Myrtis, Miz Denver Lee, and Mr. Powell Hampton, and they've already got three church buses from Greenwood signed up to come over on Christmas Eve. All the Nitwitts are saying that this will overtake the Miss Delta Floozie Contest in popularity as an annual event in The Square."

Marc was stirring his coffee, looking slightly distant. "I fervently hope so. It's not that The Square is on its last leg or anything like that, although you can see for yourselves that we've got a few vacancies, so to speak. They say the Mega-Mart and all those other stores out on the Bypass keep taking their toll. Those of us who are sticking it out downtown have generally been rewarded by the locals, though. In the short time since Michael and I moved from San Francisco, we've discovered that Second Creekers are fiercely loyal to their own. That's where the Nitwitt connection comes in. But it would still be nice to get a fresh infusion of out-of-towners to pad our coffers."

"So how's things at How's Plants?, if you'll excuse the grammar?" Meta said.

This time, it was Michael who stepped in with a tinge of resignation in his voice. "Oh, we made a big enough splash over the summer, thanks to Marc's mother and her friends. It got to where the first thing out of a customer's mouth was, 'I want you to know that a Nitwitt sent me to you today!' Then they'd pick out an azalea or dwarf gardenia or two and politely skedaddle. I wish we'd kept records, there were so many visits like that. And then your mother's wedding out at Evening Shadows was quite a boon to us, too, Petey. But we really haven't had a lot of repeat business. I wouldn't say we have our financial hopes pinned on the effects of Caroling in The Square, but it certainly couldn't hurt over the long haul."

Petey gave Meta a gentle nudge as he checked his watch. "I think the time's getting away from us. We're staying out at Evening Shadows this trip down, and Miz Myrtis will be worried about us. It's nearly lunchtime."

Marc's curiosity was clearly visible on his face. "You can't beat Evening Shadows for hospitality, no doubt about that. But I'm surprised you two aren't staying here in town."

"Long, messy story," Meta began, rolling her eyes. "My

mother, bless her meddling little heart, has been next to impossible about our living arrangements for this trip. We haven't even begun to fix up the second floor of our store, where we're going to live. Anyhow, she wanted me to stay with her and for Petey to stay with his mother and Mr. Choppy. But we saw no reason to be kept apart at this time in our lives. We're no moony-eyed teenyboppers, you know." Meta's facial expression became even more exaggerated.

"And even though Gaylie Girl did offer to put us up together, we decided that Mother might interpret that as taking sides early in the in-law game. Oh yes, that's a train that's hurtling down the tracks without an engineer. We just can't see the headlights at the other end of the tunnel yet. Petey came up with the solution, though. He and his sister, Amanda, had such a spectacular time out at Evening Shadows earlier this year that he just gave Miz Myrtis a call and arranged everything. She's not related to either one of us, so that makes her the Switzerland of the Nitwitts in this case."

Marc was laughing out loud. "That makes perfect sense if you know the entire group. Michael can't believe how complicated they can make their lives sometimes."

"At any rate, we need to get going," Petey added. "The food they serve out there is to die for, and we're not about to miss a bite. Not to mention that I'm angling for Miz Myrtis to pitch a wedding tent for us this spring like she did for Mother and Mr. Choppy this past Labor Day."

"Now that was a wedding!" Marc exclaimed. "Michael and I garnished it to perfection with our greenery, if you will. We supplied everything except those fireflies that showed up there at the end!"

❄

It was supposed to be your everyday, superbly prepared, gourmet meal at Evening Shadows. Though it was only midday, Myrtis had chosen another of her stunning saris to play hostess, and Sarah had once again outdone herself with place settings fit for a state dinner at 1600 Pennsylvania Avenue. Petey and Meta had arrived on time from their session on The Square, and at first it appeared that there would be nothing more taxing to contend with than keeping up with all the witty conversation that generally arose beneath the chandelier gracing Myrtis's dining table.

Then Euterpe, who had become a permanent fixture at the bed-and-breakfast after nearly six months as a paying customer, appeared at the top of the stairs with Pan at her shoulder and struck a dramatic pose. Next, she began a strange, staggered descent. Norma Desmond had been less mannered for her final deranged take in *Sunset Boulevard*.

Once she had reached the others below, she took a very histrionic deep breath. "I'm usually a very resourceful person, as you all know," she explained to the trio of bewildered faces standing before her. "But I may have met my match at last!"

Myrtis moved quickly to her side and put a reassuring arm on her shoulder. "Why, Euterpe, I've never seen you like this before. What on earth has happened?"

Myrtis briefly gestured to the others. "Everyone, please take a seat, won't you?"

When they were all settled in and Pan had been lowered to the floor to curl up quietly beneath the table, Myrtis resumed her tone of concern. "Please share, dear. Perhaps we can help."

Never one to mince words, Euterpe uttered a succinct but mysterious phrase: "Bring a torch! Or, as the French put it: *un flambeau!*"

"I'm not following," Myrtis said with a forced smile.

"Everything got out of hand so quickly," Euterpe continued. "This, after everyone was getting along so well. That was my biggest concern, you know. That the egos of all those choirmasters would get in the way of a successful caroling event. I've always detested having my greatest fears come to pass. Fortunately, that hasn't happened often in my life."

Myrtis waited for Sarah to finish filling the last of the water glasses before replying. "But I thought you said everything was going smoothly. Why, just last week you said you'd made the rounds and that all the rehearsals were a joy to attend. Everyone was in perfect voice and all that. We can't afford to be having any trouble less than two weeks out. We've got church buses booked and lots of interest from people all over the Delta. Our ads and radio spots seem to be doing the trick. We're even working hard on getting up a shuttle from Delta Sunset Village to get our dear Wittsie over here. Keep your fingers crossed on that one." Myrtis took a sip of her water and frowned severely. "What's all this business about torches? Are we going to storm a castle and flush out a monster somewhere? Stop being so evasive."

"Oh, it was that French Christmas carol—'Un flambeau, Jeannette, Isabelle'—that started it all. That loosely translates into 'bring a torch, Jeannette and Isabella,' in case your French is a little rusty."

Myrtis was nodding now. "It's not exactly polished, but I remember that song quite well. We sang it in high school French class eons ago. A little ditty from Provence and quite charming, as I recall."

"Yes, well, I don't know how it occurred to him, but somehow that Lawton Bead at St. Luke's got it into his head that his choir needed to have an international carol to sing for their segment. Strictly domestic just wouldn't do any longer. You'd think he was talking about champagne the way he carried on. Oh, that man's priorities! Anyway, he told me he wanted to substitute 'Un flambeau' for 'O Holy Night.' I didn't see the harm at the time and agreed to it, but word got around to the other choirmasters that 'O Holy Night' was now available."

"I must confess I wouldn't have seen the harm either," Myrtis put in.

"Who would? But apparently this touched a hidden nerve of some kind. It seems all of them had originally wanted 'O Holy Night' in their repertoires but had agreed to let the Episcopalians have it. Probably due to Lawton Bead's expert bullying. Now, the Presbyterians and the Baptists and the Church of Christ are all feuding over whose choir gets to sing it. They all say they're willing to drop another carol to make room for it, so what's the big deal? I just wonder if I have the energy to be Ecumenical Euterpe and sort this thing out. We're trying to avoid repetition, as you know. If they all sang it, it wouldn't be very special, but it may yet come to that."

Just then Sarah appeared with a silver platter of Caesar salads, and Myrtis perked up in accomplished hostess fashion. "Ah, at last! Here's our first course!"

"Who knew religion could be this much fun?" Petey observed just before digging into his salad. "Although I do recall that I raised more than a little hell back in my acolyte days."

Euterpe sounded inconsolable. "*Hell* is the word that comes to mind right now. These choirmasters are unexpectedly wired over this. Who would have guessed? I understand their interest, but I really can't fathom their intensity all of a sudden. Everyone was so compliant up until now. It's become the sort of competition I could have sworn was beneath them all, but here it is upon me, nonetheless. For once, I just can't seem to get my magic metronome ticking, and I feel as if I'm letting everyone down."

Over the main course of grilled tilapia, saffron rice, and steamed zucchini squash, the group continued to plumb the depths of Euterpe's problem. At the moment, Meta was holding forth. "I know this sounds terribly secular, but couldn't you just have a simple drawing to see who gets to sing 'O Holy Night'?"

Petey offered a conspiratorial snicker. "Or better yet— how about the proverbial coin toss?"

It was Myrtis, however, who rose above the jocularity with a serious suggestion. "Do I need to repeat the name twice, Euterpe? Laurie Hampton. We all have her on speed dial for just such occasions. After all, she *is* the 9-1-1 of the Nitwitts. I'll give her a jingle as soon as we've finished our lunch. Oh, and Petey, I'll bring your mother—otherwise known as Caroling Central—up to snuff as well."

Petey leaned over and winked at Meta. "I think we're going to like living down here, sweetheart."

· *Seven* ·

The Go-to Couple

I nside the municipal chambers on the second floor of
the courthouse, an informal council was convening on
a blustery Friday just ten days out from Christmas
Eve. But Mayor Hale Dunbar Jr. and his councilmen were
nowhere to be found. Instead, all of the Nitwitts were participating in a special session with the choirmasters of First
Baptist, First Presbyterian, and the Second Creek Church
of Christ. It was virtually unheard of for the average citizen to have such access to official municipal facilities, but
then the average citizen did not have the advantage of marital bliss with the Mayor. The old truism about politics and
strange bedfellows enjoyed a kinder, gentler interpretation
in this instance.

"All I ask is that you give us a half hour or so one afternoon when you and the councilmen have nothing else on

your agenda. And you can spare me, of course," Gaylie Girl had suggested to Mr. Choppy in the office a few days earlier. "I don't have to tell you how important this caroling project is to me and the rest of the girls. And ultimately to the well-being of The Square. As its Mayor and First Lady, we both need to take the long-range view of this and do everything we can to promote the uniqueness of Second Creek."

His response had been pitch perfect. "Still workin' on that Santa Fe feelin' of yours for Second Creek, right?"

"Oh, how I love a man who really listens to a woman!"

Mr. Choppy had readily conceded her argument, checked his schedule and those of the councilmen, and penciled her in without fanfare. Gaylie Girl's reasoning for the request had been that the three choirmasters would be more amenable to Laurie's "O Holy Night" resolution once off their own particular religious plantations, and furthermore that it would add that genteel touch of authority to the presentation. Now the time had come for the reveal that the Nitwitts were praying would keep Caroling in The Square on Christmas Eve on track.

President Renza had officially opened the meeting with each of the other Nitwitts rising from "their" padded councilmen's chairs as she introduced them to the choirmasters. Then she gestured for the men to rise together as she consulted her notes. "I'm well aware that some of you ladies already know these gentlemen, but let's cover all bases anyway. To your left there in the front row is Choirmaster Kenneth Styles of First Presbyterian."

Mr. Styles offered up an awkward little nod and hesitant smile. He was, in fact, an inordinately thin, shy man whose chronic stuttering only disappeared when he was singing. Therefore, his penchant for more choir practices than most of his charges thought necessary. It was perhaps the only part of his personality that could be considered tenacious and the likely reason he had allowed himself to become embroiled in the "O Holy Night" brouhaha.

"G-good, af-afternoon, ladies," he managed as the Nitwitts acknowledged him politely.

"And standing next to him we have Choirmaster Walker Billings of First Baptist," Renza continued.

The somewhat overfed Mr. Billings, who was the temperamental opposite of his Presbyterian counterpart, usually spoke up so loudly that it made most people cringe.

When informed to tone it down a bit by some of the church elders over the years, he always had the same reply: "I want to be sure every choir member can hear me—even the ones in the back row. Projecting is a big part of praising the Lord, you know." Surprisingly, he settled for a simple and reasonably modulated "Hello, ladies!" this time out.

"And last but not least, we have Choirmaster Lincoln Headley of the Second Creek Church of Christ," Renza concluded.

The homely Mr. Headley actually bowed to the Nitwitts sitting in a semicircle below him in the well of the chambers, and even though he had not yet uttered a syllable, the sarcasm of his gesture escaped no one. It was strengthened further by the words that followed: "I'm still wondering if all of this was really necessary, ladies. Couldn't we have resolved this over the phone?"

It was Euterpe, absent her Pan, who replied as pleasantly

as possible. "You will recall that I tried that, Mr. Headley. I spoke with all of you about this business several times. But there was a great deal of zigging and zagging among the three of you. Just when I thought I had all of you in agreement, someone would raise another objection of some kind or change course. I wanted to see if there was a way we could satisfy all of you, and I trust we've hit upon a solution."

"Very well, then," Mr. Headley replied, cutting his eyes to one side. "Let's hear it. I'm sure we all have our choir practices to get to."

Once the men had seated themselves, Renza turned the floor over to Laurie, who rose from her chair once again, this time with a thin stack of papers in her hand. "Gentlemen, these are handouts," she began, displaying them briefly before setting them back down on the table. "If you'll allow me, I'll explain what they're all about and then pass them out to each of you."

The stage was now set. Laurie quickly glanced one final time at the note she'd made to herself atop the stack before taking the plunge. It consisted of five words: *international, spirit, close the deal.* She and Powell had worked on the presentation long and hard over the past couple of days, and she was certain that it would do the trick, as her schemes had done so often over the years.

"First, gentlemen, we'd like to suggest the idea of including an international carol in each of your repertoires. As you all know, the choir of St. Luke's will be singing 'Un flambeau, Jeannette, Isabelle,' and we're wondering if other selections like that might not lend just the right touch of diversity to our caroling event. People will be coming for miles around to hear our music in The Square. Why not give them a surprise or two? We've prepared a well-researched list of such international songs in these handouts, complete with lyrics. After you've looked them over, we'll be happy to field any questions you may have."

It was Mr. Headley who stepped up to distribute the lists, and he was also first up with a question after a hurried scanning. "Miz Hampton, there are two ways I can choose to look at this. Either this foreign-language carol business is really something you're serious about, or it's just a thinly veiled ploy to get us to give up singing 'O Holy Night' altogether."

Laurie thought on her feet, striving for a bit of semantic humor. "Do you mean the one word *altogether* as in totally, or the two words *all together* as in the three of your choirs simultaneously?" She immediately saw Mr. Billings crack a smile, and Mr. Styles appeared to be mentally reviewing her question with a slight frown. But there was only a terse, deadpan response from Mr. Headley.

"Both, I suppose."

"I assure you we're serious about our suggestion," Laurie continued. "Why, look at all the choices you have there! 'Au Royaume Du Bonhomme Hiver'—that's the French version of 'Winter Wonderland,' as you can see. Then there's 'El Santo Nino,' the Puerto Rican version of 'The Holy Child.' And how about 'Noel Blance'—'White Christmas'? Or 'Promenade en Traineau'? Everyone will be enchanted to hear 'Sleigh Ride' sung in French. And don't forget the one at the bottom—"

"Yes, Miz Hampton, I see it. 'Vive Le Vent'—which

somehow translates into 'Jingle Bells.'" His expression and tone remained dour. "What makes you think everyone in my choir can sing French off the bat? Or Spanish for that matter?"

"I don't think it'll be that difficult. The lyrics are all written out phonetically there," Laurie replied. "It might be fun for your choir to give it a try. I'm sure they could master it in a few days, don't you think?" Then Laurie's knack for diplomacy kicked in. "There's nothing they couldn't accomplish under your patient direction, I'm quite certain."

That seemed to settle Mr. Headley down at the exact moment the stentorian Mr. Billings chimed in. "What's the story on this one with *Australia* and *New Zealand* in parenthesis next to it? 'Down Under Santa Gets a Suntan'? Is that supposed to be a joke, or is that actually a song?"

Laurie allowed herself a restrained little giggle. "Oh, no worries. It's an actual carol, all right. We just thought we'd include that one in case one of you might like to have a humorous number in your program. Apparently, they do sing it in those two countries. I'd put it in the 'I Saw Mommy Kissing Santa Claus' category, myself. You see, gentlemen, we just wanted to show you that you have many more options than 'O Holy Night.'"

"I'm c-confused," Mr. Styles said. "What's w-wrong with any of us s-singing 'O H-Holy Night'?"

"Nothing, of course," Laurie replied, pausing to further collect her thoughts. "We are not here to tell you that all three of your choirs cannot perform that song, if that's the way you want to go when all is said and done. But gentlemen, I think you may have lost sight of the goal here. If this event is to be truly memorable and bring people back year after year the way the Miss Delta Floozie competition does, we have to inject an element of originality here. Already, one Nitwitt after another has done just that. First, our Gaylie Girl Dunbar came up with the concept of Caroling in The Square itself. Then Euterpe Simon thought outside the box and came up with performing on the balcony. I think we've all applauded that most creative setting."

Out of the corner of her eye, Laurie saw Denver Lee's hand shoot up, waving back and forth for attention. "Oh, yes, and our Denver Lee McQueen is still offering her taped organ accompaniments for the convenience of any and all of your programs, should you require them for your practices."

Mr. Headley finally broke the awkward silence that ensued. "So you actually think these foreign-language carols will enhance our performances? You don't think people will hear them and say to themselves, 'What the heck was that?'—if you'll please pardon my English?"

Laurie quickly glanced down at the second word in her note to herself—*spirit*—and regrouped. "Yes, I honestly think the crowds will be charmed and greatly entertained. And let us fervently hope and pray that we have crowds to entertain. But I'd like you gentlemen to consider something else as well. Although this is being staged as a tourist event, it will also be a genuine manifestation of the season. At this point, I have to say that I'm a bit disappointed that the three of you don't seem to be approaching this with the Christmas spirit in mind. We are supposed to be celebrating a miraculous event instead of quibbling over petty details such as who gets to sing what. Your churches rely upon you to bring the musical traditions of the season to life. It's not a part of your mission to fuss and fight with each other. So, I ask each of you to consider all of my points in that spirit."

Laurie's barely disguised reprimand seemed to have had the desired effect, and it was Mr. Billings whose attitude crumbled first. "Well, when you put it that way, Miz Hampton . . . maybe it would be a novelty to include one a' those foreign carols. Or even that Australian song about the suntan, even though that's not a connection I'd ordinarily make around this time a' the year. Hey, but whoever said you can't have a little fun with Christmas? Besides, my choir members are quick studies."

Mr. Styles immediately followed suit. "I'm-I'm on b-board, too, I guess. W-we could t-try one or the other at F-First P-Presbyterian. I'm s-sure Reverend G-Greenlea w-would approve."

That left the ever-recalcitrant Mr. Headley to draw himself up and declare: "Then if it's all the same to the rest of you, the Second Creek Church of Christ will include 'O Holy Night' in its medley as we had originally intended. The gist of this seems to have been that you ladies want us all to perform something different, and it looks like that's going to happen now."

Laurie maintained rigid eye contact with the choirmasters, remembering her final directive to *close the deal*. "Yes. And I trust you gentlemen implicitly not to let us down and to work everything out in the Christmas spirit. That said, I believe our work here is done."

❄

"I just can't say it enough. You were beyond magnificent, Laurie!" Gaylie Girl exclaimed as the Nitwitts settled in around one of Vester Morrow's largest tables at the Victorian Tea Room.

Since it was nearly five o'clock when their chamber session had successfully concluded, they all decided that a celebratory cocktail or two was in order. Not that they would have passed up the opportunity had things not gone so well. Thus, the short jaunt en masse to their favorite restaurant and watering hole just off The Square. On the way, Gaylie Girl and Renza had briefly lagged behind and peered into one of the windows of 18 Courthouse Street North to monitor the progress of the wiring crew. It appeared that they had caught them on break, however, since what they saw was two men in overalls huddling around a space heater, one warming his hands and the other reading a newspaper.

"Well, nothing to report to Petey and Meta there," Gaylie Girl had observed to Renza as they walked away, thinking it wiser not to barge in and bust up the crew's downtime. "But the last time I spoke to Petey over the phone, he indicated that things were flowing smoothly for Meta, Unlimited, Art Gallery."

At the moment, however, nothing could have been flowing more smoothly than the libations the Nitwitts were enjoying during the Tea Room's official two-for-one happy hour. It was currently Renza's turn to praise Laurie's flawless performance at the courthouse.

"You know, I still think we should put this issue to bed of who our next president will be by installing you for life, Laurie. I wish I'd had one-tenth of your tact and patience as president these past six months. Those choirmasters were putty in your hands this afternoon. Well, all except for that Mr. Headley. He was just full of horse apples the whole time."

Euterpe was nodding enthusiastically after taking a sip of her white zinfandel.

"You do have the touch, Laurie. I was just caught in a loop with them these last few days. But you made it look so easy."

Laurie briefly allowed herself to savor her Bloody Mary and kudos together but soon put down her drink and drew herself up with some authority. "I have to level with you, ladies. I really can't take all the credit. My Powell engineered most of this for me when I asked for his input. He ends up being in on all of our schemes sooner or later because we do make a good team. Which reminds me—I've been halfway serious about this with Powell, but I think I'd like to propose it now in earnest to all of you. What would you think of making him the first male member of the Nitwitts?"

That caused an audible and visible ripple around the table, and Renza said: "You say you've mentioned this to Powell before? Well, I'd love to hear what his reaction was."

"It was a very respectful 'thanks, but no thanks.'"

Renza's brows lifted dramatically. "I think I can read between the lines and appreciate his position. Shouldn't that be the final word then?"

"Ordinarily, I would say yes," Laurie explained, pressing

on. "But I have a slightly different take on this, if you'll hear me out. My idea was to put him in a special category. He'll be a member of the group but not actually a Nitwitt the way we are. Instead, his title would be our official Go-to Guy, capitalized and with a hyphen thrown in there somewhere. Because the truth is, that's what he's been for us the last couple of years. We've gone to him for all that wonderful ballroom dancing and then writing radio spots and press releases and now this latest. I really do think he'd appreciate the recognition in this very unique way."

After a brief period of everyone sipping while mulling things over, Novie said: "Shall we take a vote on it then? As usual, I have my trusty secretarial notepad in my purse."

A few minutes later, Powell Hampton had been unanimously appointed the Go-to Guy of the Nitwitts' Club of Second Creek, Mississippi.

"You're on a roll, Laurie," Gaylie Girl said. "And that makes you and Powell our official Go-to Couple. Next question. Do you think Powell will accept?"

"I'll go out on the proverbial limb and say yes. He's really very fond of all of you, as I'm sure you know, and I think this concession to his masculinity will seal the deal for us."

Denver Lee and Myrtis were whispering and giggling next to each other, and Laurie couldn't help but notice. "What on earth are you two plotting over there? You're acting like a couple of schoolgirls."

It was Myrtis who answered with a naughty smile. "That's not far from the truth. We were just saying to ourselves how nice it would be if we both had our own personal Go-to Guys at this time in our lives."

"I second that!" Euterpe exclaimed. "It's been a while since my David rode off into the sunset."

Then Laurie crisply raised her glass. "Let's have a toast, then." The others quickly hoisted their drinks. "To all those wonderful Go-to Guys in our lives—past, present . . . and why not hold out hope for the future, as long as we're at it!"

· *Eight* ·

The Best-Laid Plans

The on-again, off-again bus trip, which would carry some of the residents of Delta Sunset Village to Caroling in The Square on Christmas Eve, was now officially off for good. On a rainy Sunday morning a mere eight days out from the event, Dr. Curtis Milburne had just phoned Gaylie Girl and interrupted her breakfast with the bad news.

"I told you from the beginning that I would give this careful consideration, Mrs. Dunbar," he had begun. "I made no hasty judgments. But I have an obligation as the facility's physician on call to look after the best interests of our residents. And, yes, I'm aware that those who don't require scooters and walkers were good candidates to attend your event. But it would still be a logistical nightmare with some undesirable side effects. You just don't realize how much our people depend upon routine. Maybe *require* is a better word than *depend*. Routine becomes an old friend to them in their retirement years—and we particularly wouldn't want to upset them at Christmastime. Even for something as special and inspirational as this caroling sounds like it will be."

But Gaylie Girl chose not to leave it at that, thinking on her feet with Laurie Hampton's constant example for inspiration. "Perhaps we've been looking at this the wrong way around, Dr. Milburne."

He listened patiently while she suggested that if the residents couldn't go to The Square, then perhaps The Square should go to the residents. "How disruptive would it be to have one of the choirs perform their program over there between now and Christmas Eve? All the residents and patients would have to do would be to come down from their rooms into the lobby," she concluded.

Dr. Milburne's reaction was a distinct mixture of support and relief. "I think that's a wonderful suggestion. I don't much relish being thought of as the bad guy in all this. Give Lisa a call as soon as we hang up and see if she can wedge something into the activities schedule. It may not be too late."

Fortunately, Mrs. Lisa Holstrom, the crisply efficient director of Delta Sunset Village, found an immediate opening on the upcoming Thursday schedule. A much-anticipated presentation from a husband-and-wife Christmas storytelling team had fallen through at the last minute, and booking a choir would be the perfect replacement.

Next, Gaylie Girl continued her flurry of activity with a call to choirmaster Press Phillips of the Second Creek First

United Methodist Church, recalling his exceptionally affable nature. And Mr. Phillips had eagerly agreed to Gaylie Girl's spur-of-the-moment proposal.

"I don't have to think twice," he assured her. "We would be happy to go over and deliver some musical cheer to the residents. We Methodists are very good at our bus trips, whether to the Smokies or the outskirts of Greenwood!"

All that had been accomplished in the space of twenty or thirty minutes, but Gaylie Girl was determined to go for more. "I'd like to round up the girls and have us all go over for Sunday brunch with Wittsie. I can't wait to give her the good news," she told Mr. Choppy as he was finishing up his breakfast of buttered grits and blueberry pancakes.

"Best move I ever made—hookin' you up with the Nitwitt ladies!" he quipped.

After that, Gaylie Girl was glued to the phone the rest of the morning. Her efforts, however, were spotty at best. Denver Lee, Myrtis, and Euterpe insisted they had other plans that could not be broken, although none of them chose to reveal what they were. Of course, they all wanted it understood that they were not abandoning Wittsie and would see her during their weekly lunch outings. Novie was having Marc and Michael over for a Sunday brunch of her own, while Laurie and Powell had committed to a theater trip up to Memphis for a performance of *Chicago* they'd been anticipating for months now.

That left Gaylie Girl with Renza as her solitary traveling companion, and she was approaching the short trip from Second Creek to Greenwood with no little trepidation. The reluctant in-law issue kept rearing its annoying head even after she got behind the wheel and they had left Second Creek in the rearview mirror. Would she be in for yet another session of second-guessing from Renza about the impending marriage of their two children? Perhaps she could forestall the possibility with small talk and not give Renza an opening. As the rain was slacking up a bit, she switched the wipers to intermittent and bravely took the plunge.

"I meant to tell you. I got a long-distance call from my daughter, Amanda, yesterday."

Renza barely seemed to be paying attention. "Oh?"

"Yes. It seems she's not going to be able to swing coming down for Caroling in The Square since it would mean spending Christmas down here instead of up in Chicago. She said the children just wouldn't like it, and I totally understand why they'd feel that way. Besides, she and Richard are trying to patch things up, so I gather she wants to hold on to what's more comfortable and familiar. There was talk of divorce this summer right around the time of my wedding." As soon as she'd let that last sentence slip out, Gaylie Girl mentally cringed. That was hardly where she wanted to go, inadvertently offering Renza another opportunity to pounce.

"It's funny that you brought that subject up just now. I'm speaking of divorce, of course," Renza observed without missing a beat.

Gaylie Girl was steeling herself for another shot across the bow. "Yes?"

"What I mean to say is . . . well, I've been wanting to tell you something . . . and I haven't been able to find the right time and place—not to mention the words. But this is long overdue."

Renza's hesitant tone caused Gaylie Girl to cut her eyes sharply to the side for just an instant—no small risk considering the spray being thrown against the windshield from a passing semi. Amazingly, these were not the abrasive sounds of the Renza they all knew so well. Instead, there was a suggestion of vulnerability, tentatively poking its head out from deep inside her protective shell.

"I'll just come right out and say it. I've carried on abominably from the very beginning about our children's engagement," she continued, while adjusting her fox furs and tugging at her seat belt as if it were too tight. "I've said some snippy things to you about Petey and his previous marriages. And I honestly regret that. Could you . . . would you please forgive me? I don't want the two of them to start out married life with us at each other's throats. Marriage is hard enough without in-law trouble of any kind. I should know—my mother-in-law was the original Gorgon Medusa. Believe me, she had everything *but* snakes growing out of that mangy scalp of hers!"

Gaylie Girl sat stupefied by the sudden intensity, unable even to steal another quick glance in Renza's direction. Somehow, focusing on the rhythm of the wipers enabled her to recover and avoid further awkwardness. "Of course I forgive you, dear. I'm sure this whirlwind affair caught us both off guard. But I have good instincts about this, I really do. I think both our children are mature enough to know what they really want out of life now, and we have an obligation to respect that."

Renza instantly morphed into the picture of gracious relief. "Of course you're right. Why, just the other morning

I woke up and said to myself, 'What on earth is wrong with you, Renza Belford? You should be thrilled Meta is finally settling down after all these years of you worrying to death about her. And to someone who comes from a very nice family like Gaylie Girl's and is quite solvent to boot!'" She softly chuckled to herself. "Every once in a while, I need a reality check, I'm afraid."

"Don't give it another thought. Let's you and I just concentrate on having a nice brunch with Wittsie and making her day."

Now Renza was wincing. "I hope she's having one of her better ones. She's been so blank lately. Even her long silences seem like a foreign language to me lately."

※

At first it appeared that Wittsie might just be grasping what Gaylie Girl had finished telling her about the Second Creek First Methodist Church choir coming to sing at Delta Sunset Village on Thursday afternoon. There was a discernible excitement in her voice and animation in her body language when she immediately reacted.

"Oh, I love choirs . . . I've always loved choirs . . . I used to sing in one when I was a girl and—" Then she stopped abruptly, as if an invisible hand had covered her mouth. Gaylie Girl and Renza both waited patiently for more, but Wittsie had nothing further to add.

They had all just returned from helping their plates in the brunch buffet line and were settled in once again around their cozy corner table. Gaylie Girl had been unable to restrain herself, leading with the choir news before anyone had taken a first bite. But after the prolonged silence from Wittsie, Renza put an end to their fast, spearing two of the ripe cherry tomatoes that adorned her veggie omelet and polishing them off quickly.

"I went through my cherry tomato phase a few years back," Renza explained, looking extremely pleased with herself. "I wanted to see if I had a green thumb, but I didn't want to go all out with those big tomato plants that have to be stalked to the sky. Someone told me that you had to spend hours picking off those awful worms that look like they could sting the fire out of you. So I figured maybe I wouldn't have to do that if I just stuck with cherry tomatoes in manageable little pots." Renza was shaking her head in genuine amusement.

"Of course, that was a huge horse apple fantasy on my part. The first time one of those nasty little worms appeared— and God knows how it managed that since my pots were out on the back screen porch—I screamed at the top of my lungs and took a big whack at the pot with my garden shears. It broke right in two—or three or four probably. There were shards all over the place. In other words, I threw out the baby with the bathwater. The plant was no more. I was a brave little trooper, all right, but with way too much pent-up energy. So, that was the end of my attempt to grow something in the dirt and then serve it up proudly as a garnish to all my Nitwitt friends when they came over for Bloody Marys."

Gaylie Girl was laughing brightly, but Wittsie was looking at her with the strangest expression on her face.

"What is it, Wittsie?" Renza said, exchanging concerned glances with Gaylie Girl.

But Wittsie still had nothing to say, continuing to shake her head as she appeared to be mouthing several words.

"Why don't we all dig into this wonderful brunch?" Gaylie Girl put in quickly, thinking it best to move on. "I can't wait to try this huge slice of spinach and cheese quiche I've helped myself to. I hope my eyes weren't bigger than my stomach. And look there, Wittsie, that's a wonderful piece of ham you have with all those cinnamon apples and yummy grits on the side. I've practically become a grits gourmet, thanks to Hale and his mother's cookbook. One of these days, I'm going to invite some of my Lake Forest friends down here and introduce them to all this very special Southern food."

Wittsie continued to stare down at her plate but eventually broke her silence. "Is this . . . what I ordered?"

"We didn't order, dear. We all went over to the other end of the room and served ourselves," Gaylie Girl pointed out. "Remember how your friend, that lovely Mrs. Norris, commented on your pretty blue dress? And now that we've all gone to this trouble, we shouldn't let our food get cold."

Wittsie picked up her fork and put one of the sliced apples in her mouth. "I like it," she said. But she seemed to be grimacing as she swallowed. Then: "What happened to my . . . cherry tomatoes?"

"You didn't get any, dear," Renza explained. "I had a couple, but I've finished mine. Both the tomatoes and my little story about them are gone. But I'd be happy to go over and get you some, if you'd like."

"Yes . . . I think so."

Renza dutifully excused herself and headed toward the

buffet table, while Gaylie Girl kept Wittsie engaged. "Mrs. Holstrom tells me you're not eating as well as you were when you first got here. You must keep up your strength. This food is really so delicious that it shouldn't be a problem."

Wittsie was smiling again. "Yes . . . I like the food here . . . I gained weight, you know . . . when I first came . . . I don't know when that was . . ."

"The extra pounds looked good on you, too, sweetie."

"I . . . have trouble . . . keepin' weight on . . . have since I was a girl . . . I used to sing in a choir, too . . . did I tell you?"

"Yes, you told us."

Renza returned with a small bowl filled with six cherry tomatoes and put it to the side of Wittsie's plate. "I think this should be more than enough for the three of us. But if not, I'll go back for more. They've got tons over there. At least somebody has a green thumb around here."

From that point on, eating their brunch slowed to a crawl, as Gaylie Girl and Renza did not want to finish way before Wittsie did. But it finally became quite clear that Wittsie did not intend to eat very much, so that tactic fell through.

"I . . . don't swallow the way I used to . . . sometimes it's hard," Wittsie offered out of the blue, pointing to her throat.

The alarm clearly registered on Gaylie Girl's face. "Have you spoken to Dr. Milburne about this?"

"I'm not sure . . . I may have . . ."

Equally distressed, Renza reached over and patted Wittsie's hand. "We'll mention it to Mrs. Holstrom on the way out, sweetie. I'm sure they'll look into it for you."

Shortly thereafter, the brunch came to an end, and the three Nitwitts proceeded to the front, where an orderly was waiting to escort Wittsie back to the memory care wing. But the enormous Christmas tree in the center of the lobby halted their progress. It reached up to the second floor of the atrium and had been decorated in Victorian fashion with red- and gold-felt bows instead of ornaments. Scattered beneath it atop a red, circular skirt were mounds of gift-wrapped packages of various shapes and sizes—some of them real and others added by the staff for effect. Wittsie stood before it all like a child on Christmas morning.

"Did they put all this up . . . while we were eating?" she said, but she seemed more delighted than puzzled by it all.

Gaylie Girl seized the moment almost like a professional. "Now that you mention it, I believe they must have, dear. There really is nothing they can't do around here, is there?"

Just then the smartly dressed, impeccably coiffed Mrs. Holstrom emerged from her office and motioned to both Gaylie Girl and Renza. "Ladies, if I may have a word with you before you leave, please."

And finally it was time to let Wittsie go her way.

"We loved being with you, dear," Gaylie Girl said as the orderly took Wittsie's arm and began leading her down the corridor. "And Renza and I will be coming over again on Thursday to hear the choir with you."

Wittsie turned and looked back at the last second. "Choir?"

Gaylie Girl and Renza just smiled and waved, realizing there was nothing more to be said except good-bye.

❄

"Unfortunately, our dear Miz Wittsie is approaching the last stages of the disease," Mrs. Holstrom was saying to Gaylie Girl and Renza as the three of them sat together in her office. "Some of her vital functions are beginning to be problematic. Dr. Milburne knows about the swallowing problem, I can assure you, and you'll be pleased to know that she'll be made as comfortable as possible. But the patients forget how to do the simplest things. The brain forgets so the body forgets. It's one of the most heartbreaking aspects of Alzheimer's to have to observe. I've been around it for almost two decades now in my work managing communities like these, and I never get used to it."

Gaylie Girl was dabbing at her eyes with a piece of Kleenex. "How much longer do you think she has, if you don't mind my asking?"

Mrs. Holstrom leaned in, her smile generous and full of empathy as only a trained professional's could be. "Of course I don't mind. That's what we're here for. She has a few more months, perhaps. It's hard to be more specific. But we'll keep you fully informed of any drastic changes."

"This will be Wittsie's last Christmas, won't it?" Gaylie Girl added, gathering herself a bit.

"In all likelihood, yes."

Gaylie Girl took a deep breath and then turned to Renza. "Then perhaps we should all come over here and make the most of Thursday. We can all gather around Wittsie and sing along with the choir and drink whatever you're serving. By the way, what are you serving? Now there's a Nitwitt question for you."

"Nothing stronger than mulled cider and hot chocolate, I'm afraid," Mrs. Holstrom replied with a wink. "Alcohol and so many patient medications just don't mix, though I can assure you that most of our residents would adore a little jigger or two of something every night if we'd let them. Oh, every once in a while we have a watered-down Mimosa or wine social. We just don't tell them about the watered-down part." She paused briefly with an expectant look on her face. "Then we'll see you again Thursday for the caroling?"

"You can bank on it," Gaylie Girl said, leaning over to lightly rap her knuckles on Mrs. Holstrom's desk. "Every one of us Nitwitts will be here for our Wittsie."

❄

The nasty weather had finally cleared up, so the ride back to Second Creek was far less stressful for Gaylie Girl than the trip over. Few things annoyed her more than driving in the rain. She and Renza had remained unusually quiet so far, carefully sifting through all the information Mrs. Holstrom had given them. They were both lost in thought, in fact, when a muffled ringtone gave them a slight start.

"Oh, that would be my cell phone," Gaylie Girl explained, gesturing toward the backseat. "It's in my purse. But let it ring, please. I never use or answer it while I'm driving. There ought to be a law against that, in my opinion. It's the addiction of the millennium the way all these people run around in traffic yakking up a storm like they're hosting talk shows. I simply refuse to do any of that. Besides, it's probably just Hale checking to see when I'll be getting home. And if it's not, whoever it is will leave a message."

"Then would you mind if I check to see if there's a message for you when it stops ringing?" Renza inquired. "Just in case it's an emergency of some sort. After all, my hands are certainly free."

The ringtone finally ceased, and Gaylie Girl gave permission with a hasty nod, followed by a snicker. "I hope you can actually find it, though. I've got everything in there except last year's tax return."

Renza retrieved the bulky handbag and opened it slowly, drawing back slightly as the contents came to light. "You weren't kidding, were you? There's an infomercial's worth of cosmetics in here. But no sign of a cell phone." Renza rummaged around further, making all sorts of mixing and clicking noises. "Ah, here it is! It was hidden by this little package of Kleenex you shamefully tore right through in Mrs. Holstrom's office."

Gaylie Girl gave her a prolonged sideways glance. "Now don't pretend for a moment that your eyes were exactly dry, Renza Belford. You are a big fake behind all that prickly bravado and horse apple expletives. I saw you turn away from me every time I tried to make eye contact. This whole business about Wittsie is getting harder and harder to take as we get closer to the end."

Renza shrugged and waved her off and then flipped the phone open, staring at the screen for a while. "Don't worry.

I think I can figure it out. I can tell it's got a similar menu to mine."

Gaylie Girl alternated between keeping her eyes on the road and sneaking glances at Renza's intricate maneuvers with her thumb. Finally, Renza put the phone to her ear and began to listen in eager anticipation. The first words out of her mouth were mundane enough: "Yes, it's from Mr. Choppy— I mean, your Hale."

But Renza's expression changed suddenly and drastically. The severest of frowns appeared first, followed by an audible intake of air. Then Renza paused to replay the message before closing the phone with a decided snap.

Gaylie Girl felt an initial wave of panic moving through her. "For heaven's sake! Don't keep me in suspense! What is it? What did Hale say?"

Renza took another deep breath and spoke slowly. "He wants you to meet him at the hospital right away. He says Henry Hempstead just called to say his wife had gone into premature labor, and they're trying to save the baby right now with a C-section. That's the secretary you've been filling in for, isn't it? That sweet little Cherish Hempstead?"

"Yes, it is," Gaylie Girl said, but her emotions prevented her from commenting further. They were all caving in on her, reminding her of how fragile everything had suddenly become. First with Wittsie. Now with Cherish. This just couldn't be happening to the Hempsteads again. They had been so careful this time around, taken such elaborate precautions, and Gaylie Girl had been an integral part of helping them implement their best-laid plans.

"Do you want to go to the hospital with me? I'd really appreciate it if you would," Gaylie Girl managed, once the initial shock had passed.

Renza reached across and gently rubbed her shoulder. "I most certainly will. In-laws should make it easy on themselves and stick together."

Nine

Vigil Aunties

H enry Hempstead's face looked drawn and haggard
as he stood just inside the doorway of the Second
Creek Baptist Hospital waiting room. Despite
his recent emergency ordeal, he managed a somewhat pre-
sentable smile as Mr. Choppy, Gaylie Girl, and Renza came
forward to offer him their further support. Their vigil had
begun with their arrival some thirty minutes earlier, when
they had discovered that it was a slow afternoon and they
had the entire room to themselves. They had managed to
keep their nervousness at bay by making small talk, swilling
bad vending machine coffee and thumbing through worn,
gossipy Hollywood magazines while Henry was being
allowed his first visit to the neonatal intensive care unit.
There he would be getting his first glimpse of his newborn
child. In the interim, a rather plump surgical nurse sporting

green scrubs and a flowered shower cap had ventured out and explained that Cherish was still in the recovery room after her traumatic but successful C-section. Now they were about to receive the prognosis for "baby boy Hempstead" from Henry himself.

"Dr. Cameron says it's just too early to tell how things'll turn out. We're just gonna have to wait and see. He also says the next twenty-four hours'll be real crucial. After that, it still might be days before we're completely outta the woods," Henry explained, his voice catching. Then he moved his index fingers toward each other until they were nearly touching. "But I've never seen anything so tiny. I can't get over it. My son is just barely three measly little pounds. Doctor says that's not too bad for twenty-eight weeks old, but that doesn't change the fact he's nearly two months premature."

Now Henry's eyes seemed to be searching the room for a place to focus as he rambled on about the predicament that was clearly threatening to overwhelm him. "I just never thought anything could be so tiny and still be human. I mean, it's almost like he's not real but some kinda doll. The nurse wouldn't let me stay too long, and I had to put on a surgical mask just to enter the room. He's hooked up to all these tubes, and there's this ventilator thing to help him breathe. It looks so scary to me—"

"Come over here and sit down, son," Mr. Choppy interrupted, nudging him toward the sofa where they had all been biding their time. "You've been through a helluva lot over the last coupla hours. You need to catch your breath."

Ordinarily composed, not to mention sturdy of frame and jaw, Henry was too shaken to resist the suggestion, immediately doing as he was told while the others gathered around him solicitously.

"One of us would offer to go and get you some coffee, Henry, but you really don't want what they're serving up in that machine out in the hallway, believe me. I may never get this nasty aftertaste out of my mouth," Gaylie Girl said, patting his hand after settling in next to him. "Have you had anything to eat? I bet you've forgotten to. My first husband, Peter, lost at least ten pounds worrying about me both times I delivered our children. Oh, he'd come into my hospital room and tell me that he'd eaten, all right, but he was just plain lying about it. Maybe I could go and get you something from the cafeteria?"

"That's okay, Miz Dunbar. We ate our big Sunday dinner together after church as usual, and then about an hour or so later, Cherish started getting these pains in her stomach. We both thought it was indigestion at first, especially since it was too soon for the baby, you know. Cherish had some bad indigestion all durin' the pregnancy."

Mr. Choppy was shaking his head now. "Well, I know for a fact that you and Cherish did everything you were told to do this time. All I ever got was good reports from the both of you. I know this is a big shock to you right now, Henry, but I got a feelin' that your baby boy is gonna do just fine. I'm sure he's a fighter just like his daddy is."

Henry suddenly leaned forward on his elbows, hanging his head between his legs before it snapped back up after a brief interlude. "Whew! I felt kinda sick there for a second, Mr. Choppy. But it passed. Why do these things keep happenin' to Cherish? Plus, I'm thinkin' about too many things at once. Like my supervisory shift out at the catfish plant. It starts in a few more hours, and I'd really rather be here in case somethin' happens. I'd—I'd want to be here for Cherish in case—" His voice broke off.

Gaylie Girl was squeezing his hand now. "I'll call up my Petey and tell him what's happened. He's still here in town, staying out at Evening Shadows with our Myrtis." She managed the softest of chuckles. "Petey and Euterpe have become her permanent fixtures, it seems. Anyway, I'm sure he'll be happy to appoint someone else to manage your shift so you can stick around and monitor things here."

Henry's pleasant features brightened for the first time. "Oh, that'd be great, Miz Dunbar. I'd really appreciate it. And since I have the chance now, I'd like to tell you what a pleasure it's been to have your son as my boss now. I think everyone here in Second Creek is so happy he bought the plant. He's truly given Pond-Raised Catfish new life."

"I'll pass all that along to him, and I'm sure he'll enjoy hearing it. But meanwhile, you have to take care of your-self, young man. You're a father now, and you have to keep up your strength for Cherish and your son. And that means you can't get by with no food or rest or breaks," Gaylie Girl continued. Then she turned toward Renza, who was sitting beside her. "I have an idea. Let's you and I go to the ladies' room together, shall we?"

"But I just went a few minutes ago."

Gaylie Girl repeated part of what she'd just said with a pronounced emphasis. "I said—I . . . have . . . an . . . idea."

Renza got the message this time, so up and off they went, promising to return soon and leaving the two men alone together.

✳

Mr. Choppy wasn't sure this was the right time to bring it up, but some instinct kept tugging at him to chance it; that it might be just the thing to give Henry the additional hope and strength he surely needed for whatever lay ahead. Still, two or three minutes of awkward silence passed before he actually broached the subject.

"I don't mean to pry into your personal business right now, Henry, but I was wonderin' if you and Cherish—" For a brief moment, he lost his nerve but soon regained it as he kept his goal in mind. "Well, son, I'm confident this is gonna turn out just fine for the two of you, as I said. We'll all watch that boy a' yours grow up strong and healthy just like you are. So, here's the thing I wanted to get to. Have you and Cherish thought about namin' a godfather?"

Henry turned his head dramatically, looking happily surprised. "Why, no, Mr. Choppy, we hadn't thought about it at all yet. Maybe we would have if we'd known the baby was gonna come along so far ahead a' schedule. Were you thinkin' a' runnin' for that the way you did for Mayor?"

Their laughter eased the tension a bit, and Mr. Choppy said: "Well, I was for a fact, son. I don't mind tellin' you that I've thought of your Cherish almost as a daughter since just after she came to work for me back in May. What a ray of sunshine she's been for me since day one! No better secretary anywhere, although my wife's not half bad either. I'd just be honored if you'd let me pay you back in such a special way."

"Hey, you'd get my vote for sure, Mr. Choppy. And when they finally let me go see Cherish, I'm bettin' she'll be thrilled to vote for ya, too."

Mr. Choppy quickly reflected, leaning back in his seat with a smile on his face. "My, my. I guess I'm blessed four times over then. Mayor, husband, stepfather, and now godfather all in the same year. How often d'ya think that happens in life?"

"Not often, I expect, but I know this much. I couldn't a' named a nicer fellow for it all to happen to."

That triggered another question that no one had asked yet. "Speakin' of names, had you and Cherish come up with any for the baby before all this happened?"

Henry was nodding his head slowly. "Actually, we had. We went around and around the way most parents do, and we'd pretty much picked out two that we liked the best. Lauren Margaret if it was a girl, and Riley Jacob if it was a boy. Those really weren't from either of our families, by the way. We just went down to the library and checked out one a' those baby name books. *1001 Baby Names Your Child Can Live With Later*, I believe it was. That nice Miz Grubbs just led us straight to it."

"Riley Jacob," Mr. Choppy repeated slowly. "I like the sound of it, my boy, and I'll be very proud to be his godfather."

That provided the two men a few minutes of what could

have passed for peace of mind, but Henry's worry soon got the better of him. "You think it's bad luck for us to be jumpin' the gun on this namin' and godfather business?"

Here, Mr. Choppy was in his element, gently resting his arm on Henry's shoulder. "I most certainly do not. You need to go on the assumption that this son comin' into your life is meant to be and never let go a' that. I know what I'm talkin' about when I tell you that you gotta hold on to the things that mean the world to you, no matter what. I finally got married to the only woman I've ever loved after fifty years of bein' by myself. But I never gave up. Somewhere deep down in my soul, where I lived and breathed, I knew it was ordained for me somehow. Just you never stop believin' when it comes to the life of your precious boy."

Henry was tearing up despite his best efforts to conceal it by rubbing his eyes with the tips of his fingers. Then he sniffled and cleared his throat for an encore. "Oh, man, Mr. Choppy, you're gonna be one helluva godfather."

"If I have anything to say about it, I will. And I have one thing more to point out to you. I predict the only problem you and Cherish'll have with young Riley Jacob is that he'll complain to you every year about his birthday bein' so close to Christmas. That is, if you try to combine the two. My mother, Gladys, had a cousin who was born on Christmas Eve, and she told me that Saundra Kaye always felt cheated when everything kinda got blended into one big celebration."

"I can't see us doin' that," Henry observed. "I already know it'll mean the world to us just to see our son's first birthday come to pass. And then we'll have Christmas to give thanks for that."

Not too long after their conversation had quietly wound down, another nurse—this one in her best starched whites— appeared in the doorway, and Henry immediately sprang up from his seat. "Mr. Hempstead, your wife has been transferred to her room now," she told him. "She's still a little groggy, but she's doing just fine. You should be able to visit with her briefly in about thirty minutes or so."

"And my son? Any change?"

"Not to worry. Still safely in the NICU and stable was the last report I received."

Henry sat back down slowly after the nurse left, allowing himself what for all intents and purposes was a deep, cleansing breath. It coincided exactly with the return of Gaylie Girl and Renza, who immediately bombarded the men with questions. Mr. Choppy gave them the latest update and then added: "What have you both been up to all this time? You didn't really go to the ladies' room, did you?"

Gaylie Girl gently nudged Renza with her elbow, looking triumphantly smug. "We've been outside rounding up the girls on our cell phones, haven't we?"

"That, and probably catching pneumonia. A cold front's moved through behind all that rain we had earlier in the day," Renza added.

Gaylie Girl was waving off her complaint. "Oh, nonsense. We were bundled up enough. Anyhow, Mr. Henry Hempstead, we have a very special Nitwitt proposition for you, and we trust you'll be smart enough to take advantage of it."

Henry and Mr. Choppy exchanged perplexed glances before Mr. Choppy said: "Translate, please. I can't wait to hear what this is about."

Both women resumed their seats, and Gaylie Girl began speaking in rehearsed fashion. "Very well. I believe I have this mostly committed to memory. It is hereby declared that one Mr. Henry Hempstead of Second Creek, Mississippi, has imminently qualified for benevolent care and feeding from all the members of the Nitwitts. Now, let's see—oh yes. They will in turn check in on him throughout the vigil ahead in specific shifts assigned to each one. Furthermore, they will make sure that he has not dwindled away to nothing, exposing him to sufficient food and drink, and forcing him to go home now and then to get some much-needed rest." She quickly searched her memory before dredging up the finale. "And last but not least—each Nitwitt on duty, so to speak, will also spell him during certain periods and agree to notify him at once if there are any significant changes to report concerning either mother or child. That way, there is no possibility that anybody will miss anything."

Henry's delight could not be contained, and his generous laughter allowed him to blow off steam. "You came up with all that just for me, Miz Dunbar?" he finally managed there at the end.

"Just for you."

But Renza was wiggling her fingers in front of Gaylie Girl's face. "The name. You forgot the part about the name. I think that's the best part."

"Oh, yes. How in the world could I forget? For this particular Nitwitt project of ours, we've decided to refer to ourselves as your dear, sweet Vigil Aunties." She spelled out the last two words as Henry and Mr. Choppy followed along in genuine amusement. "It sounds terribly corny, but wouldn't you know? Laurie Hampton said it came to her in a flash as I was talking to her over the phone a few minutes ago. She's just so good at these things. Of course, there was no way I could resist using it, and every one of the ladies has agreed to help you out until we're over the hump. Well, all except our dear Wittsie Chadwick. So, what's your verdict, Henry? Will you let us help you get through this without exhausting yourself? After all, 'tis the season."

Henry stood up and embraced Gaylie Girl and Renza in turn. "You bet I will. I'd be more than proud to have all you ladies as my sweet aunties for as long as you want me."

"Your sweet Vigil Aunties," Gaylie Girl reminded him, pulling back to hold him at arm's length. "God, how I do love being a Nitwitt! And, of course, I'll be taking the first watch this evening." She reached over and grabbed Mr. Choppy by the sleeve. "Come on, Hale, let's hurry home so I can whip up one of Gladys Dunbar's best recipes for Henry."

❄

Gaylie Girl was amazed. No woman who had just endured an emergency C-section should be looking the way Cherish Hempstead looked. Propped up on several pillows, her long, blond hair falling to her shoulders, she was nothing short of a smiling angelic vision nestled in a hospital bed.

"It was so good of you to visit me, Miz Dunbar," Cherish was saying as Gaylie Girl moved to her side to hold her hand. Henry stood on the other side, gazing down at his wife adoringly. "Henry's told me all about your latest little

Nitwitt project. It takes a load off my mind to know that you ladies will be takin' care of him until I get back on my feet. Which I trust will be very soon. They tell me all my vital signs are pretty much normal considerin' what I've just been through."

She pointed to the screens beside the bed keeping digital tabs on her. "That little incision they made in my belly just needs to heal up, and they say I'm home free. I've been assured there won't be much of a scar." But her mood and expression suddenly darkened. "Our little Riley Jacob is another matter, though. I've haven't even been able to see him yet because they don't dare take him out of that neonatal intensive care unit. I don't know why it is, but I seem to have had all sorts of trouble bringin' new life into the world. I wonder if somebody's tryin' to tell me somethin'."

Gaylie Girl gave her hand a brief but firm squeeze. "Don't you even think that way. Maybe we're not meant to be able to figure out everything that happens to us. That way we try harder and take things seriously. I had two C-sections with both my children, and back then, they cut you up pretty good to get the baby out, compared to the way they did it with you today. But from the very beginning I always felt my scars were worth it. Oh, yes, I missed the old figure and the way all my clothes used to fit me so well, but the important thing was I had my son and daughter in place by my side. The rest was now going to be up to me and my husband, Peter. So you and Henry just concentrate on how you're going to raise little Riley Jacob, and it will all fall into place."

"You and Mr. Dunbar have just been so nice to both of us," Cherish replied, her spirits clearly lifted by Gaylie Girl's subtle cheerleading. "You've been almost like parents, since both ours are gone, you know."

"And what your son's done for me, Miz Dunbar!" Henry added. "Givin' me the next four days off with pay is really goin' the extra mile. We've got our expenses comin' up with what the insurance doesn't cover."

"It was Petey's pleasure," Gaylie Girl explained. "He told me from the beginning that he wanted to provide incentives for his key employees to produce the kind of leadership it takes to keep a company running successfully." Then she reached into her coat pocket and drew out a piece of paper, handing it over to Cherish. "I wanted you and Henry to have a copy of this so you'd know exactly what to expect over the next few days. I've written out the schedule of all your Vigil Aunties. It's not twenty-four hours a day, you understand, but I think it will help at this critical time."

Cherish smiled brightly and began scanning it silently, but Henry requested that she read it out loud. So she started all over. "Sunday evenin'—6 to 9—Gaylie Girl Dunbar." She stopped to acknowledge Gaylie Girl's presence with a nod of her head. "And here you are. Then we have Monday mornin'—8 to 11—Laurie Hampton. Monday afternoon—1 to 4—Renza Belford. Monday evenin'—6 to 9—Novie Mims." Cherish worked her way through the rest of the Aunties and their schedules with a discernible awe in her voice. "I can't believe you're all doin' this for us. You Nitwitts really are the true spirit of Second Creek, what with your

Caroling in The Square on Christmas Eve comin' up this weekend, too. I've been lookin' forward to it so, but I prob'ly won't be allowed out to see it now."

"There'll be another one next year to go to," Henry pointed out. "Assumin' this first one'll be the big success everyone thinks it'll be."

Gaylie Girl's laugh was prolonged and thoroughly cavalier. It was clear that she felt she was at the top of her game. "I don't see how it can help but be. Our choirs have been polishing up their selections every day and are just champing at the bit. We're even going to have Lady Roth spotlighted on the widow's walk of the courthouse roof and dressed up as the Star of Bethlehem. Won't that be a sight to see?"

Henry leaned in and gave his wife a peck on the cheek. "Don't worry. I'll take pictures for you, honey. Especially some of Lady Roth up there. I remember how much you enjoyed her as Susan B. Anthony during the election campaign."

Cherish cocked her head, apparently reviewing those arresting, once-in-a-lifetime images and performances. "If Mr. Dunbar hadn't been runnin', I might've voted for her she was so convincin'. And now she'll stand as a symbol for all who travel far and wide to Second Creek at Christmastime. She must be beside herself."

"I often think that very thing about her," Gaylie Girl added, not bothering to elaborate. "But no matter. Let's just assume everything will go our way—from the choirs singing on the balconies to Lady Roth shining on the roof to your little Riley Jacob coming home soon. What a wonderful Christmas present all of that will be for us!"

Ten

A Wailing of Sirens, a Gnashing of Teeth

aylie Girl realized she was in the midst of a dream, but she was nonetheless being royally entertained. As so often happens in such cases, the plot of her unconscious drama made sense one second and morphed into utter nonsense the next. Time and place had been deliriously jumbled, and people no longer alive popped in and out of the mise-en-scène at a moment's notice. But it was all being staged in vivid color and was holding her attention every bit as effectively as a much-acclaimed movie in a first-run theater.

First, there had been that sequence in the manse at Lake Forest. She was seated at the grand piano in the drawing room, only there was a metronome beside her on the bench, ticking away noisily.

"See? I can play now," she was telling her late husband, Peter Lyons, who was standing over her. There was the sense that he was eagerly anticipating her newly found skills. And then she began playing but could produce nothing more than a cacophonous din. As it turned out, she was literally banging on the keys with her fists, and he had started laughing.

"I thought you said you could play," Peter Lyons had told her then. "You mean I came back to listen to this?"

"You shouldn't have left Petey and Amanda all that money when you died!" she replied, flashing on him. "It's only gotten them into trouble and spoiled them rotten. Why else do you think I'm banging on this piano? It's the only way I could get your attention!"

Whereupon the scene instantly shifted to Second Creek. She found herself atop the courthouse on the widow's walk, helping Lady Roth arrange her elaborate Star of Bethlehem costume. The wind was blowing fiercely around them, and she kept getting caught up in the voluminous folds of the dress. They were sticky to boot, akin to the threads of a spiderweb, and she felt trapped.

"Hurry up, it's almost time for my solo!" Lady Roth was shouting.

And that was when Gaylie Girl was overcome with a sensation of defeat. Despite everyone's herculean efforts to prevent it from happening, Lady Roth began singing to the crowd that had gathered in The Square below.

Perhaps singing was too kind a word to use. It seemed to Gaylie Girl that it was more like screeching—even a coloratura gone mad with a high-pitched wail that could have shattered glass. Not only that, it appeared that Lady Roth

had disdained a traditional Christmas carol for an unidenti-
fiable rock-and-roll ditty.

"Myrtis Troy gave me the sheet music. It was from her
husband's old record shop!" Lady Roth continued.

It was then that the lighter, more humorous tone of the
dream instantly disappeared, replaced by a sense of something unexpected and menacing. Something foreboding that
seemed to be lurking around The Square—as yet unseen but
frighteningly felt and inevitable . . .

The bedside phone rang in the physical flesh and blood
world, jarring Gaylie Girl to wakefulness. It was Mr. Choppy who answered it, however. But not before clicking on
the lamp and groaning quite audibly when he glanced at the
neon-blue numbers on the digital clock. 2:33, it read.

It blinked to 2:34 even as he was reading it.

"Who the hell is callin' me up this time a' night? There's
no way this can be good news!"

He briefly fumbled with the cordless phone, removing
it from its stand and putting it to his ear. All the way over
on her side of the bed, Gaylie Girl could clearly hear the
loud and agitated voice as well as high-pitched background
noises emanating from the other end. Suddenly, the bad feeling that had crept into the last scene of her dream began to
grip her as she sat bolt upright and said the first thing that
popped into her head.

"Please don't tell me that's Henry Hempstead calling
from the hospital!"

Mr. Choppy shook his head emphatically while continuing to listen intently to his caller. But soon enough he put an
end to the conversation with a hurried "I'll be down there

as soon as I can get dressed! Save what you can!" Then he ripped the covers off his side of the bed and headed for his closet across the room.

"I know something horrible has just happened," Gaylie Girl said. "I even have the creepiest sensation that I was about to dream just exactly what it was when the phone rang."

The brief sentence Mr. Choppy uttered seemed to register in the marrow of Gaylie Girl's bones as well as the adrenalin shooting through her veins: "The Square's caught on fire!"

Gaylie Girl closed her eyes and shuddered, trying to completely crowd out of her mind what he had just told her. But all she had to show for her efforts was a strange little whimper, followed by further confusion. "I'm not even sure what day this is supposed to be. But I know I went to bed early when I got back from my first Vigil Auntie shift at the hospital. Is it Monday?"

"Yes, and that was Garvin Braswell, my fire chief. He says the fire's gotten outta hand quickly since all those buildings are smack dab right up against each other, as you know," Mr. Choppy continued while stepping into his pants. "That's the downside to buildin' rows like that. If one burns, the others frequently do, too. There's just no wiggle room."

Gaylie Girl was trying her best to visualize it. "Are all four sides burning?"

"Just the north side for now, but Garvin says it's spreadin' west. They've got all the brigades in the county either down there or on the way. I could hear some of the sirens as we talked." Mr. Choppy was throwing on his heavy coat now.

"The north side is where Petey and Meta's building is!" Gaylie Girl suddenly exclaimed.

"Yes, it is, as I recollect."

"Shouldn't I let Petey know?"

"You can, but whatever you do, tell him not to go down there right now. It's dangerous, and there's nothin' he can do but get in the way. Garvin says there are already enough gawkers as it is, even though the whole area's been cordoned off. Damned rubberneckers! He says no deaths so far, thank God, but someone could end up gettin' killed that way!" He grabbed his car keys from the nightstand and stuffed them into his coat pocket, then momentarily froze in place. "Meta hasn't moved any of her artwork into their buildin' yet, has she? There's nothin' to save, right?"

"That's right. Renza says she went down to St. Augustine this week to close the gallery and make arrangements to have everything shipped up here. She was bound and determined to have an opening of some sort for Caroling in The Square even though they still haven't completely finished with all the wiring." Gaylie Girl's sigh of relief summed it up perfectly. "At least there's that to be thankful for."

Mr. Choppy quickly moved around the bed and gave her a parting kiss. "I'm sure I don't have to tell you to stay right here. Don't you even think about venturin' out. I'll give you a call on my cell when it's finally under control." He produced one last caveat.

"Oh, and tell all your Nitwitt ladies to stay put, too.

Because I know you'll wake every one of 'em up and get your little network goin' into the wee hours. No, scratch that. We're already in the wee hours. You ladies'll be at it until the crack a' dawn."

Gaylie Girl met his somewhat patronizing monologue with a light touch. "You do see that I have to, don't you? They'd revoke my Nitwitt membership if I didn't call. Renza will want to know because of the gallery, and Novie will want to know because of Marc and Michael's plant boutique, and as for Euterpe—"

Mr. Choppy interrupted, though he made a point of softening his tone this time. "Miz Renza could stand to be kept in the dark for a few hours every once in a while. And How's Plants? is on the other side of The Square away from the fire. So far it's not bein' threatened. And if you're gonna bring Euterpe's studio into this, my old Piggly Wiggly hasn't moved since I leased it to her. It's still one block off The Square on the east side. Just make sure none of you goes down there on a lark. I want y'all safe and sound, and I don't wanna read about any of you in the *Citizen* obits tomorrow. The news'll be bad enough as it is."

For some reason she decided to give him a playful salute and that brought the briefest of smiles to their faces. "Yes, Mayor Dunbar," she added with a wink.

He leaned down and gave her another quick kiss for good measure. "All we can do is hope for the best, but it sure sounds like our beloved Second Creek is takin' a big hit tonight."

She grabbed the sleeve of his coat almost as a reflex action. "You be careful, too, while you're down there, sir."

"Will do, First Lady, will do."

With that, he was out the door and on his way.

❄ .

The last time Mr. Choppy had been so mesmerized by a fire was in the darkened balcony of the Grand Theater during the very first Second Creek screening of *Gone with the Wind*. The lengthy "Burning of Atlanta" sequence had been so ablaze with eye-searing oranges and yellows that the movie rat extraordinaire and part-time Piggly Wiggly stock clerk in training had been forced to turn away from the screen now and then to get some relief. Though he had no trouble grasping the fact that the massive conflagration was only a clever and spectacular Hollywood trick, it had neverthe-less traumatized his eleven-year-old brain. He had endured nights of fitful sleep in the weeks that followed, offering up his childlike prayers that nothing and no one he loved or admired would ever be destroyed by such a voracious catastrophe.

And yet here it was happening to the very heart of his beloved Second Creek—the only home he had ever known and now the one he lovingly shepherded from the Mayor's office. By the time Mr. Choppy had reached The Square and begun huddling with Garvin Braswell behind the lines— both men yelling over all the noise and mayhem just to be heard—the entire block of Courthouse Street North had been engulfed. Half of Courthouse Street West was well on its way to the same fate. The hoses of three different trucks were taking dead aim at the ravenous flames rising high into the cold December sky, but the fire seemed to have taken on a life of its own, lapping up the incoming streams of pressurized water like some unquenchable demon.

"The north side is a goner, but at least we've stopped it from spreadin' east!" Garvin Braswell shouted, producing visible bursts of frosty breath. "It's gonna be touch and go how far down the west side she goes now!" The ordinarily implacable fire chief, who boasted a quarter-century of firefighting experience, took a moment to crane his neck, squint his eyes, and shake his head. "This might be the worst I've ever seen, Mr. Dunbar! This one's gonna take a while to snuff!" Then he was back to barking orders at his charges as they struggled mightily to save buildings that would more than likely be standing in ruin before the sun came up.

Mr. Choppy just couldn't take it all in. It was one thing to have stores fail and remain sadly vacant due to competition from chains like the MegaMart and the newest Bypass shopping centers full of their slick neon look-alikes. There was always the hope that some enterprising businessman or -woman might step into the historical vacuum and give The Square the old small-business try. Marc Mims and Michael Peeler had been the latest to give good account of themselves in doing just that.

It was even possible to gut it up and block out the deplorable zoning practices of the previous Hammontree administration. Possible but not easy, considering that Mr. Floyce had bent the rules to the breaking point and fattened his own coffers even as that doomed irreplaceable landmarks to extinction.

But this disheartening destruction of what had always been an integral part of what made Second Creek a special place to live in and visit was more than Mr. Choppy could bear. He didn't see how things could ever be the same again. Even if the various brigades—working together as hard as they possibly could—succeeded in preventing further damage by halting the fire right this very moment, there would still be no way that the integrity of The Square would not be seriously compromised.

And all this just a few days out from Christmas and the original initiative his Gaylie Girl had taken to leave her mark on Second Creek and bring people together at the same time. He knew in the pit of his stomach that it was now as simple as this: her Caroling in The Square on Christmas Eve had just gone up in flames. Would there be anything left of Christmas for Second Creekers?

❄

Just as Mr. Choppy had predicted, the Nitwitt network was up and running throughout the night, and Gaylie Girl had become Conflagration Central by virtue of her getting all the girls out of their beds at the ungodliest of hours. Not an easy feat to accomplish. From time to time, Mr. Choppy had given her updates on his cell phone as he had promised, always careful to include the status of How's Plants? and Euterpe's studio. There, at least, the news continued to be good. Neither had been remotely threatened at any point, and the fire had finally been contained and restricted to the north and west sides of The Square after a grueling two-hour battle.

"Please come on home now," Gaylie Girl pleaded to Mr. Choppy over the phone as his four-fifteen report rolled around. "You need to take the advice you've been giving everyone else from the beginning. There's nothing more you can do right now. You've done your duty as Mayor and stood on the front lines for the troops longer than most elected officials would ever think of doing. But now it's time for you to get some rest, Hale. You're going to need a clear head and your wits about you in the days ahead. We all will."

He had finally conceded his exhaustion and told her he would give up his terrible vigil. "I don't know where we go from here, though," he concluded just before hanging up.

In truth, Gaylie Girl didn't either. But her ordeal had been made more bearable by Petey's appearance at her doorstep around three-fifteen in rumpled clothes, his eyes half lidded.

"I don't care what you say, Mother, I'm coming over to be with you," he had insisted over the phone earlier. "I haven't been able to get back to sleep since you called the first time. If Myrtis and Euterpe are any indication out here at Evening Shadows, your Nitwitt friends are looking to you for answers every fifteen minutes, and I don't think you should be handling that all by your lonesome. Last time I checked, you weren't on the CNN payroll as a correspondent, and this isn't exactly 9/11. Though it probably feels like it to most of us. Besides, I need some advice myself. I'm dreading breaking the news to Meta about the gallery when it gets to be a decent hour. She's going to be devastated. So I'll be over in a few."

Sipping their coffee at Gaylie Girl's kitchen counter some twenty-five minutes later, mother and son resumed their conversation, trying their best to make some sense of it all.

"It's so weird, Mother," Petey was saying, running his hand through his disheveled hair. "I've been down here in Second Creek off and on for only six months, and I feel the pull of the place in a way I would never have imagined. Oh sure, I know I've bought Pond-Raised Catfish as an investment, and running it has gotten all my executive juices flowing but good. And, yeah, Sis and I have both been set straight after having our noses in the air about Hale and anything connected with the state of Mississippi. But we finally saw the light this past summer during all your wedding hoopla, thanks to you and your Nitwitts. I give all of you full credit for shaking the snobbery out of us. You know as well as I do that the sun had always risen and set in Lake Forest and environs for me. That seems like decades ago now, though. I want to know how this little town has gotten to me so fast."

Gaylie Girl was stirring her coffee while looking past him, and then she decided to tell him all about her Santa Fe feeling. "I was so surprised at how well your father and I treated each other when we were out there vacationing in New Mexico together. The town brought out the best in us somehow, and the same thing has happened to me and Hale here in Second Creek the second time around. I also think it's happened to you and Meta. It's just part of what makes this place tick."

Petey gave an ironic little chuckle and gazed up at the ceiling. "Meta and I were just looking forward so much to opening up her gallery and then fixing the upstairs as our cozy little love nest. We were going to walk out on the balcony every morning with our mugs of steaming coffee and gaze out over The Square as it slowly came to life. That old brick and lacework building was beginning to seem like an old friend we hadn't seen in a while, and we were determined to lift its sagging bones. It was going to symbolize our spiffy new life together."

"I know, son, I know. But just be thankful you hadn't moved any of your things in yet." Gaylie Girl took a sip of her coffee while searching for something to lighten the mood and soon found it. "You were insured, of course. You won't take the loss."

"Yes. But you know money's not the issue here. I know we can buy something else downtown and start all over. Seems funny to be putting it that way when we hadn't even really begun, though. It's just that—well, I trust this fire wasn't any kind of omen for my third trip to the altar."

Gaylie Girl's maternal instincts kicked in, and she moved forward to wrap him up in her arms, letting the strength of her hug speak for her. The result was that neither of them was willing to let go for quite a while.

"Mother, I really want things to work out this time," he said, pulling back slightly to give her an earnest smile. "I freely admit I blew it with Sharon and Marny big-time. If this doesn't work out with Meta, I think I might be permanently headed toward 'rich but lonely old codger' status."

His self-deprecation generated some much-needed laughter. "That's not going to happen, son. Renza and I have reached an understanding as future in-laws, and we came to the conclusion that the four of us are definitely a match."

Petey brightened further. "Yeah, Meta told me that her mother's finally come around and has stopped reading her the riot act about all her choices in life. Yesterday evening, she said she had the best conversation she's had with her mother in years, and that's saying something. If you had anything at all to do with that, I thank you from the bottom of my heart."

"Just one more thing a mother is supposed to do for her children," Gaylie Girl added, taking a cute little bow.

But Petey did not remain upbeat for long, as a thoughtful frown crept into his face. "Who's going to tell Sis about this? I'll call her up later after I talk to Meta, if you want."

Gaylie Girl was emphatic, however. "Let me do it. Your sister and I have been keeping in touch constantly about the caroling progress. Amanda just adored The Square on your visits down this summer. That's what really won her over to Second Creek. You know how she is about architecture and historic buildings. She'll be every bit as heartbroken as Meta will, I'm sure. But I want to be the one to handle it."

"Speaking of the caroling, what are you going to do about it, Mother? All those choirs practicing so hard, all that elaborate planning and coordination, not to mention those church bus tours that are in the bag. And now this. Can you salvage something?"

Gaylie Girl's sigh was clearly full of pessimism as she tied her terry-cloth robe at her waist and folded her arms. "Hale has already told me most of The Square will definitely be off-limits for a long time while the cleanup is taking place. After that, it's up in the air as to what gets rebuilt and restored, but that kind of thing always takes money and patience. I don't see how we can pull off Caroling in The Square with all that to contend with."

"Hey, you thought outside the box to come up with the event in the first place. Maybe you could do it again and surprise the hell out of everybody with something brilliant," Petey said, offering a ray of hope.

"I suppose I could try." But her reply was as subdued as her resolve. For much like The Square, itself, she was substantially burned out.

※

Though they both needed to get at least a few hours of sleep before heading down to the courthouse and officially tackling the aftermath of the devastation the night before, Gaylie Girl and Mr. Choppy were unable to do much more than lie in bed and stare at the ceiling once he'd finally returned. She winced at every one of his plaintive sighs as he tossed and turned, and she was hardly more relaxed herself. But it was that conversation she'd had with Euterpe somewhere in the midst of their Nitwitt networking that kept resonating with her in particular, and she needed to bounce it off someone to clear the decks.

"As long as we're both not sleeping, sweetheart," she finally ventured, "I wanted to run something past you."

He wrestled with his pillow for the umpteenth time and slid down to face her squarely. "If your brain is still runnin' on like mine is, we might as well. I just can't get the images of that fire outta my head. It felt like the end of the world to me. Or maybe some bad dream."

Gaylie Girl inched closer as his last words spurred her

on. "That's exactly what I wanted to talk to you about—the dream I had tonight that started turning into a nightmare. It's receded in my memory a bit now, but I could swear I was on the verge of having it all leaked to me somehow."

"Havin' what leaked to you?"

"The fire. Or more precisely, the fact that it was headed full speed for The Square." She gave him the details of her dream just before the phone call from Garvin Braswell had awakened them both. Then she awaited his reaction.

"A strange coincidence, maybe?" he offered after a brief silence. "Who can explain dreams?"

She told him about Euterpe winning the Denver Lee McQueen sweepstakes a while back with her fevered dream about frantic dancing that came very close to what had actually taken place among the Nitwitts that particular Saturday. "Euterpe and I discussed the significance of both our dreams a couple of hours ago, and she once again expressed the notion that there is something out there in the universe always looking after us whether we acknowledge it or not."

"I can go along with that," Mr. Choppy answered. "My mother sure believed it, and that was the way she raised me. I have to say that my faith in somethin' greater than myself kept me goin' all those decades we were apart and I was still very much in love with you."

Gaylie Girl snuggled right up against the warmth his racing blood was generating and kissed him gently on the lips. "And I was just thinking that I wasn't much prone to probing beneath the surface of my life of luxury until we got reconnected. Euterpe says you have to be open to the universe to receive its messages when they come your way.

Still, I think there are some things I'd be frightened to know about ahead of time. That sort of ignorance would surely be bliss. Euterpe seems to be able to deal with her prescience very well. I'm finding my way with mine, I suppose. If that's what it is, I mean." Then she pulled away slightly as her philosophical ramblings ended with an unexpected exit line. "You didn't mention your father."

"What about him?"

"You said you got your religious beliefs from your mother. Didn't your father believe in anything?"

Mr. Choppy managed a surprising little chuckle. "Heh. My dad believed in sellin' groceries and doin' a damned good job of it at the Piggly Wiggly. And that also meant being there to hand out free food and water for Second Creekers in time of disaster. Lotsa folks thought of Hale Dunbar Senior as his own private Red Cross whenever one of our gruesome tornadoes and other violent storms practically wrecked the town. You could also say my dad was the kinda man whose deeds always spoke louder than his words. Everybody else might be gnashin' their teeth when the weather turned against Second Creek as it so often has over the years, but he just rolled up his sleeves in workmanlike fashion and got busy helpin' people every time out."

"Like father, like son, Mister Mayor!"

They embraced further, wrapping their arms around each other. But they were far too tired and burdened to undertake anything more physical, sensing that tomorrow and too many days thereafter were going to take a lot out of them.

· *Eleven* ·

Ashes and Switches

And so it came to pass in the dwindling days of 2002 that the sun came up on Monday morning as it always did. But the sight it greeted below in Second Creek, Mississippi, was hideous to behold. Where once had stood unique brick and lacework structures all in a row and fashioned by artisans long dead from a simpler era long past, there were only gutted, blackened ruins. Ashes covered everything from charred beams to The Square sidewalks like a fine gray snow, eerily draining much of the color from the landscape. Even buildings that had not actually burned showed evidence of water damage from the pressure hoses, and the overall effect was of a war zone reeking of acrid, lingering smoke.

For as long as it had burned and even after it had finally

been doused, the fire had been the ruthless victor. But sadly, the spoils belonged only to the broken hearts of Second Creekers. It was perhaps not an understatement to say that the Spirit of Second Creek had been seriously wounded. Not fatally, of course. Nothing could take Second Creek out that easily—not with its proven resilience and fortitude. But on this cold, drab December morning, here was yet another unexpected disaster to overcome in a history replete with them.

Mr. Choppy was in the midst of scanning the two-page Second Creek Fire Department incident report that Garvin Braswell had left on his desk earlier that morning. It was just past ten o'clock, and he was still feeling the impact of too little sleep and too much stress. His Gaylie Girl Friday soon appeared in the doorway looking drained and disconsolate as well.

"Any surprises?" she said, collapsing into one of the armchairs across from him as he put down the stapled papers and sighed.

"No. Business as usual. It was first called in at 2:14. Police car patrolling The Square caught the first glimpse. Braswell's company was the first to arrive three minutes later. It took an hour and fifty-one minutes to get it under control. Too soon to determine area of origin or heat source or any of the rest a' that. There's gonna be plenty a' damage with at least a dozen buildings affected—in the millions, I'm afraid. Only upside is no injuries or fatalities, which is to be expected considerin' the hour. Thank God it didn't happen in the middle of the day with The Square up and runnin' full blast. And then Garvin's note he's clipped on here says it'll take a coupla days to do a complete investigation into the cause. Can't imagine it would be arson, but stranger things've happened."

Gaylie Girl caught his gaze intently. He knew exactly what she was going to say, and it made him squirm in his seat for an instant or two. "Give me a bottom line here, Hale. Is Caroling in The Square officially kaput?"

"Sweetheart, we just can't have people wanderin' around out there anywhere near that mess, I can tell you that right now. I'm just as sorry as I can be to have to say it, but The Square isn't gonna belong to the public for a while now. We'll need a staging area for the demolition crews, so this'll hurt the businesses that weren't even damaged. No, I think you'd better make some other arrangements for those choirs now that this has happened. Oh, and break it to Lady Roth gently that we're not gonna have her up on top of the court-house roof now. We gotta check out every structure around The Square anyway. That'll be just as good an excuse as any to use."

Gaylie Girl was touching her eyelids with the tips of her fingers and shaking her head slowly. "You're right to remind me about her. She's just as likely as not to insist on appearing as the Star of Bethlehem anyway. Knowing her, she'll view the fire as a plot to throw a wrench in her illustrious career. We'll be making her give up the role of a lifetime."

"Yeah, she probably won't go quietly, but if she gives you too much trouble, you just tell her to come to me," Mr. Choppy added, allowing himself a brief smirk. Then he leaned in and assumed a more stoic attitude. "You're just gonna have to postpone that 'Santa Fe' feelin' for a while longer. I don't know why either of us thought Second Creek would change its spots when we got into office. Just when you think you've got this town tamed and purrin', it likes to bare its claws, doesn't it?" He made a sudden sour face. "Hey, what am I sayin' here? Second Creek's no alley cat. I've got no business puttin' that kinda face on this gentle place I love so much. It's just that it's smudged with all that soot today."

But Gaylie Girl chose not to answer. Instead, she seemed to be adding things up in her head with a restless fervor, cutting her eyes this way and that as she moved her index finger back and forth in midair. At some point, the hint of a smile crept into the corners of her mouth.

"I'm doing a diagram of The Square in my head," she finally explained. "All of the choirs chose the north and west balconies for their caroling, and those are now mostly gone. Couldn't we try to move everything to the south and east sides? I know there aren't nearly as many balconies along those blocks, and there's some cleanup over there, too. So it would all be more difficult logistically. We'd have to okay it with those merchants here at the last minute and get all the choirs on board, but maybe you'd let the Nitwitts give it the old college try?"

Mr. Choppy conjured up a polite smile, but his tone was unyielding. In that respect, he was granting his wife no special quarter. "It's my responsibility to make judgment calls for the safety and well-bein' of all Second Creekers as well as the tourists that come here, Gaylie Girl. I just can't in good conscience let people mill around out there as if it was our everyday, charmin' little Square with souvenirs aplenty available. And I hate to say it, but human nature bein' what it is and all, I betcha you'd have more people showin' up to gawk at all the damage than there'd be payin' attention to any carols within a five-mile radius."

"Oh, I know you're probably right," Gaylie Girl said, sounding completely resigned. "I was just hoping against hope for a reprieve of some kind."

"My daddy once told me that you can always find more people wantin' to look at car wrecks out on the highway than at new cars in the showroom. I've gotta err here on the side a' prudence. If anything happened to anybody as a result of my decidin' to let this go on, I couldn't live with myself. Not to mention that the city would probably be liable. I don't have to tell you that folks run to trial lawyers these days when somebody sneezes on 'em and they come down with a cold."

"So it's a big fat definite 'no'?"

"Afraid so, sweetie."

Gaylie Girl rose from her chair without saying anything further, heading back to the reception desk. Mr. Choppy watched her glacial pace from afar and winced, her usual boundless energy and confidence substantially drained from her body.

"Then I guess I'd better get started discussing this with Laurie and Euterpe pronto," she muttered, not bothering to turn her head as she spoke. "We'll have to contact all the choirmasters and decide what to do next. They're all going to be horribly disappointed, of course."

❄

An emergency meeting of everyone involved in Caroling in The Square on Christmas Eve had been hastily called for six o'clock that evening in Gaylie Girl's immaculately kept drawing room on North Bayou Avenue, and it was now under way. It had required a monumental effort, but she, Laurie, and Euterpe had managed to round up the rest of the Nitwitts, their newly appointed Go-to Guy, Powell Hampton, and all the choirmasters for the brainstorming session. Only Novie had been unable to attend, since her Vigil Auntie shift for Cherish, Henry, and baby Riley Jacob at the hospital would begin at six and end at nine. Meanwhile, Mr. Choppy had asked to sit in to offer the mayoral viewpoint on any proposals that arose. His would be the final word regarding anything involving activity in The Square.

With less than a half hour to prepare after rushing home from her secretarial duties, Gaylie Girl had just enough time to put out a store-bought spinach-artichoke dip and several bowls of crackers, pretzels, and nuts around the room. She had thought better of making a big to-do of the usual elaborate Nitwitt libations in deference to certain denominational viewpoints on the subject of alcohol that would be entering her house. Instead, she offered only bottled water and soft drinks. Not surprisingly, there were a few disgruntled expressions among the ladies, but she did not let that faze her. After the meeting, she reasoned, any of the Nitwitts having extreme withdrawal symptoms from the lack of Bloody Marys, mimosas, or something straight up and stronger flowing through their veins could throw one or two or three together at the wet bar and go home happy.

"So, Mayor Dunbar," Lawton Bead of St. Luke's Episcopal was saying from his corner armchair, "let me get this straight. You remain unalterably opposed to letting us switch any of our performances to other balconies farther away from the fire? You don't think we can salvage something here?"

Mr. Choppy, who was standing in the doorway in a kibitzing mode and sipping a ginger ale, drew himself up and cleared his throat. "I would dearly love to, Mr. Bead. I, above anyone else, know how much plannin' and rehearsal this has taken, since my wife here was the spirit behind it from the start. But I just don't think the city of Second Creek should take the risk. I think we'd all readily agree that the venue has been drastically altered overnight anyway. It's pretty much an eyesore right now." He nodded in Powell's general direction. "So, if you'll put together one of your state-of-the-art press releases for the ladies on the official cancellation and get it to *The Citizen* tomorrow mornin', it'd be much appreciated, Mr. Hampton."

"Will do. After all, I'm Mr. Go-to now."

"So that's the end of it?" Mr. Bead continued, thrusting out his jaw in a combination of defiance and disgust. "Do we just blow off everything we've done just like that?"

Interestingly, it was the amenable Press Phillips of Second Creek United Methodist who quickly stepped into the fray just after grabbing his second generous handful of cashews. He'd been noshing ever since entering the room. "Well, I just wanted to say that things haven't changed at all for our choir. Not where it matters. We still intend to go over to Delta Sunset Village in Greenwood and perform for the residents on Thursday afternoon. And I've discussed the aftermath of the fire with our pastor, and he thinks we should perform our caroling selections for our own congregation at the church on Christmas Eve. We already have the program well rehearsed, so even if we can't sing it in The Square as we all originally intended, we can still sing it there. And we can get the word out to the general public that they're perfectly welcome to attend. There's still time for another press release for *The Citizen*'s 'Community Doings' column. Why don't we all consider what I've just said? It's seems very simple to me."

"And very much like a letdown to me," Lincoln Headley of the Second Creek Church of Christ added. "We're all splintering into a lot of separate little events which may or may not be well attended. And what about the bus tours? Are those going to be canceled, too?"

This time, Gaylie Girl took the floor, rising from her sofa in the center of her friends. "I managed to get in touch with all the out-of-town churches this afternoon, and I told them about the Mayor's decision to cancel the event. They were pretty definite about several things. First, they wanted to pass along their sincerest regrets about the fire. Some of them had no idea, since everything happened in the middle of the night and there was next to no news coverage. They also said they intend to keep us in their prayers for a timely recovery. And unfortunately, they regretted to say that they don't think the interest will be there any longer for the bus trips now that the balconies around The Square won't be the focus of the caroling. I know for a fact that that's what attracted them in the first place."

"And surely Lady Roth shining down on them from above," said Renza, frowning into her Perrier and lemon.

"Well, Press's idea is about the best we can do at this point," added Walker Billings of First Baptist in his booming voice. "I just wanted to make sure there was no chance we could pull off this balcony business, as we've all come to call it. Hey, Press, maybe our choir could come over with yours to that retirement home?"

But it was Gaylie Girl who addressed the suggestion. "Oh, I can tell you there wouldn't be enough room, Mr. Billings. Every bit of space in the Delta Sunset Village lobby will be taken up by the Methodist choir and the seating for the residents." She paused to give him the politest of smiles. "But what a nice gesture. Certainly in the spirit of the season."

Mr. Billings shrugged. "Hey, you do what you can!"

Gaylie Girl impulsively decided to inject a positive note. "Maybe we should all keep in mind that there's always next year. I trust The Square will have been restored to its former glory by then."

Mrs. Vergie Woods of the Marblestone Alley Church of Holiness spoke up next.

Gaylie Girl noted that she was dressed once again from head to toe in purple, as she had been the first time the two of them had met at her church. Perhaps it was her signature color. "Miz Dunbar, I just wanted to say that maybe we should be talkin' 'bout how we can help that former glory thing get here a little bit sooner. There's not a' one of our churches that can't hold a bake sale to raise money for a good cause. Why, we do it all the time at Marblestone Alley Church of Holiness."

"I think that's a marvelous idea," Gaylie Girl said. "What do you think about it, Hale?"

Mr. Choppy gripped his glass of ginger ale a little tighter and managed a tense little laugh. "I think it's gonna be a long, hard road back for The Square. It'll take loads of money and plannin' and maybe even a guardian angel or two to get us to where we once were. There's a part of me that wonders if we'll ever get there. But, by all means, let's try anything— bake sales, concerts, raffles—anything we can think of to make The Square a desirable destination again."

On this, there was unanimous agreement, and the spirits of the group seemed to lift ever so slightly. "It's at least something to work toward," Press Phillips offered, tossing back the last of his cashews. "Even if it doesn't feel much like Christmas right now."

❆

Novie's Vigil Auntie shift in the hospital waiting room started out uneventfully. First off, she asked Henry if there had been any change to report, and he answered calmly enough.

"Cherish is her usual angelic self, thank God. I've just been in to see her. If there was such a thing as an advertisement for the perfect hospital stay, she'd be it—all propped up in bed smilin' and not so much as a hair outta place. But behind that pretty picture I can tell you Cherish is plenty worried because our Riley Jacob's still on the ventilator.

That's the key, the doctor says. If they can just get him off it . . ."

Novie conjured up her most reassuring demeanor. "I'm sure they will soon, Henry. Now, it's time for you to run on home and get something good and homemade to eat. You'll find your plate on the bottom shelf of the refrigerator. Just zap it in the microwave for a minute or so. Not too long, though. About a minute should do the trick. You don't want my wonderful cuisine nuked to a crisp!"

"Mind tellin' me what's on the menu?"

"Ah! Well, for your dining pleasure this evening I have lovingly prepared for you several slices of pork tenderloin with a light gravy, a generous helping of smashed red potatoes, and lots of buttered green beans with slivered toasted almonds. I always have that when Marc and Michael come over for dinner. They both rave about it. You know, it's very satisfying for a woman to see the men in her life enjoying her cooking."

Henry was beaming and rubbing his belly at the same time. "Man, you Nitwitts sure know how to treat a fella!"

Indeed, the details they had worked out for their Vigil Auntie shifts were far beyond the call of duty. In exchange for a copy of the key to Henry's modest little bungalow in New Vista Acres, each Nitwitt would be dropping by before her watch to deliver a full home-cooked meal or at least a delicious little snack for him to enjoy on his much-needed breaks from the hospital. No fast-food or vending-machine indigestion for this young father with the weight of the world on his shoulders!

"As I explained, it's no more than I'd do for my Marc,"

Novie added, grasping his hand warmly. "Now, you run right along and take some downtime, young man. Vigil Auntie Novie's orders. I'll let you know immediately if anything changes."

It was about five minutes after Henry's departure that the NICU nurse on duty, a short plump woman with big hair, came shuffling out in search of him. "Has Mr. Hempstead left?" she said while looking around the room.

"Just a few minutes ago," Novie answered with a hint of trepidation in her voice. "I'm his friend, Novie Mims, and I'm holding down the fort while he goes home to have a little bite to eat. Is something wrong?"

The nurse was smiling and shaking her head at the same time—a professional affectation she typically indulged with all her patients. "We think it's under control now, but there have been a couple of episodes of apnea in the NICU."

An alarm went off in Novie's head. "Apnea? Isn't that when someone stops breathing? Has the baby stopped breathing?"

"Relax, Ms. Mims. It's under control. It can happen sometimes with babies this young who are being weaned off ventilators."

"Should I call Mr. Hempstead and let him know? I promised to do that if anything came up."

"Frankly, I'd let him go ahead and enjoy his dinner. As I said, the situation is under control, and there's nothing he could do if he rushed back here. I just came out to keep him informed."

Novie thought for a moment. "Does Mrs. Hempstead know about this? Perhaps he'd like to be here for her."

"She knows. Actually, she was in the NICU watching the baby when it happened. Just her second visit, it seems, so it was quite distressing for her. But the doctor has given her something to calm her down. She'll be all right, especially now that we've told her the baby's apnea episode has passed."

"Can she have visitors? Perhaps I could go in and be of some comfort to her."

The nurse broadened what was already an understanding smile. "Not just yet. We'll let her rest just a little while longer. Then I'll come out and take you to her room for a nice little visit."

❋

Cherish couldn't seem to get the image of her baby son not breathing out of her head. "It was so frightenin', Miz Mims," she was explaining some thirty minutes later from her recumbent position in the hospital bed. Novie was standing beside her holding her hand and gently smiling down at her. "How could I know it wasn't . . . well, the end? I panicked for a while there. You watch those hospital shows on television and the equipment starts makin' all those funny hectic noises, and you know good and well it means somethin' is drastically wrong."

"I know exactly what you mean, dear. Those shows are so dramatic. There's a crisis around every corner of the hallways. Of course, they do it for the ratings."

"I'm sure they do, but what I felt an hour or so ago was real. My heart just dropped to the soles of my feet. It was like bein' on the roller-coaster ride at the state fair in Jackson."

Novie loosened her grip and patted Cherish's hand gently. "No need to dwell on it, though. I've been assured things are back to normal."

"If bein' on a ventilator and bein' almost two months premature can be considered normal for a baby," Cherish stated in a monotone, while averting her eyes.

Then she gave Novie an earnest glance. "Miz Mims, would you mind if I asked you somethin'?"

"Why, of course not."

"Do you think it's possible I'm not a good person?"

Novie drew back slightly, both surprised and perplexed. It was the last thing she expected to hear from a young woman that Gaylie Girl had once precisely described as eternally optimistic and relentlessly cheerful. "I—uh, don't quite know what you mean, dear."

Cherish was looking off to the side now, allowing herself a rueful little smile. "I was just thinkin' about Christmas nearly bein' here and all. Henry told me about the terrible fire in The Square last night and all the devastation, and that's just made everything worse."

"I'm still not following you."

Cherish sat up a bit straighter against her pillows and sniffled. "Oh, I know I'm not makin' much sense. But they say bad things happen to bad people, and I think everyone would agree that miscarriages and premature babies aren't exactly good news. So the way things have gone for me, I sometimes wonder if I'm bein' punished for somethin'. Do you think that's possible?"

Novie grasped Cherish's hand again, this time more firmly. "I most certainly do not, young lady. I don't know why you would even get a notion like that into your head. This is a challenge you've been given for whatever reasons, and you and Henry will just have to be strong enough to work your way through it. Now, I've seen for myself how much you both love each other, and I have no doubt this whole thing will turn your way very soon."

"So you don't think everything is an omen? What about the fire in The Square? When I was a little girl, my mother used to tell me that if I wasn't good all year, I'd get ashes and switches for Christmas. I can't help thinkin' about all those ashes Henry says The Square is covered with now. He says it's so ugly he can barely stand to go anywhere near it. I guess I keep waitin' for the switches to show up."

Novie's voice stayed on the gentle side, but there was a hint of impatience about it. "My mother told me the same thing, Cherish, and I told my Marc when he was just a little boy. It's not meant to be taken seriously. As for the fire, I spoke with Gaylie Girl Dunbar this morning, and she says they won't know the likely cause for another couple of days. They're investigating it right now. But whatever the case, you can rest assured it will be something scientific. There'll be no mysterious omen to explain away. It's just one of those things that happens from time to time."

"I know I'm bein' silly about it, Miz Mims. I guess I'm just depressed. Christmas is supposed to be such a joyous time to celebrate your beliefs and bein' with your friends and family, and it seems like that's not goin' to happen this year in Second Creek."

Novie took a deep breath and reflected. To a certain extent, Cherish was right. It wasn't turning out to be the special Christmas they'd all been so judiciously planning the past few months.

❄

"You'll never guess who that was," Gaylie Girl said to Mr. Choppy. He had sauntered into the kitchen just as she was hanging up the phone.

The emergency meeting she'd called had been over for twenty-five minutes now, and all the choirmasters and Nitwitts had long retreated to their homes. Of course, some of the Nitwitts had partaken of various spirituous concoctions for good measure. Now it was time for Gaylie Girl to think about getting dinner together, but the phone call promptly put that task on hold.

"I give up. Practically everybody we know was just here," Mr. Choppy replied. "A telemarketer, perhaps?"

"You're forgetting about Lady Roth, Hale."

Mr. Choppy put the palm of his hand to his temple and sighed. "Oh, no."

"Oh, yes. She demands a meeting with both of us tomorrow at the office to discuss the status of her role as the Star of Bethlehem. She insists that she be allowed to depict it despite the fire. Oh, I knew this would happen!"

Mr. Choppy was now patiently massaging his temple with the tips of his fingers, his face a mask of stoicism. "What did you tell her?"

"That we'd see her around two. You know there's no way around it. We'd have to face her sooner or later. What are you going to do—get a restraining order?"

The phone rang again, startling them both, and Gaylie Girl said: "I'm afraid to answer it. It's brought us nothing but grief the past twenty-four hours."

Nonetheless, she picked up the receiver gingerly, said hello, and listened. "Why, yes, how delightful to hear from you," she began. "Your Mrs. Woods was just here and contributed quite a bit to our discussion. I think everyone agreed she had some positive ideas to contribute to a situation that was a bit depressing, to say the least."

There followed a long period of silence in which Gaylie Girl did little more than nod and say things like "Uh-huh" and "She did?"

Mr. Choppy stood quietly at the counter, drumming his fingers and trying to figure out what was going on from Gaylie Girl's end of the conversation. But to no avail.

Finally, she said: "Let me check with the Mayor. Please hold on a minute." Then she covered the receiver, turned to him, and said: "We've just gotten the most offbeat dinner invitation I could ever imagine in a thousand years, and I think I'd like to accept."

"Dinner? Where?"

"Here, if you can believe it. It's Reverend Quintus Payne of the Marblestone Alley Church of Holiness. He says Mrs. Woods called him up and told him and his wife, Yolie, that we needed some cheering up immediately because of the damage to The Square and the cancellation of the caroling. He says we're not to even consider fixing dinner tonight.

They'll be bringing some inspirational food for the four of us. The gist is they have something they think will help us move on. Well, I don't know about that, but I'm positively intrigued by the boldness of it all. I say, 'Let's do this.'"

Mr. Choppy was rolling his eyes and licking his lips at the same time. "Is his wife the one who made that incredibly delicious bread pudding with the buttered-rum drizzle you brought home for me a coupla months ago? I've never had anything so tasty in my life."

"One and the same."

"Then by all means, don't keep the man waitin' any longer. Tell him we can't wait to sink our teeth into whatever they've cooked up for us. Oh, and not to forget that bread pudding for dessert."

Gaylie Girl promptly relayed all the instructions and hung up after the usual polite sign-off. Then she impishly wagged her brows. "I don't know about you, but I can't wait to see how the rest of our evening is going to go."

Twelve

A Little Cream of Courage

Gaylie Girl had not remembered Yolie Payne being this stylish and striking on her visit to the Marble-stone Alley Church of Holiness a few months back. Oh, she had noticed that the woman was tall with a model-thin figure easily enough. She seemed the perfect match for her equally lanky and lean husband. But the large apron Yolie was wearing that afternoon while turning out pans of her superlative bread pudding had inadvertently prevented Gaylie Girl from making any sort of definitive judgment on the woman's taste in clothes.

Now, with this spur-of-the-moment but convivial dinner engagement for a backdrop, there was nothing to stand in the way of such a fashion appraisal, and Gaylie Girl's ver-dict as Yolie Payne entered her foyer was that her ensemble was stunning. It wasn't just the dress, either, though the alternating bands of crimson and muted gold with matching accessories were breathtaking to behold. Gaylie Girl was certain the last time she had encountered this sophisticated an outfit on anyone other than herself was on a visit to Evening Shadows to have a cocktail with those two elegants Myrtis and Euterpe. Either or both of them might have something like this—perhaps several like this—hanging in their extensive closets.

But neither of them could match Yolie Payne's flawless, ginger-colored skin, full, bright red lips, and coiffure of luxuriant, relaxed curls. Altogether, the woman was a feast for the eyes, and it flashed into Gaylie Girl's head that someone ought to do a portrait of her while she remained in full bloom this way.

"You're probably wonderin' about all these things we're bringin' up in here," Yolie said, after all the perfunctory greetings. "Let me put you in the loop then. This industrial-strength thermos I have here is our main course, and Quintus has my yeast rolls all wrapped up in foil there in his right hand, and the bread pudding the Mayor requested in his left. And that's what we're all havin' for dinner."

"Please. Mayor seems a little too formal. Just call us Hale and Gaylie Girl," Mr. Choppy said.

"And you just call us Yolie and Quintus. He gets tired of the Reverend title all the time, even though that's his business, and that's who he truly is." Yolie turned to Gaylie Girl, handing over the large thermos while taking the rolls and bread pudding from her husband. "Let's head on back to your kitchen, and I'll show you what we got in here. Meanwhile, I hope y'all are hungry 'cause I know we are."

"Hungry and intrigued," Gaylie Girl said. "I don't know when I've looked forward so much to having dinner. And what wife wouldn't like to have a night off from cooking? Hale, you'll offer Quintus something to drink from the bar, won't you? And what about you, Yolie?"

"I think I'll wait until we eat, if you don't mind. I always like a little wine with my dinner."

Then the women left the men to their own devices in the drawing room and headed to the kitchen. Halfway there, Yolie said: "I can imagine you were plenty surprised to get our phone call. I know I would be in your shoes. After all, we did invite ourselves over without a care in the world, and that's not the way you're supposed to do things. But our Miz Vergie just insisted we could do some good here tonight, and we intend to prove her right."

Once in the kitchen Gaylie Girl retrieved a large saucepan from one of the overhead cabinets and poured out the contents of the thermos, admiring the aroma and appearance of the thick, creamy concoction that emerged. "This looks absolutely heavenly. I can tell it has to be homemade. Don't tell me—a treasured family recipe, right?"

Yolie looked thoroughly amused as Gaylie Girl began stirring with a big slotted spoon. "It is, as a matter of fact. I was a Hazlip from over in Indianola, you see, and my family all called this their cream of courage soup."

"Oh, I love the sound of that. I can't wait to hear what's in it. Meanwhile, I think I'll throw together a little romaine and tomato salad with croutons for all of us while you talk about your recipe," Gaylie Girl added, momentarily abandoning the burner to pop the yeast rolls into the oven to warm.

Yolie took over the stirring duties from her and began explaining with great enthusiasm while Gaylie Girl retrieved her produce from the refrigerator. "It's not so much what's in my cream of courage as the story behind it. Now, as far as the ingredients are concerned, I could rattle 'em off in my sleep. You got your cut-up chicken breast, half-and-half, butter, mushrooms, carrots, peas, potatoes, a dash of celery salt, and a secret ingredient I won't tell you about. I never had to write any of it down, though—I just watched my mama makin' it at the stove, just hummin' away and havin' herself a good time. Originally, it was handed down by my grandmama and she just called it her chicken pot pie soup. But that name got thrown out because of somethin' that happened when I was growin' up."

Gaylie Girl leaned against the granite marble counter with the biggest smile on her face. No two ways about it— she was hooked, putting her hunger on the back burner as Yolie's story continued to unfold.

"You see, I had these two pitiful fools for older broth- ers. They couldn't stop fussin' and fightin' with each other. I cain't tell you the number of times they got punished for it. Anyway, one Christmas mornin' they both got BB guns under the tree, and do you know what those two fools up and did? They went out in the backyard and stood up in front of each other and one of 'em said, 'I'm gonna shoot you!' And the other one said, 'Not if I don't shoot you first!' And then they both aimed those guns and shot each other in the arm like a scene from *Gunsmoke* or somethin'. Nothin' serious, you know what I'm sayin'. Silly flesh wounds. But all the same, it was still two fools talkin' trash to each other and swappin' BBs."

Gaylie Girl was trying her best to suppress her laughter, but she couldn't quite manage it.

"Oh, go ahead and laugh, girl. It's funny when you look back on it now, but my mama didn't think it was so funny back then. She lit into my daddy, sayin', 'What the hell was you thinkin' about givin' those boys those guns for presents, Joseph?' Oh, she went on and on about how somebody was gonna get an eye put out one of these days if this family didn't straighten up and fly right. She'd had her fill of foolishness and let everybody know it."

"What did she do next?"

"Well, she got all the family together and sat us all down around the dinner table. Then she came out and ladled her latest batch of chicken pot pie soup to everybody. But she wouldn't let us touch a drop until she'd said her piece. 'You boys are gonna be the death of me yet the way you carry on so. Now, I been prayin' to God to give me the strength to deal with you two. But I think he musta gone deaf, or you wouldn't've shot each other with those sorry guns. So now I'm servin' up this recipe that the women of this family been fixin' generation after generation, but I'm callin' it my cream of courage from now on. I need every bit of strength I can put in my body to keep me from takin' those guns to you boys myself. Now, I'm not gonna waste my breath with anymore warnin's. Y'all eat my cream of courage soup and give me somethin' to be proud of, you hear me? Otherwise, I'm gonna have to just give up and turn both y'all out into the street!"

Gaylie Girl was enjoying the story so much, she almost felt like clapping as Yolie came to the end. Instead, she pursued her natural curiosity. "So you think Hale and I could use a little cream of courage at this point, do you?"

Yolie looked up from her stirring and winked. "Couldn't hurt. Because I mean to say those two brothers of mine did straighten up after that. I believe it was somethin' in my mama's tone of voice—she put the fear of God in 'em. They could tell she was at the end of her rope. And Miz Vergie told us she thought you and your husband might be gettin' there with everything goin' wrong the way it has. 'Go serve 'em up some of your cream of courage, Yolie!' she said to me. So here I am, and here it is just about ready to serve."

❄

Out in the drawing room, Mr. Choppy and Quintus Payne sat at either end of Gaylie Girl's pristine Belter sofa, sipping Delta Lady dry muscadine wine and discussing the distant past. It was the good Reverend, in fact, who had led them down that particular path.

"I never told you this when you came to my church seekin' my support for your campaign earlier this year, Hale, but you had me in your back pocket even if you'd never shown up. Or even if young Kenyatta Warner hadn't spoken so highly of the way you helped him out all that time he was baggin' groceries and stockin' the shelves for you at the Piggly Wiggly."

Mr. Choppy took another swig of his wine and offered up an almost fatherly grin. "Ah, yes—Kenyatta Warner. I got a little note from him just the other day tellin' me that he's still enrolled at Delta State. Hasn't decided on his major yet, though. I think he was halfway expectin' me to come up with some suggestions the way I always did when he had a problem at the store. He's a good kid."

"Never missed church, I can tell you that. Anyhow, it didn't surprise me that he looked up to you so much. So many folks in this town do."

Mr. Choppy seemed to be blushing now. "Enough to vote me into office, at least. Well, I'm sure you know I'd never take anybody or anything for granted. That's not the way I operate."

"No, sir, you wouldn't. And neither did your daddy. You see, my family owes your family a debt of gratitude goin' all the way back to the Tornado of 1953. I was just a little boy back then, but we were hard-hit by the storm. Our little house out on Lower Winchester Road was directly in the path, and there was nothin' left of it but a pile of bricks after it passed over. I mean, we lost everything from toys to weddin' pictures to all our clothes 'cept what we had on our backs. My mama and daddy and sisters and myself moved into the church to have a place to stay. Had to sleep on cots in the social hall for quite a spell there. That's when I first became interested in the ministry. The way Marblestone Alley Church of Holiness took us in made me want to give somethin' back. And that's what I hope I've done."

Mr. Choppy nodded thoughtfully, lost in his memories of the destructive event that had torn off and carried away part of the steeple of First Presbyterian Church. The very same finger pointing to heaven he had somehow managed to hunt down, retrieve, and showcase in the backyard of his new home. "I'll never forget all the misery that storm brought to Second Creek. I was twenty-two or twenty-three at the time. Daddy couldn't bear the thought of people goin' hungry or not havin' anything to drink in the aftermath, so he handed out free staples and soft drinks to as many as he could during those first few days."

The Reverend hoisted his wineglass as if getting ready to make a toast. "That's the debt I'm talkin' 'bout. Between the church and your daddy, we got by until we could get back on our feet. But it was goin' downtown to the Piggly Wiggly with my mama and my sisters that I remember most." He settled back even more comfortably in his chair, his gaze almost worshipful.

"Your daddy had a way of smilin' at people the minute they stepped into his Piggly Wiggly. He acted like it was his home, and everybody who came to shop was his guest of honor. My mama, she never did stop talkin' about him on the way back to the church carryin' her paper bag full of Vienna sausages and pork and beans he'd handed out to us. 'That man is a child of God,' she would say to all of us over and over. 'I want you chirren to be just like him when you grow up.'" He leaned forward a bit, downing the last of his wine as he capped off his tribute. "And I like to think I am just like him, Hale. I like to think I am."

Mr. Choppy was struggling with his emotions but ultimately opted not to hide the fact that he was tearing up. "Oh, my," he began, sniffling a couple of times. "You'll have to forgive me. Thinkin' about my daddy's kindness gets to me every now and then. He sure was special. You'd think I'd never forget it, but sometimes you just get too caught up in the moment."

Just then Gaylie Girl and Yolie appeared together in the doorway. "Time to eat, gentlemen. Shall we adjourn to the dining room? We're having cream of courage," Gaylie Girl announced.

Mr. Choppy looked puzzled but smiled big anyway. "Uh . . . bring it on. Whatever it is."

❄

"You simply have to give me your secret ingredient, Yolie," Gaylie Girl insisted, as the two couples were sitting around the table, finishing up their cream of courage and salads. "Otherwise, when I try to make this on my own, it will lack that last little bit of zing. Not that I would ever expect it to be as good as yours."

But Yolie was having none of it, tossing her head back saucily. "Just cain't do it, I'm afraid. My mama swore me to secrecy. She was like that, you know. Her recipes were sacred. Especially the ones she called her comfort food. And this was her favorite one."

Gaylie Girl kept savoring her last spoonful, working her mouth and lips in an attempt to guess at the last ingredient. "Is it fennel? I'm getting an almost licorice taste there at the end."

Yolie shook her head with a mischievous smile.

"Basil, then?"

"You'll never guess."

"Gaylie Girl has been a whirling dervish at the stove ever

since I gave her my mama's recipe book," Mr. Choppy put in from his seat at the head of the table. "And she's become an excellent Southern cook, by the way."

Gaylie Girl winked smartly, catching the gaze of both her guests. "Even if I am a Yankee from Lake Forest." Then she put down her spoon and assumed a more serious demeanor. "But I've been bound and determined to blend in down here, learn the ways of Second Creek—that sort of thing. I had hoped my Caroling in The Square project would be the first mark I'd leave on the town. The first of many. But it doesn't look like that's going to work out."

Quintus leaned in with a solicitous smile. "That's really why Yolie and I wanted to come over here tonight. Miz Vergie told us you were takin' that fire pretty hard, and nobody can blame you. Downtown looks even worse than it did right after the Tornado of 1953 came through, and I didn't think I'd ever see anything more terrible than that as long as I lived."

"It's hard to see right now how it's all gonna be built back, Quintus," Mr. Choppy said, settling back in his chair with a sigh. "There'd be so many different owners involved. Would they want to rebuild the stores the way they were, down to the doorknobs? It might be easier and less expensive for some of 'em just to raze and try to sell their lots. I think what's really gettin' to me—and Gaylie Girl, too— is that The Square may never come close to bein' the way it was, no matter what's decided. I feel like I've lost a part of my soul, in a way."

Mr. Choppy's words seemed to energize the Reverend Quintus Payne in a very memorable way. He brought his hands together prayerfully and nodded gently at Mr. Choppy and Gaylie Girl in turn. "That's why you need to use that cream of courage to fortify your faith that it will all work out. This is the season for miracles, for the victories, big and small. Keep believin' that, and The Square will rise from the ashes. That's what we came here to tell you both tonight."

Mr. Choppy and Gaylie Girl caught each other's gaze, and she was the first to answer the minisermon they had both just received. "Second Creek really is a remarkable place to have people such as yourself deeply involved the way you are."

"And you're just as involved in the right way—you and your husband both," Quintus replied. "But not Mr. Floyce all those years he ran things. Everybody knew he was up to no good all the time. He was just in it for himself with all those deals he made under the table. Of course, nobody could prove it, but everybody knew it just the same. Maybe he's found his end of the rainbow out there in Las Vegas, where he said he was movin' to. But you two need to remember that you represent the best of Second Creek. And Second Creek's gonna come through for you. Just wait and see."

❄

It was after Quintus and Yolie had left that Mr. Choppy reflected on the remarkable dinner they had just eaten. In one sense he could almost feel the effects of the cream of courage surging through his veins. Or was it more the good Reverend's inspirational words?

"We can use all the help we can get with that mess in The

Square," he said, as he helped Gaylie Girl clear the table. "But let's start with the little things that are much more doable."

"Such as?"

They both headed toward the kitchen with their plates and silverware, and he said: "Lady Roth, for instance. We have that appointment with her tomorrow afternoon. I've just had a brilliant idea on how to handle her."

Gaylie Girl was smiling as she stacked her dishes on the counter and then took his as well. "The inspiration from the Paynes is infectious, I see. I'm not sure when I've had a more surprising evening. So what's your idea?"

He watched her scraping the plates as he patted his belly. "I think I'll wait and tell you about it when we get to the office tomorrow. That'll give me time to sleep on it, not to mention a few more hours for all this cream of courage and bread pudding to settle."

The front doorbell rang insistently, startling them both.

"Who could that be?" Gaylie Girl said. "I wonder if the Paynes forgot something?" She surveyed the kitchen thoroughly and shrugged. "No, I'm positive they left here with that enormous thermos and all their trays. Would you go answer it, sweetheart? I'm right in the middle of this, and my hands are all wet."

It did not take Mr. Choppy long to return with a worried-looking Novie in tow. "I tried to call you before coming over," she began as Mr. Choppy helped her off with her coat. "But my cell phone's been on the blink all evening. I'm always forgetting to charge it. Anyway, I wanted to tell you all about my first vigil at the hospital. A little too much excitement for my taste."

"Oh, no bad news, I hope?" Gaylie Girl said, putting the dishes on hold and drying her hands quickly. "Would you like a cup of coffee?"

"No to both questions. Especially to the coffee. I've had enough of that bad vending-machine variety as it is. I may never sleep again. I should take a tip from what I'm doing for Henry and make sure I get the proper food and drink myself."

Then the three of them sat around the kitchen table, and Novie told them about the frightening apnea episode that baby Riley Jacob had endured in the neonatal intensive care unit. "Henry was so upset with me when he returned from eating that delicious dinner I fixed for him," she continued. "At first, he said I'd let him down by not telling him about it immediately. But the nurse helped me calm him down a few minutes later. She backed me up that there was really nothing to be gained by telling him at that point, except to give him indigestion. Or get him so upset he wouldn't eat at all. And that's what the Vigil Aunties were trying to help him avoid, weren't we?"

Gaylie Girl reached over to pat Novie's hand gently. "Of course that's what we're trying to do. You did the right thing, and I'm glad Henry saw it your way eventually. How do things stand now? With the baby, I mean."

"He's still on the ventilator. They're not going to try and wean him off for the time being. The thing is, as long as he's on that ventilator, he's definitely not out of the woods.

The nurse said getting him to breathe on his own would be a huge step toward stabilizing him. She said there's just no telling when that might happen. It's touch and go. So there are still some anxious days and nights ahead for all of us."

"But for now my godson-to-be is hangin' in there, right?" Mr. Choppy said, the concern clearly evident in his tone.

"The nurse believes he still has every chance to get over the hump."

"And how's our Cherish doin'?"

Novie seemed suddenly guarded, taking her time answering, and Mr. Choppy was alarmed. "She hasn't developed any complications, has she?"

"No, no. Not the way you mean. It's just that this is hard on her emotionally, of course. It would be on any mother. At one point, she needed someone to lift her spirits, and I believe I came through for her. Perhaps the two of you could drop by when you can find a moment in your office routine tomorrow. I know it would help."

Mr. Choppy's response was immediate, with no lack of conviction. "We'll make the time."

Gaylie Girl rose from the table and moved with all deliberate speed to the refrigerator. "Meanwhile, Novie, you need a little something to lift your spirits the way Hale and I have just had ours lifted." She opened the refrigerator, peered in, and retrieved a small plate wrapped in foil. "It just so happens that we have a little piece of unbelievably sinful bread pudding left over from our dinner tonight. They—well, the Reverend Quintus Payne and his charming wife, Yolie, that is—invited themselves over on the spur of the moment and served us a homemade dinner."

Novie couldn't have looked more perplexed, cocking her head while she made small quizzical gestures with her open palms. "They did what?"

Gaylie Girl quickly explained what had happened after the meeting with the choirmasters and the rest of the Nitwitts had adjourned, ending with the entertaining story from Yolie Payne about the history of cream of courage soup.

"I could have used a cup of that stuff at the hospital," Novie quipped, craning her neck as Gaylie Girl removed the foil from the bread pudding and hovered near the stove with it.

"As for this, Novie, the kitchen is still open. Would you prefer it warmed or microwaved?"

"Oh, I've died and gone to heaven!" Novie exclaimed, ignoring the question. "That was the best bread pudding I've ever tasted the day you and Laurie and I drove out to that Marblestone Church in the Alley, or was it The Holy Church of Marblestones—oh, I forget what they call it. Whatever. I've been wishing there was a way I could have a piece of it again ever since then."

Gaylie Girl pointed rather dramatically to the plate of bread pudding she was still holding. "Well, here's your wish come true, Novie, dear. Now, which will it be—stove or microwave?"

"Let me at it. Microwave, please."

It was only after Novie had begun to dig into her steaming treat with great relish that she came up for air long enough to ask for an update on the meeting with the choirmasters that she had missed.

"They took the cancellation reasonably well for the most

part," Gaylie Girl explained. "Oh, a few squawks here and there from Lawton Bead and Lincoln Headley, but that was to be expected. Basically, the choirs are going to sing for their congregations and open the caroling to the public in their own churches. Powell Hampton will write a press release to that effect for *The Citizen*. But as to the future of my Caroling in The Square idea—"

"It may not be possible this year," Mr. Choppy interrupted, not wanting to let go of his inspirational feeling. "But we've got to find a way to make it happen for next Christmas. Because if we don't, it will mean that The Square's down for the count for good. We just can't let that happen. Quintus Payne is right, you know. This is the season of miracles, and more important, this is Second Creek."

Thirteen

Sparks and Other
Heat Sources

*I*ncendiary was the best word to describe the exchange
currently raging between Mr. Choppy and Lady Roth
around two-fifteen Tuesday afternoon in his office.
Sparks were definitely flying. The Star of Bethlehem simply would not be moved from her mission of light. Gaylie
Girl sat off to one side taking notes as Mr. Choppy made
repeated attempts to placate her.

"Back to the safety issue, Lady Roth," Mr. Choppy was
saying. "I'll be receiving the final investigation report from
my fire chief late this afternoon, but Mr. Braswell's already
told me there's lots of soot and debris up on the widow's
walk. That'll have to be cleaned up before anyone walks
around up there."

Lady Roth turned up her nose while adjusting her

turban and remained an unmovable object. "How long will that take?"

Mr. Choppy leaned in from behind his desk, his face clearly showing signs of frustration. "It's not somethin' we'd want to rush. And, as I said before, we'd have to set up your spotlight on one of the balconies on the other side now. And I can't emphasize enough, Lady Roth, there will be no caroling down below. It'd be just you by yourself up there in the whippin' wind."

"How do you know it will be windy? Have you seen an extended forecast yet?"

Gaylie Girl glanced down at her notes with a subtle shake of her head. Mr. Choppy's "brilliant" idea for dealing with Lady Roth that he'd slept on had fallen on deaf ears. Her scribble was a gossipy testament: *Hale asks L.R. to consider portraying The Star at the various churches instead of on C-house roof... L.R. cops usual histrionic attitude... says out of question... no dramatic effect in that, no spotlight in that... Hale smiles that smile when he's had enough of something or somebody, only they don't know what it means like I do... trouble ahead... Hale tells L.R. not safe up there on widow's walk... must err on side of caution... why doesn't somebody just tell L.R. the truth once in a while... she's a royal (term used loosely here) pain... this could go on all morning... oh, my God, this reads like a teenager's diary... poor Hale!... L.R. won't let this go... uh, oh, something's up... I've seen that look on Hale's face before... when he chewed out workman who pasted drawing room wallpaper on crooked in our new house... must stop now... this could get good...*

Mr. Choppy drew himself up and began speaking the way Powell Hampton had taught him for all his election campaign speeches. Every syllable was evenly paced and projected with great force. "Lady Roth, I am making an executive decision here. This is the way it is going to be. You will not be allowed to portray the Star of Bethlehem atop the courthouse on Christmas Eve. Period."

Gaylie Girl watched with bated breath during the awkward silence that ensued. She could not move a muscle, even to lift her pen to record her ongoing reactions as she'd been doing all morning for her amusement.

Finally, Lady Roth leaned forward in her chair and intently caught Mr. Choppy's gaze. Amazingly, it was with a smile. "I knew my vote was not wasted on you, Mr. Choppy. I knew you had the best interests of Second Creek at heart, or I would not have agreed to portray Susan B. Anthony on your behalf during the campaign. And I want you to know that you are the first person since my parents arranged my marriage to Heath Vanderlith Roth who has taken a firm stand with me. I say it's about time. It's amused me no end to watch people kowtow to me all these years."

Mr. Choppy and Gaylie Girl exchanged flabbergasted glances, and then he allowed a genuine smile to light up his face. "Well, Lady Roth, this is a true revelation, I must say. Almost as revealin' as the time you first told me about your actress ambitions."

Lady Roth was laughing now. Not anything forced, not even anything ladylike. It was a hearty laugh that sounded like it might be decades in coming. "Isn't it, though? The truth is, I started making all these demands of mine just to see what would happen. And when people started giving me exactly what I wanted all the time, I saw no reason to stop.

The entire town of Second Creek has been enabling me all these years. How refreshing to actually have someone stand up to me!"

"Then you agree that your standin' up there in the widow's walk with nothin' else goin' on down below is an idea whose time has not come, right?"

"Oh, heavens, yes! I wasn't even looking forward to it when Caroling in The Square was on. I just like to see how far I can take things. It's the ultimate revenge against my parents for planning my life the way they did."

Gaylie Girl was finally able to move her pen again and wrote: *Unbelievable stuff . . . like a scene from a Georges Feydeau farce . . . wonder if Hale knows what that is . . . bet L.R. does . . . bet she would have given her eyeteeth to star in Hotel Paradiso under that hokey stage name of hers . . . Vocifera P. Forest, if I recall correctly . . .*

Lady Roth then rose from her chair and winked at both Mr. Choppy and Gaylie Girl. "This will just be our little secret, Mayor and Mrs. Dunbar. I think I'd enjoy continuing to play my greatest role to the hilt until I croak."

"Of course," Mr. Choppy said, reaching across to shake her hand. "You've taken me into your confidence before, and I've respected that."

Gaylie Girl stood up and offered her hand, too. "The same goes for me. And my offer still stands for you coming into town so the two of us can go out to lunch from time to time at the Tea Room or someplace else."

"I shall definitely take you up on that. And now, I must bid you adieu. I have a thousand errands to run around town, including many an unwary salesman to terrify."

Gaylie Girl showed Lady Roth to the outer office, tacked on another good-bye, and returned quickly. "Well, that made my day. It was almost spooky, though. There I was busily taking stream-of-consciousness notes all morning and wishing you would just shut down all her foolishness, and that's exactly what you did. I'm very proud of you, Hale. You took a big risk because we both know she could have made lots and lots of trouble for you."

"I think I'm still very much in the cream-of-courage mode from last night," he explained, shrugging his shoulders. "I wouldn't exactly call what just happened a miracle, but it's a good starting point considerin' what's ahead of us."

❄

Two hours later Mr. Choppy had just finished reading the fire investigation report that Garvin Braswell had laid on his desk a few minutes earlier. He looked up from the document and called Gaylie Girl into his office. Then he handed it over to her.

"Read it first. Then you can tell me what you think we ought to say to Petey and Meta."

Gaylie Girl began scanning quickly, focusing in on the gist. . . . *And it appears that the fire probably started in the center of the block known as Courthouse Street North . . . remains of space heater found in burned-out building . . . tax records show building as 18 Courthouse Square North . . . winter and space heaters go together to make fires . . . not conclusive, but possible heat source . . . no evidence of arson found, however . . . could have been combustible material near space heater left running as the culprit . . .*

Gaylie Girl came up for air and said what they were

both thinking. "Petey says they were still working on the wiring up until the day of the fire. I remember that Renza and I looked through the window once and saw that same space heater the workmen were gathered around. Who could blame them? It's been such a frigid December. Petey's hinted to me in a couple of conversations that he's been suspicious all along the fire could have started in their building. And Petey said poor Meta started blaming herself as soon as he called her up and told her about it. You see how easily this sort of thing can get out of hand."

"Then maybe we shouldn't tell them about the report. No one's been cited as bein' at fault here."

Gaylie Girl reflected a moment and said: "I don't know. Petey's a big boy. It might be better to pin this down definitely for him rather than have him wondering forever. As for Meta, he'll just have to remind her that the building was insured, and they still have plenty of options."

"I can understand why she'd be upset, though," Mr. Choppy added. "Some of the other building owners may not have so many options. The future of The Square is on the line here."

❄

Petey came down from his suite to join Myrtis and Euterpe for dinner around eight o'clock that evening at Evening Shadows. The house was festively decorated from bar to banister, and there were scores of scented candles tucked away in every nook and cranny. Here, the aroma of apples and cinnamon prevailed. There, a hint of vanilla tantalized. Even the Waterford crystal chandelier above the dining-room table was part of the show, sporting several sprigs of mistletoe and holly for that extra holiday touch.

Petey's mood, however, was solemn and withdrawn, as it had been generally since he had received news of the loss of his building. But this time there was something even more drastic reflected in his expression, and Myrtis in particular picked up on it.

"Now that has to be the saddest face I've seen in a long time. What do you think of it, Euterpe? Is it one for the ages? Quick. Haul out the charcoals and let's have a sketch of it for posterity."

"In musical terms, I'd have to call it a funeral dirge face."

Both women laughed gently, and Petey himself cracked a smile. "Am I that transparent tonight?"

"I'm afraid so, dear boy. You haven't rented my Mimosa Suite all this time and not given me an advanced course on your body language. But it's nothing that can't be remedied with some of my gourmet food and sparkling conversation," Myrtis explained. "Sarah's outdone herself again tonight. She's serving a corn bread–stuffed chicken breast with a hot cranberry-and-pear compote. But until that arrives, wouldn't you care to lighten your load? As you surely know by now, Euterpe and I are marvelous listeners, aren't we, dear?"

Euterpe offered up one of her silvery chuckles. "I'm never tone-deaf when it comes to empathy."

Petey picked up his glass of Delta Lady sweet muscadine wine and took a sip, finally managing a shrug. "It's the same old song. Just a new verse. Mother just phoned about an hour ago and said the fire investigation report showed that it could have started in Meta's art gallery. Or at least what was supposed to be her art gallery. It makes me feel responsible for what happened, even though there was no definite conclusion. But the workmen were rewiring the building, after all."

Myrtis's vigilant ear had picked up on the out for him, however. "If I heard you correctly, the report said that it *could* have started in the gallery and there was no definite conclusion. Is that not right?"

"Yes. Of course, I didn't actually see the report myself. I'm only going by what Mom said."

Myrtis continued to put the best face on the situation, something her trained hostess instincts handled with customary aplomb. "Then my advice is to let it go. And don't tell Meta about it either. You've got her flying into Memphis tomorrow, and I'm sure she feels bad enough about everything as it is. You need to make every effort to have the merriest Christmas you can in spite of what's happened. You go up there and meet her plane with a new plan in mind. You find the spark you need to bravely forge ahead. Really, we all need to do that, considering what's happened to our beloved Square."

Petey toyed with his marinated hearts of palm salad for a few moments, and suddenly his demeanor seemed to do a one-eighty. He speared a bite and popped it into his mouth, chewing with an energy that had been patently absent heretofore. "You're absolutely right!" he proclaimed after another sip of wine. "We can't let this defeat us. Mom and Hale and just about everyone else have all been down in the dumps about this, but we don't have to be. Not if we look at this long-range, we don't."

Sarah appeared with a silver tray of entrées and served them up promptly, temporarily interrupting Petey's train of thought. But after a forkful of the chicken breast he was simply unable to resist, he picked up where he had left off. "I've already made quite an investment in Second Creek as the owner of Pond-Raised Catfish. Meta and I have got to get on with our dreams."

Myrtis responded to the excitement in his voice with some in her own. "Oh, I love dreamers. My Raymond was one, you know. I've never told anyone this part before, but the real reason he bought the record shop was because he actually fancied himself a rock-and-roll singer himself at one point." She was giggling now, thoroughly enjoying herself.

"Imagine. My dignified Raymond, the upstanding, well-established attorney, having that kind of a dream. Unfortunately, it was not to be. He may have wanted to take a stab at sounding like his favorite, Frankie Valli, and he could even do a few bars in falsetto by hook or crook. But his normal singing voice was like a chain-smoker gargling with gravel. And I didn't make that up about him either—those were his exact words. If he couldn't be the next Elvis or Pat Boone or whoever, though, he told me he'd settle for the next best thing. And that was selling records to the up-and-coming generation. 'It'll help keep me young!' he would say to me. And, you know, I truly believe it did. I think it added another ten or twelve years to his life."

"I'm feeling better about everything by the minute,"

Petey said. "By the time we finish dessert, I'll have that new plan in place."

"How exciting!" Myrtis exclaimed. "Now that's the Petey Lyons we've all come to know and admire around here."

"I must admit it's been great fun having you here at Evening Shadows to keep us ladies of a certain age company," Euterpe put in, sighing there at the end. "If I were only a couple of decades younger, I keep telling myself during my daydreams . . . oh, did I say that out loud?"

Myrtis gave her a naughty glance and wagged a finger. "You know good and well you did." Then she put down her fork and took a deep breath.

"I'm not quite sure where this came from, but I'd like to take this opportunity to thank both of you for these past few months of marvelous companionship. I know it's not going to be a permanent arrangement, but I just can't help it. It feels like a family to me. Every morning when I get up and walk down the upstairs hallway to help Sarah in the kitchen, I glance at the Mimosa Suite and know that the dashing Mr. Petey Lyons is in there sleeping in my four-poster. And then I glance at the Bloody Mary Suite across the hall, and I know my sophisticated friend and fellow Nitwitt—not to mention piano teacher—Euterpe Simon and her precious Pan are getting their beauty rest in there. I really don't get the chance to know the guests who come and go overnight for the most part." She paused briefly to dab at her eyes with her napkin. "Oh, I wonder if I'll have withdrawal symptoms after the two of you are gone."

It was Euterpe who spoke first. "This may come as a

surprise to you, but I'm not so sure I'll ever leave, Myrtis. You've made it so easy for me to live here in high style. Where else could I enjoy such elaborate meals and impeccable living quarters all rolled into one? I've toyed with finding a place of my own, of course, but, Myrtis, I'm leaning strongly toward the two of us making a go of it out here together. I end up doing miniconcerts at the piano for your guests all the time anyway. What would you think of our sitting down with a lawyer and making this bed-and-breakfast a partnership of some kind?"

Myrtis gave a little gasp of surprise, followed by the grandest of smiles. "Why, Euterpe, the thought never occurred to me. But I must say that I'm intrigued. This is an awfully big house, and it was terribly lonely for me after Raymond died. That's why I finally came up with the bed-and-breakfast idea. At least I could have some company now and then. Other than Sarah in the kitchen, I mean. But what would become of your music studio? Would you give it up?"

"Absolutely not. I am, after all, the Mistress of the Scales, and I assure you she can handle both."

"Well, I think it's just an extraordinary idea!"

"Is that a yes, no, or a maybe?"

Myrtis took a healthy sip of her wine for courage. "Well, I think it's a 'let's sit down and explore it seriously' after the holidays."

Then Petey joined in, obviously delighted by the developments. "Now you have a new plan, too, Myrtis. Which reminds me—I haven't really had the chance to tell you how much the wedding you staged for my mother meant me to me and my sister, Amanda. Meta and her Florida friends were just as crazy about it, too. You went all out here at Evening Shadows, and we all agreed that we'd never been more impressed with a reception. That tent you put up was to die for. So, Meta and I were wondering if you'd be willing to do the same for us. That is, if we finally come around and set an actual date."

"Well, it seems Christmas has come early for me this evening," Myrtis said. "I'd be honored to host your wedding and reception, Petey." Then she leaned in and began talking in a stage whisper. "And rumor has it that Renza has been trying to get her only daughter married off for years. I'm sure she'd foot the bill without a hint of her usual prickly pear behavior."

Petey managed a little smirk. "Meta and I didn't think she'd come around at first, but she has. Last time Meta talked to her over the phone she brought up the subject of grandchildren. Oh, yes, she's definitely on board now."

Over the dessert of tiramisu and coffee, Myrtis reminded Petey of his promise to unveil his new plan for himself and Meta. "Are you ready to share? Unless the wedding here at Evening Shadows was the plan."

"Of course the wedding is part of the plan, and I know Meta will be thrilled to hear we're having it out here. I don't think she envisioned anywhere else but here. But I have something more comprehensive in mind for Second Creek," he explained. "The details have to be ironed out, though. First, I have an important phone call to make to Amanda up in Chicago. Then I have to run a few things by my mother. I really don't mean to sound so mysterious, but I promise you I'll have something in place by Christmas Eve."

❅

Just past nine o'clock, Mr. Choppy and Gaylie Girl left the hospital after visiting with Cherish and Henry and getting the latest update on baby Riley Jacob. Denver Lee had just wound up her Vigil Auntie shift and tagged along, but none of them were in especially high spirits.

"It must be just awful for Henry and Cherish to have to wait it out like this with no change in the status of that precious little baby. Every hour must seem like an eternity to them," Gaylie Girl remarked as they headed out into the cold to the hospital parking lot. A brisk wind brought tears to their eyes as they hugged their coats and picked up the pace to their cars.

"Anyone want to go for some decent coffee and have a little talk before we head home?" Denver Lee called out just as she reached her Cadillac. "I believe the Town Square Café is still open."

Her suggestion met with everyone's approval, and soon they were thawing out with their cappuccinos at a corner café table.

"I don't know why I keep coming here," Denver Lee was saying. "Oh, of course I do. Their bear claws are such a temptation for me, and I just can't afford the sugar bomb. I have no business putting myself in harm's way."

"We'll remind you if you get the sudden urge to order one," Gaylie Girl replied with a wink.

Mr. Choppy was craning his neck, staring at the café's big picture window that overlooked The Square. He seemed about to make a comment when March Ventress, the tall, gangly owner of the Town Square Café, approached their table.

"Sad sight out there, isn't it, Mayor?" March said, shaking his head and then whistling through his teeth for emphasis.

"How's it affected your business so far, March? Not too much, I hope," Mr. Choppy asked, wanting to know.

"Well, it's funny. We've actually had a little spike here lately. People comin' to The Square to see all the damage that's been done, and then they see we're open and come in for a cup of coffee or somethin' to get outta the cold. But I really don't expect that kinda business to last. Even our burned-out stores aren't that spectacular to gawk at, ya know. I'm sure word'll get around that there's just not that much to see." March surveyed the table quickly. "My waiter taken good care of you here? Got everything you need?"

"Service was just fine, March," Mr. Choppy said. "Thanks for lookin' after us."

After March had stepped away, Mr. Choppy returned to his contemplation of The Square. "I'm really worried about the long-range effects. We have such a monumental re-buildin' task ahead of us."

Gaylie Girl put down her coffee cup and nodded. "I did talk to Novie the other day, and she said that it's too early to tell how much the fire will affect Marc's business at How's Plants? She also said that he and Michael really needed to have a banner Christmas to make up for lagging sales the past few months. The reality has to be that this terrible fire can't help things. But I feel sure that Caroling in The Square would have been a boon. We were so close to establishing a new Square tradition."

Mr. Choppy leaned over and nudged her. "We gotta remember our cream of courage, right?"

Denver Lee blinked a couple of times. "What?"

"Oh, long story," Gaylie Girl said. "I'll fill you in another time over a Bloody Mary or two."

Then Denver Lee let out a long and plaintive sigh. "Do you know that I actually had a couple of the choirmasters take me up on my organ accompaniment tapes? It was that nice Press Phillips at First Presbyterian and that sweet Mrs. Vergie Woods of that Marblestone Whatchamacallit Church. And they both got back to me and said what a tremendous help my tapes were during practice. I custom made them, you know. I really felt like I was contributing to the success of your project, Gaylie Girl. And now, all we have to show for our efforts are these awful ruins. This is the sort of thing that drives me to powdered doughnuts!"

Gaylie Girl wagged a finger with a supportive smile. "Willpower, dear, willpower."

Denver Lee straightened up in her chair and crisply tossed her head back. "You're absolutely right. I must be strong. We all must be strong—for ourselves, for Second Creek, and for Henry and Cherish and their little son. The fact is, we could all use a little resolution at this point. Well, at least we have the caroling at Delta Sunset Village to look forward to as a definite. That, and seeing our dear Wittsie is sure to put us back in the Christmas spirit."

Gaylie Girl reached over and grasped Mr. Choppy's hand. "I sincerely hope so. Hale is giving me the afternoon off from my secretarial duties so I can be there with all of you. I'm sure it will be good for our souls."

Fourteen

All Ye Faithful

"Miz Wittsie is having her best day in months!" Mrs. Holstrom was explaining to Laurie and Powell, the first of the Nitwitt contingent to arrive for the afternoon caroling event at Delta Sunset Village. They had left Second Creek a good fifteen minutes before the others and had happened to walk into the enormous atrium lobby just as Mrs. Holstrom was finishing up directing the arrangement of folding chairs for the audience of residents and their friends and families.

"I really think the fact that you're all coming to see her at once has sparked her interest. She hasn't forgotten a thing all day. It's pretty remarkable in a way," Mrs. Holstrom continued. "You're aware she's had that trouble swallowing, of course. It's been a rough couple of weeks for her. But she seems to be all there today. Just as bright-eyed and bushy-tailed as I've ever seen her. It's somebody's Christmas wish come true."

Laurie gazed at Powell briefly and then offered Mrs. Holstrom her brightest smile. "Maybe ours. I'm referring to the Nitwitts, of course. I'm sure we've all been praying for her every day."

Mrs. Holstrom smiled and then checked her watch with her usual efficiency. "Mr. Phillips called just before you came in and said they were running a tad bit late, but he expected the choir bus to be here any minute. We've still got a half hour before it's all scheduled to start. But as you can see, we've got some curious early birds. Our people have been talking about this for days on end. I'm just hoping we have enough chairs. I just finished having the staff put out some extra. Some of the residents have invited as many family members as they can get hold of. It's probably going to be an overflow crowd. I'm fairly certain we wouldn't have gotten this kind of reaction if the Christmas storytelling couple I had booked originally had shown up. Sometimes what looks like a bother and a problem turns out to be a blessing in disguise."

Laurie surveyed the lobby and noted the sprinkling of walkers and scooters around the edges. The faces of those using them were expectant, even touchingly childlike, and Laurie felt pangs of emotion welling up in her throat. "I wonder if that will be us in another ten or fifteen years," she said to Powell.

"As long as we're together," he answered, smiling down

at her, "I don't care where we are. And who says we can't get us a scooter built for two?"

The rest of the Nitwitts began trickling in. Future in-laws Renza and Gaylie Girl had driven over together and were next to join them in the lobby. Then Myrtis and Euterpe showed up as the Evening Shadows contingent. Denver Lee rolled in last, muttering something about almost running out of gas and having to stop at a filthy service station somewhere that charged outrageous prices at the pump and had Third World bathrooms to boot. But finally they were all there, ready to embrace Wittsie, sing along with the choir to the best of their ability, and immerse themselves in the much-needed Christmas spirit.

Next, the First Presbyterian Church choir entered en masse in their festive red-and-white robes, and Mrs. Holstrom rushed over to greet Press Phillips. There was some logistical turmoil as the choir members were directed to their proper places on the little makeshift stage the staff of Delta Sunset Village had painstakingly created especially for the occasion.

Mrs. Holstrom finally broke away and approached the Nitwitts, who were huddled together on the outskirts of the gathering crowd. "It's going to be a bit hectic in here for a while," she told them all at once. "I thought this might happen, so I've taken the liberty of reserving a small private room off the dining area so that Miz Wittsie can visit with all of you before the program starts. I'll show you the way, and one of the orderlies will bring Miz Wittsie along shortly. I've already visited with her briefly, and I can tell you that she's practically glowing today. She really seems to be rising to the occasion, so I'm sure you'll all make the most of this. Of course, if there's anything further you need, you'll let me know."

"My God, but that woman runs on," Renza muttered to Gaylie Girl under her breath as everyone followed Mrs. Holstrom down the corridor. "She ought to run for office the way she can turn out speeches like that. And she seems super efficient. I'm sure she'd be an improvement on those slick, tired politicians we've got running things from Mississippi to Washington, D.C."

"Second Creek excepted, of course," Gaylie Girl answered, tactfully lowering her voice.

❄

"Did you know my dream came to life last night?" Wittsie announced to all the Nitwitts gathered around the table.

Once they had all settled into the private room and finished commenting on the beautiful cranberry-red dress their beloved Wittsie was wearing, they began listening intently to everything she had to say.

Laurie, who was sitting next to her, took the first plunge. "What dream was that, sweetie?"

Wittsie took a little time, but when she spoke, her words were surprisingly clear and forceful. Her usual hesitation had disappeared, at least for the moment. "I saw this light. I looked out my window and there it was. I dreamed it, too."

No one made a sound for a while. Then Laurie broke the silence. "Please, tell us. How did your dream come to life?"

"I dreamed there was a bright light before me . . . never

seen anything so bright in my life. It took up all the space in my dream. Then I woke up and . . ."

"Yes?" Laurie put in with a hopeful expression on her face. "Don't keep us in suspense."

"And I went to the window . . . and the light was there. It had moved from my dream. It was there for me just like the fireflies were—outside my window this summer."

Now it was Gaylie Girl's turn to interact. "I'll remember those fireflies as long as I live, Wittsie. I just know they came to give Hale and me a send-off for our honeymoon. They even followed us all the way up to Memphis. We thought it was the most marvelous sight we'd ever seen. I had goose bumps up until the time we boarded the plane for Santa Fe."

"Those fireflies were spectacular," Myrtis added. "There must have been hundreds of them. I don't know—maybe even thousands. Everybody at the reception kept asking me how on earth I'd managed to arrange it all. They said they thought it was something I'd ordered up like the finger sandwiches and all the booze. In fact, somebody very drunk—and I forget now who it was since there were so many who were—came up to me and asked if I had found those fireflies online. But the truth is, I had absolutely nothing to do with it."

"I think Wittsie sent them, didn't you, dear?" Gaylie Girl said, her tone both pleasant and direct.

Wittsie seemed slightly unsure of herself but offered up an intriguing smile anyway. "Maybe."

Wittsie changed the subject abruptly. "I received some wonderful news this mornin' . . . my April called me . . .

she's comin' down to spend Christmas Day with me right here . . . she and my little Meagan . . . my beautiful granddaughter . . . they're comin' to see me."

Laurie clasped her hands together, and the others were tittering and buzzing as well. "Oh, that *is* wonderful news. We're all so happy for you. Your Meagan is just adorable, and I loved having her as my maid of honor in my wedding at the Piggly Wiggly summer before last. I'll bet she's quite the grown-up little lady by now."

"It was the light . . ." Wittsie resumed, completely ignoring Laurie's train of thought. "I knew when I saw the light that somethin' good was goin' to happen . . . and it did . . . this very mornin' . . ."

"And we're all here for you as well," Gaylie Girl added. "We're here to sing Christmas carols and remember this Christmas with you forever."

Wittsie laughed the sweetest little laugh and bobbed her head up and down.

"Wish I could carry a tune better."

"Don't worry, dear. You aren't the only one who can't warble," Renza quipped, cutting her eyes at Denver Lee. "But the choir should cover all of us up nicely whether we have the gift or not."

"By the way, Euterpe," Laurie said, "do you know what the choir is going to sing this afternoon?"

"I do indeed. It's the same program they would have sung from the balconies had everything gone as expected. They'll be opening with 'Adeste Fideles,' which I think is very appropriate since all of us Nitwitt faithful are here.

Then, 'The Little Drummer Boy,' which has always been one of my favorites, followed by 'I Saw Three Ships Come Sailing In,' 'Silver Bells,' 'Feliz Navidad' for their international carol, and finally 'We Three Kings of Orient Are.' Unless Mr. Phillips has changed something up on me. Of course, he may have. I didn't want to seem unyielding in all of this. It's not like he was one of my pupils prepping for a recital and I was completely running the show."

Wittsie was nodding with a certain reserve. "I like all those carols . . . but did I tell you . . . I get to spend Christmas with my daughter, April, and my granddaughter, Meagan?"

Laurie patted her hand gently and brushed right past the repetition. "That was a wonderful Christmas present for you, wasn't it?"

Wittsie's interest began to flicker. "It was . . . but April doesn't come to see me very often . . . I don't know why."

"It's probably because she can't find a day one of us Nitwitts isn't over here completely monopolizing you," Laurie added, trying for levity. "Truth is, we want you all to ourselves. But what does that matter when your daughter and granddaughter will be with you this Christmas, as you say. That's the most important thing this time of the year."

Just then Mrs. Holstrom appeared in the doorway. "The choir will be starting in about ten minutes. Perhaps you'd all care to go out and take your seats. Just a heads-up, but we're filling up fast. They're practically having scooter races out there for the best spots. I think this could be standing room only."

Several of the Nitwitts and Powell rose to their feet, and

Gaylie Girl said: "Then by all means, let's adjourn and head on out. We've been waiting for months to hear those angelic voices."

❄

From Gaylie Girl's perspective, seated right next to her, it appeared that Wittsie's voice was getting stronger with each carol that Press Phillips and his choir performed. She had been following along with no trouble, not missing a single word of any of the lyrics. The entire experience seemed to be transforming her into someone who was very much in the world and present in the moment.

"I thought you said you couldn't carry a tune," Gaylie Girl said, leaning over as the choir finished up "I Saw Three Ships." "I wish I could sing half as well as you are right now."

"She's doing marvelously well, isn't she?" Laurie added from her perch on the other side of Wittsie.

"Don't know what's gotten into me," Wittsie answered them both, turning her head first one way and then the other. "But . . . maybe I do."

"Have you been practicing up?" Gaylie Girl asked. She leaned back into the row behind her, where the rest of the Nitwitts were sitting. "Euterpe, I didn't know you were offering voice lessons now. Have you been sneaking over here behind our backs?"

Euterpe snickered. "Nope. Can't take credit, I'm afraid."

"It was . . . the light," Wittsie said, nodding emphatically.

Then Euterpe leaned forward and offered her insights. "I put great store in dreams, you know. I believe our Wittsie has had a vision. And what a wonderful time of the year to have it."

Wittsie said nothing for a while. But shortly before the choir began singing "Silver Bells," she turned to Gaylie Girl and said in her strongest voice yet: "Don't worry. It will be restored."

Gaylie Girl was puzzled but smiled anyway. "What will be restored, Wittsie?"

Wittsie closed her eyes briefly and said: "I know from the light. It will be restored."

The choir began singing, and Wittsie joined in immediately, saying nothing further. She continued to sing along, her voice ringing out among the Nitwitts, even startling them with her power. This was a woman that none of them had ever seen or heard before, not even in the formative period of the Nitwitts' existence. It was as if something had broken through the Alzheimer's shell that had been hardening around her, and a brand-new Wittsie had emerged to rejoice a few days out from Christmas.

When the program had ended and the applause of the appreciative residents had finally died down—Wittsie being one of the last to desist—everyone moved to the refreshment tables that had been set up nearby. The Nitwitts homed in on their favorite nibbles and sweets but had to graciously resign themselves to unadulterated fruit punch and mulled cider to wash them down.

"I just wanted to congratulate you on such a lovely program, Mr. Phillips," Mrs. Holstrom was saying as she circulated throughout the crowd. "Just the right length, too. Some of our residents do like their naptime, you know."

"I understand perfectly," Press Phillips replied, munching blissfully on a handful of cheese crackers. "Perhaps we can make this an annual event. I think all of us choirmasters aren't going to pin our hopes on another Caroling in The Square on Christmas Eve considering all the damage done over there."

"Yes, it does seem daunting, bordering on the impossible, that The Square could come back the way it was. Of course we'd be delighted to have you again next year, regardless."

A kibitzing Gaylie Girl monitored their conversation with great interest. Something began resonating strongly with her. But this was not the time and place to discuss it. Not with the other Nitwitts and Powell, not with Mrs. Holstrom, not with anyone here. No, she would say good-bye to Wittsie, giving her a heartfelt hug and farewell. Then perhaps when she got home she would run all her suppositions past her husband. In the short time since her return, he had become her only true Second Creek touchstone.

She finally tracked Wittsie down just as one of the orderlies had shown up from the memory care unit. Though he was a tall, imposing man, he took Wittsie's arm as if it belonged to a delicate little doll and spoke to her in a gentle, reassuring tone—even complimenting her on her dress.

"That has to be the prettiest red color I've ever seen on one of our residents, Miz Wittsie. Sure reminds me that it's almost Christmas. But it's time for you to go back to your room now. We don't want you to tire yourself out before dinner later."

Wittsie's response was disheartening. "Dinner? Isn't this

dinner?" She was pointing to a small paper plate she had filled with crackers and grapes and a strawberry or two. But she had not taken a bite.

"No," the orderly answered with a smile. "Dinner's not for another couple of hours. This was just a snack Miz Holstrom and the staff put out for everybody after the choir sang."

"The choir?"

Suddenly, Gaylie Girl realized that the old disoriented Wittsie had returned in full force. The fact that she was fading quickly was all there in her expression. Gone was the vigorous voice that had kept up with the choir note by note. Gone was the confidence she had exuded when relaying the details of her intriguing dream come to life. Whatever focus she had been generously granted earlier in the day had evidently been withdrawn now just as unexpectedly. Wittsie's brief shining interlude was over.

Gaylie Girl and the other Nitwitts each embraced Wittsie in turn and said their good-byes, tearful as that turned out to be in some cases. For on Wittsie's part, it was as if they'd all just arrived, and she was seeing them for the first time that day. More than once she was saying, "Why, I didn't know you were here!" without the least bit of hesitation.

The orderly flashed them all an understanding smile as he finally led Wittsie away. Gaylie Girl had the disquieting notion that he was taking away part of the Christmas spirit they had all worked so hard to encounter and indulge. She was looking forward more than ever to getting home and discussing everything with her Hale.

※

"I have the most wonderful news!" Mr. Choppy exclaimed as Gaylie Girl entered the kitchen and tossed her car keys on the counter with a metallic, jangling noise. "It's about my godson. They were able to take him off the ventilator several hours ago without any a' those apnea episodes. Little Riley Jacob has been breathin' on his own all afternoon. I just hung up with Henry after a long conversation. It's finally lookin' pretty good for his little family. Talk about one excited father—and godfather, for that matter!"

"That is good news," she said, but there was a hint of caution in her voice. "Then is the baby finally out of that depressing intensive care unit? Cherish says it makes him look even more vulnerable hooked up to all those tubes."

"Not just yet. He may be in there a while longer. But this is the first step he had to take to have a shot at a normal life." Mr. Choppy gave her a big hug and a warm kiss and then held her at arm's length. "And I have another little surprise for you. I'm going to make us dinner in honor of this smallest of miracles—a baby step, if you'll pardon the pun. How do omelets and cheese grits sound to you? That was the first Southern dish I taught you to make, remember?"

"Ah, yes, the beginning of my transformation from an inveterate Yankee out of suburban Chicago into a li'l ole Southern belle, y'all." She glanced at the clock on the wall and saw that it was early yet. "Let's sit and have a little something to drink first. Pour us some wine. There's something I need to tell you. It happened this afternoon at Delta Sunset Village."

"Comin' right up."

She watched him open a bottle of Delta Lady dry muscadine and fill two wineglasses to the brim. Then they sat across from each other at the kitchen table and took a couple of thoughtful sips. "Your news fits perfectly with mine now that I think about it," she began. "In fact, I've been thinking about the whole thing all the way back from Greenwood. Renza thought I was upset with her, I was so quiet. She's so used to upsetting people, I think it comes with the territory for her. But I just told her I was thinking about Wittsie, and she said she understood. That was partly true, by the way. I was thinking about Wittsie—just not the way she thought I was thinking about her. Oh, that sounds like double-talk, doesn't it?"

Mr. Choppy shot her a skeptical glance but tempered it with his best grin. "Seems like your news is a bit more complicated than mine. Either that, or you're becomin' more and more of a genuine Nitwitt every day. Now you know I love every one of you ladies, and I owe the club a helluva lot with all the support y'all have given me. But I'm glad I don't go to your get-togethers like Powell sometimes does and try to follow the ebb and flow of everything y'all discuss."

"Uh, thanks for the compliment . . . I think. But what I have to tell you definitely needs clarification of some kind. That's where you enter the picture. I want your intuitive opinion here."

Mr. Choppy took a big sip of his wine and braced himself. "Okay, shoot. Whatever you have to say can't possibly be as complex as all this buildup. Let's get to it."

Gaylie Girl told him about Wittsie's dream and its surreal

waking aftermath, particularly the way she had kept emphasizing her fascination with the light.

"Sounds like one helluva dream," Mr. Choppy remarked in a somewhat detached fashion. "My dreams are sometimes all over the map, too. That is, when I can recall 'em."

"You don't sound very interested in this."

"No, you're readin' me wrong. Of course I am. So you want me to give you my interpretation of the light? Is that it?"

She shook her head and waved him off. "No, no. There's something else I haven't told you. That's the part that really intrigues me. It was something Wittsie said to me a couple of times. She made a point of leaning over and saying it to me and only me. At least that was my interpretation. She said, 'It will be restored.' And then later she said that the light had told her that 'it would be restored.' When I asked her what 'it' was, she wouldn't say. But I think I know what she meant." She paused for effect, so long in fact that Mr. Choppy became slightly agitated.

"Well, for heaven's sake, what do you think she meant?"

"I think she meant that The Square would be restored. And she had this dream to back her up. Now, what do *you* think she meant?"

Mr. Choppy took his time, twitching his mouth and cutting his eyes from side to side. "If I were living in an ordinary town, maybe I'd say that she meant nothing. That she was sufferin' from Alzheimer's, which she is, and can't think straight anymore. That'd be the conventional interpretation.

But I don't live in an ordinary town. I live in Second Creek, and I've seen too much happen here over the years that convinces me there's more to life than conventional wisdom has to offer. Like those fireflies last summer. What was that all about? And Wittsie was somehow involved in that, too. Don't know how, but my gut instincts tell me she was." He paused for another swig of wine and to catch his breath.

"And so, what I'm gonna say to you is that your explanation probably makes as much sense as anything anybody else could come up with me—includin' me. Not only that, but I hope your explanation is right. Because if it is, we'll have a bigger miracle on our hands than a premature baby bein' taken off a ventilator. If The Square is actually restored to its former glory, then we can breathe a huge sigh of relief and go on with our lives. You'll prob'ly get that second chance at Caroling in The Square on Christmas Eve after all. And Second Creek will continue to be the tourist attraction it's always been. Now, how's that for an answer?"

Gaylie Girl quickly rose, moved to him, and planted a big kiss on his lips. "Spoken like a true, native-born Mayor of Second Creek. I couldn't have put it better myself."

"We seem to be gettin' it from all sides," Mr. Choppy reflected suddenly.

"What do you mean?"

"I mean, all the faithful keep showin' up everywhere, don't they? I know you haven't forgotten the taste of that cream of courage."

"Ah! Good point."

He put down his wineglass and caught her gaze. "So. Where do we go from here?"

Gaylie Girl's laugh was a series of delicate, staccato tones that made her sound like she couldn't possibly have a care in the world. "I say we settle back and wait for something miraculous to happen. Or maybe we make it happen ourselves."

Fifteen

The Square Deal

Christmas Eve had finally arrived. Mr. Choppy was taking only a half day at the office, and then he and Gaylie Girl were heading out to an afternoon holiday party at Evening Shadows that Myrtis seemed to have thrown together at the last minute. He was actually suspicious of the entire affair, since Gaylie Girl had disappeared the previous evening for an emergency meeting of the Nitwitts at Renza's house.

"What are you all up to now?" he had asked her just before she left, as frisky and conspiratorial-looking as he had ever seen her as she headed for the door.

"I'm not telling. You'll find out soon enough."

And they had left it at that.

But now it was the next day, and Mr. Choppy was more curious than ever as the noon hour approached and his half day at the office came to an end. He summoned Gaylie Girl just before quitting time and had her take a seat on the other side of his desk.

"I know good and well that this is not one of Myrtis's usual shindigs," he began, bearing down upon her with his eyes. "That's not how she works. You ladies talk about her parties for weeks leadin' up to 'em. I know this has somethin' to do with that last-minute Nitwitt meetin' yesterday. Why won't you let me in on it?"

Gaylie Girl looked supremely smug as she lifted her profile dramatically. "Now, Hale, what good is a surprise if I tell you about it in advance? And don't ask me to tell you anyway so you can fake it. In a way, this will be my main Christmas present to you."

Mr. Choppy was smiling in spite of himself. "It ought to be good, then. You've been on the phone constantly and runnin' off to visit with practically everybody we know twenty-four hours a day lately, it seems. Out to Evening Shadows to see Petey. Over to Renza's to see Meta. On the phone with Amanda up in Chicago. And on and on. If I ran things like Mr. Floyce did, I'd have my spies everywhere around town on the lookout and then they'd skulk up the stairs and spill the beans in some midnight rendezvous. But we all know I run a clean ship. Well, I guess I'd just better resign myself to the fact that I'm not gonna know anything until we get out to Evening Shadows." He glanced at his watch and got up from his desk. "And now I believe you and I are officially on Christmas break. Let's turn off the lights and head on home."

As they headed down the corridor after locking things

up, Gaylie Girl turned to him and said: "I will tell you about one piece of business we put to bed at our meeting last night. We decided to officially wind up our Vigil Auntie shifts at the hospital. As you know, the baby's been off the ventilator for two days now. Henry says he'll be eternally grateful for all the support—and especially the delicious food we fixed for him—but the worst seems to be over now. And he says Cherish will be home in time for Christmas, too."

There was almost a boastful quality in Mr. Choppy's elaborate sigh. "So it looks like my chances of becomin' a godfather are gettin' pretty good. I can't wait to do all the things godfathers are supposed to do."

"Oh, you'll do fine, I'm sure."

They had just reached the parking lot when Mr. Choppy took one last stab at undermining Gaylie Girl's resolve. "You sure you won't tell me anything more? Not even a teensy-weensy hint?"

"For heaven's sake, Hale, you're just like a child on Christmas morning waiting to get at the presents. Anything worthwhile is worth waiting for. Let's get on home and change. If everything is on schedule, Myrtis and the gang will be putting the finishing touches on everything right about this time."

❄

Mr. Choppy had not been mistaken when he had jokingly called out Gaylie Girl for being in contact over the past twenty-four hours with just about everyone they knew. With very few exceptions, they were all present on Myrtis's glassed-in back porch overlooking her famous boxwood maze. As in years past, the elaborately trimmed puzzle was decorated with a sea of twinkling Christmas lights, and it made an enchanting backdrop for those already enjoying nibbles and cocktails while engaging in their small talk. And true to her fascination with rock-and-roll hits that her Raymond had exposed her to over the years, Myrtis had the original 1957 recording of Bobby Helms's "Jingle Bell Rock" spinning on the turntable. She and Euterpe were even doing a silly imitation of the Twist to the music in the far corner of the room.

All the other Nitwitts except Wittsie were present, of course. But they were generously augmented by Petey and Meta, who had returned from St. Augustine a couple of days earlier, all of the city councilmen, Marc Mims and Michael Peeler, Vester Morrow and Mal Davis of the Victorian Tea Room, March Ventress of the Town Square Café, the Reverend Quintus and Yolie Payne, all of the choirmasters except Lawton Bead and Lincoln Headley, and several other owners of businesses on or around The Square, including many whose buildings had gone up in flames.

"Are we the last to arrive?" Mr. Choppy wanted to know, as he and Gaylie Girl started to circulate around the crowded room, shaking hands and greeting people.

"Looks that way," she began. "You'll find out that this is going to be very much about you in your official capacity as Mayor. We wanted a big audience for the announcement. Oh, what time is it, by the way?"

He checked his watch and told her it was nearly two o'clock, but he couldn't resist making light of all the suspense. "You're makin' me think Santa Claus is comin' to town the way you've been carryin' on. Does Myrtis have a chimney?"

She hoisted her glass of white zinfandel with a sly grin. "No, she doesn't, but you're not far from wrong about Santa Claus."

It was then that Petey stepped out of the crowd with Meta in tow and tapped Mr. Choppy on the shoulder from behind. "Are you ready, Hale?"

Mr. Choppy swung around and greeted them cordially. Then he said: "Gaylie Girl's been playin' this mysterious game with me night and day, and now I find that everybody else here is in on whatever this is. So, yeah, Petey, I think I'm more than ready."

"Then let's do it," Petey said. He and Meta moved to the center of the porch, where she chimed a spoon on her wineglass several times.

But it was Gaylie Girl who addressed the crowd after the general chatter had finally subsided. "Everyone, please. If we could have your attention. My son, Petey, has a very important announcement to make. So if all of you could just gather around with your drinks and pick-me-ups."

Now the crowd was completely hushed as Petey motioned Mr. Choppy to move closer to him. "That's it, Mr. Mayor. You just step right on up here and get ready to receive the Christmas present of your life."

Mr. Choppy willingly complied, and Gaylie Girl accompanied him, hooking her arm through his.

"Ladies and gentlemen," Petey began, "all of you know why we are here this afternoon. In fact, our wonderful

Mayor and my understanding stepfather right next to me is the only one who's in the dark. I'm sure he's about to burst at the seams to find out what's going on. But if he'll indulge me just a bit longer, I can assure him that everything will fall into place nicely. Of course, it hasn't been easy keeping this news from him. So many of us have been sworn to secrecy, and I've been told a few of you have had a little trouble with that in the past." There was an outburst of titters as she caught the gaze of several of the Nitwitts surrounding him.

Indeed, Renza couldn't resist deflecting the unexpected attention. "If you are referring to any of us Nitwitts, you haven't a leg to stand on. Being forced to reveal secrets against our better judgment is strictly one of our bylaws. And we uphold it quite well ordinarily, I can assure you. Only not this once."

This time there was outright laughter around the room.

"As your future son-in-law, I can absolutely respect that, Miz Renza," Petey said, while exchanging affectionate glances with Meta. "But back to the announcement. As I don't have to explain to any of you, the fire that struck the historic Square earlier this week *has* threatened the very character of Second Creek as we have known it. I realize that I'm a newcomer from Yankeeland—" He broke off briefly as another wave of chuckles and giggles swept throughout the room.

"Oh, yes, it's true. I am not to the manor born, so to speak. But I now have a substantial investment in Second Creek, since I'm the owner of Pond-Raised Catfish, the single largest employer in the county. As such, I have a tremendous responsibility to the community, and that's why I've taken the steps I've taken."

He paused and gestured toward Gaylie Girl. "All of you know my mother by now—the First Lady of Second Creek. But a few of you may not know that before she became Mrs. Hale Dunbar Jr., she was married to my father, Peter Lyons, of Lyons Insole, Incorporated. Perhaps many of you have stuffed his insoles into your shoes over the years to make it a little easier on your poor tired feet. For that, my family and I thank you from the bottom of *our* soles, and you're certainly welcome to interpret that any way you want."

There was a healthy appreciation of his pun throughout the crowd.

"When my father died a few years back, he was generous enough to leave my sister, Amanda, and myself quite a bit of money. To put it bluntly, we were both set for life. Neither of us could ever want for anything. Nor could our heirs, if we played our cards right. And I freely admit I've gone through periods in which I haven't really known what to do with myself and my money. The same was also true for my sister, who is married and lives in Chicago with her husband and children. But now she and I have come to an important decision, and after all this buildup, I'd like to share it with you, the Mayor of Second Creek, Hale Dunbar Jr."

It seemed as if everyone in the room had suddenly taken a deep breath in anticipation of the words to follow, no one more than Mr. Choppy. But finally Petey said them, and with an obvious conviction.

"I'm here to tell you this afternoon that my sister, Amanda Lyons Sykes, my mother, and myself have established a fund for Second Creek to be called The Square Deal. Amanda has just been devastated by the havoc wreaked upon The Square by the fire ever since my mother called and told her about it. On her first-ever visit to Second Creek this past summer, she was absolutely charmed by the historic architecture and the unique flavor of this little town. She remarked that she'd never seen such a concentration of interesting buildings outside of Europe. Traveling to historic places is her particular thing, you see.

"And since both Mother and myself are now living down here and have made Second Creek our home, she felt the sting of the fire's destruction more than most. I gave her a call myself to discuss my concept of The Square Deal with her, and she jumped at the chance to contribute something meaningful and substantial. Therefore, among the three of us—meaning myself, my sister, and my mother—we are each contributing two million dollars, for a total of six million, to kick off a charitable fund-raising drive for Second Creek's downtown. The Square Deal will make funds available to any merchant or building owner who wishes to apply in order to start over from scratch or renovate whatever is still damaged but salvageable. This money is to be awarded exclusively to those directly affected, and we will be vigilant about its use. Along with insurance payments, we envision these funds as being more than sufficient to restore what has been lost."

Petey came up for air as the room exploded with chatter and light applause.

"Hale, I'd like to work closely with you on all the projects that are approved as a result of The Square Deal. Together, you and I can make sure that what is rebuilt conforms to the charm and authenticity of what was there before. And, of course, I encourage all of you here today, and any of your friends out there, to contribute what you can to The Square Deal. Even if it's not money—even if it's just your time. If we do this up right, we'll have our Caroling in The Square on Christmas Eve this time next year to talk about, and so will lots of tourists from around the South. We'll have our Square back better than ever."

Petey reached out and shook Mr. Choppy's hand as he said, "Well, Mayor Dunbar, Merry Christmas to you!"

Mr. Choppy swallowed hard, wondering if he just might lose it in front of everyone. But then he regained his composure, took another deep breath, and began speaking every bit as eloquently as Powell Hampton had taught him to do for his election campaign.

"I'm almost speechless," he began. "But I've got to remember that I didn't become your Mayor by keeping my mouth shut. I spoke up and promised to get things done in a new way. But honestly, I have to say I'm overwhelmed by the generosity of my wife and her family. I am privileged to be her husband and the stepfather of her children."

At that point, Gaylie Girl gave his arm a healthy squeeze and leaned into him with the biggest smile she could manage. "Don't be so modest, Hale. You bring a lot to the table yourself."

The room rewarded her remark with more light applause.

"This is the Christmas present of the ages, as far as I'm

concerned," Mr. Choppy continued. "I know already that The Square Deal will not just restore buildings, it will restore lives and broken dreams. I know what it's like to live with broken dreams. At some point you have to have resolution or you just can't keep on going. The Square Deal will keep Second Creek going, and we won't have to look back on what once was with regret. I thank all of you for getting behind this, and I look forward to working with all of you in getting The Square back on its feet again."

At that point the celebration began in earnest.

"The Square is back!" and "Merry Christmas to Second Creek!" were the phrases of choice, and people never seemed to stop chanting them as they moved around the room eating and drinking and laughing. Petey and Meta were the first ones caught smooching under the sprigs of mistletoe hanging here and there. They were followed by the Reverend Quintus Payne and his wife, Yolie, and then Laurie and Powell, who stole more than one kiss.

Lady Roth made a point of cornering Gaylie Girl and Laurie with the inevitable question. "So I'll be portraying the Star of Bethlehem after all? I'll want to know so I can have my costume dry-cleaned and put away until next Christmas."

"Yes, you go ahead and do that, Lady Roth," Laurie advised. "We wouldn't want the moths to steal your flames."

Several of the freer spirits wandered over to join Myrtis and Euterpe in dancing to the program of rock-and-roll Christmas music that Myrtis kept spinning on her turntable. Among the selections that had people really getting into a loosey-goosey holiday spirit were Elvis's "Blue Christmas" and Jimmy Boyd's "I Saw Mommy Kissing Santa Claus." Then the requests started up.

"Do you have 'All I Want for Christmas Is My Two Front Teeth'?" Councilman Morgan Player asked. "Man, that brings back memories. I think the first time I heard it, I was actually missing several of my baby teeth. I remember the tooth fairy and Santa came together that Christmas. I really cleaned up."

"I have everything that was a holiday hit," Myrtis answered. "Especially from the fifties forward."

"What about that song where the guy—oh, you know— where the guy, uh, sings with the chipmunks . . . and it sounds like they're on the wrong speed? You know—real fast," said March Ventress, who was enjoying his third cup of Sarah's rather potent spiked punch.

Myrtis had that one covered as well. "You must mean David Seville and 'The Chipmunk Song.' Raymond loved that almost as much as he loved 'Big Girls Don't Cry.'"

"That's the one."

So Myrtis played deejay as her guests indulged sing-alongs and paired off on the crowded makeshift dance floor. Then, having been abandoned by Euterpe, who had gone up to look after Pan, Myrtis herself rejoined the fray.

"You know, next year we'll have to consider including some of these oldies but goodies in our caroling program on The Square," Press Phillips was saying as he was waltzing with her to "The Chipmunk Song." "Especially now that we're reasonably sure there will be another event."

"You can count on it," Myrtis said, still slightly winded from her frantic exertions with Euterpe during "Jingle Bell

Rock." "No Nitwitt project shall ever fall flat on its face. I think it's written in our bylaws."

"By the way, I must compliment you on those cheddar-cheese balls with the pimento olives in the middle. I'm practically addicted to savory snacks like that," the choirmaster added. "I don't suppose you'd be willing to give me the recipe?"

"I would if it were mine to give. But it's Sarah's, you know. She's my indispensable cook and housekeeper. But when we finish this dance, I'll take you out to the kitchen to meet her, and maybe she'd be willing to share her secrets. No promises, though."

"You lead, and I'll follow."

"Not until this song is over, Mr. Phillips. A Nitwitt never leads a gentleman on the dance floor."

❄

About an hour later, the party had thinned out considerably. All the choirmasters, councilmen, business owners, the Paynes, and Lady Roth had left, but every one of the Nitwitts, as well as Mr. Choppy and Powell Hampton, remained. Petey and Meta had sneaked upstairs to his Mimosa Suite for a little privacy, as engaged couples in love are wont to do.

So now it was up to the inner circle to review the recent developments through the filter of much good food, drink, singing, dancing, and laughter. They had all pulled up their chairs around the turntable where Myrtis had programmed the music so efficiently, but at the moment they had reached a lull in the conversation. Then Denver Lee attempted to get things rolling again.

"I wish there was some way Wittsie could have been here with us this afternoon. She had such fun when the First Presbyterian choir went over to Delta Sunset Village on Thursday."

"But she *was* here, Denver Lee," Gaylie Girl pointed out, gazing down into her mug of Kahlúa-laced coffee. "She's been here among us as a moving spirit these last few days when we put all this together. 'It will be restored,' she said to me, just as loud and clear in between carols. She said she knew it because of her dream. And what she knew and what she was telling us in no uncertain terms was that The Square would be restored. Take it for what it's worth. But it's my understanding that this sort of thing happens all the time here in Second Creek."

"That's the truth of it," Mr. Choppy added. "No need to wonder how or why. It's enough that she was right. Second Creek now has an excellent chance to recapture its charm, thanks to The Square Deal." He turned to Gaylie Girl and gave her a gentle nudge. "By the way, who came up with the name? I think it's brilliant."

"Oh, that was Petey's brainstorm. I stayed out of that part completely and let the children work it out. He said he and Amanda were kicking around names over the phone once they agreed to do this, but he didn't much like what she came up with. She wanted to call it The Second Creek Phoenix Fund. You know, as in a phoenix rising from the ashes. Very mythological, of course. She even wanted to try her hand at designing the logo since she's been taking art classes lately."

Powell Hampton was enjoying a good laugh. "That sounds like some kind of 401(k) investment."

"Exactly," Gaylie Girl said, managing a little giggle herself. "But Petey said his name had a solid ring to it. As in square meal. The Square Deal sounded like something you could believe in and would want to contribute to."

"Well, there's a part of me that still can't believe this is actually happening," Mr. Choppy added. "Everything seemed to be goin' against us big-time. We were all sayin' that it didn't feel much like Christmas around here, and we had the burned-out Square as an ugly reminder of that feelin' every day. Hey, all I had to do was look out my office window and grimace. Funny how things can turn around so fast."

"O ye of little faith," Euterpe put in. "I still say you can put great store in dreams. They give us insights we don't know we have, and I think it's easier for someone in Wittsie's position to recognize them. Her regrettable struggle is portrayed as a diminution, but there's another way of looking at it. Perhaps it clears the decks of all the routine stuff that clogs our brains so that only the most remarkable things get through toward the end. Even things that we can't explain in logical terms."

"Heavens, Euterpe!" Renza exclaimed. "I've said it before, and I'll say it again. You do have a way with words. You and Laurie both talk like psychologists or psychiatrists or diplomats all the time. Meanwhile, I sound like an over-the-hill sorority president at a blackballing session!"

Everyone laughed good-naturedly, including Renza herself.

"Oh, cut yourself some slack, Renza," Laurie said. "We really wouldn't have you any other way. And I say that to you in the spirit of Christmas. That means I'm thankful for your friendship, and I look forward to many more years of it. I know it's a day early, but Merry Christmas, sweetie!"

Renza pointed toward Laurie and shrugged. "See what I mean? And Merry Christmas to you one day early, too."

That set off a flurry of hugs, kisses, and gushing sentiment among the ladies, the likes of which Mr. Choppy and Powell Hampton had never witnessed in their long and involved association with the group. The two of them caught each other's gaze as the Nitwitts moved to a new level of camaraderie and emotional display.

"Don't look at me," Powell said with a shrug and a smile. "I'm just the Go-to Guy."

"And I thought I was runnin' things as the Mayor," Mr. Choppy added. "But the truth is, I'm just the husband of a Nitwitt."

· Sixteen ·

A Very Piggly Wiggly Christmas

There had been no mention of it in the forecast. Not in any paper, nor on any television or radio station that catered to Second Creek. Nonetheless, they were there in all their glory on Christmas morning. Snow flurries gently floating down. No wind-driven sound to disturb things. Flakes that did not stick at first. Flakes that were too wet falling onto ground that was still too warm.

Strangely, by the time the sun had come up, the temperature had fallen several degrees to just below freezing. It was the thick cloud cover that had done it. As a result, the snow began to stick. First one inch. Then half an inch more. It was the first white Christmas Second Creek had ever experienced in the recorded history of the community, and perhaps it had never been more needed. All around town people were muttering approximately the same thing: "Second Creek weather—consistently a law unto itself!"

Unlike the February ice storm that had ultimately affected the outcome of the election between Mr. Choppy and Mr. Floyce, however, this delicate snowfall presented no real obstacle for Second Creek drivers. For the most part, they still ventured out in their cars to Christmas services or to visit friends and family without incident. Some just wanted to gawk at the rarity of it all, taking photographs with their eyes as they drove by landmarks that had been transformed into something nearly unrecognizable by the pristine layer of white coating them.

This was especially true of The Square. It was as if the breath of winter had brought forth its most fanciful invention—the snowflake—to soften the ugly reality of the burned-out buildings below. A reality that continued to knife through the very hearts of Second Creekers every second those sad ruins remained standing. For the general public did not yet know about The Square Deal. They were taking their holiday spirit whenever and wherever they could find it, and this totally unexpected white Christmas was fitting the bill nicely for the time being.

Inside the residence of Mayor and Mrs. Hale Dunbar Jr. of North Bayou Avenue, a very eventful Christmas Day had been up and running for some time now. They'd had an early breakfast of grits, eggs, and toast around eight, and now the nine o'clock hour was fast approaching. Gaylie Girl briefly wondered if they would have time to make all their rounds. Then she put all doubt out of her mind. This was Christmas after all, and nothing was going to stop them from spreading as much cheer as they could.

"We've got to keep an eye on the time," Gaylie Girl was saying, as she transferred side dishes into the Tupperware she had laid out on the kitchen counter. After they'd left the Evening Shadows' announcement party, they'd attended Press Phillips's caroling service at First Presbyterian. Then she'd spent the better part of the evening cooking up a storm at home. Mr. Choppy had pitched in and helped substantially, and they were still working as a team, though at different tasks.

"How are you coming with the wrapping in there?" she called out when she hadn't heard so much as a peep from him in quite a while.

Mr. Choppy shouted back from the den, though there was a definite lack of confidence in his voice. "It's comin'—I guess!"

What he failed to add was that he was struggling with what many considered to be a lost art. Actually, an art that had never really been found—that of well-meaning men trying their hand at gift-wrapping things for any occasion whatsoever. Gaylie Girl should have known better, but she was just too involved with spooning out corn bread dressing and yellow squash casserole and green beans with almonds to worry about it too much. Besides, she knew she could always undo at the last second whatever he had grievously done with the scissors, Scotch tape, all thumbs, and too little imagination.

"I can't get this wrappin' paper to fit right!" Mr. Choppy

called out, sounding definitely stressed. "Somethin's wrong!"

Gaylie Girl recognized the warning signs and put her work on hold. "Wait a minute. Let me come in there and see what you're doing."

She found him on his knees, mumbling incoherent things while waving the scissors at the paper like a weapon, but she tried to be as gentle as possible with her commentary. "You're using too much paper, sweetheart. That's why it looks all wrinkled like that. You've cut off enough to wrap the refrigerator."

He got to his feet and handed her the scissors. "Could you do this one for me? I've never had to wrap a photograph album before. In fact, the only thing I've ever wrapped in my entire life was a cut of meat, and this isn't exactly butcher's paper and string."

She gave him a peck on the cheek and went to work.

"Is there anything you'd like me to keep an eye on for you in the kitchen?" he offered in return, obviously grateful to be relieved of his gift-wrapping duties.

"Glad you reminded me. Yes. Go and check on the rolls, please. They should be just about ready. I don't want to be like Laurie Hampton and burn them to a crisp."

He headed for the kitchen but was back in no time. "Not quite done, I think. Maybe a coupla more minutes. Speakin' of Laurie and Powell, are we still gonna try and make their open house?"

Gaylie Girl nodded while affixing tape to her nearly wrapped present. "If all goes well. The rest of the girls will be there for their Christmas nightcaps, I trust."

"You ladies do have this Nitwitt thing down to a science, I have to admit," Mr. Choppy quipped, feeling full of himself. "Always a toast to make somewhere."

❄

The Hempstead household in New Vista Acres was just a bottom-of-the-line ranch model like most of the others in the blue-collar development. But with a huge red bow tied to the doorknocker and blinking white lights adorning the little cedar tree in the front yard on this white Christmas Day, it took on a special, welcoming shine. And it was around eleven-thirty that Henry and Cherish Hempstead welcomed Hale and Gaylie Girl Dunbar into their home for Christmas dinner. Actually, it was Henry who greeted them at the door by himself, helping them first with their coats and then the containers of food they had brought in from the car. Next, he took the present that Gaylie Girl had spelled Mr. Choppy in wrapping presentably for them.

Henry stood in the middle of the tiny but efficient kitchen, obviously in awe. "You brought us a present on top of everything else? We just can't thank you enough for fixin' all this for us." He was eyeing appreciatively the roasted turkey breast with all the trimmings in Tupperware the three of them had just laid out on the counter. "I can't boil water, and Cherish was just not up to puttin' somethin' like this together yet. She'll be out in a minute, by the way. She just wanted to make sure she was good and rested for your visit. She still gets tired pretty easy."

"Oh, we enjoyed doing it for you," Gaylie Girl answered, waving him off. "What's Christmas for if not to think up

things like this to do for people? And don't you and Cherish worry about a thing from here on out. Hale and I will
run things into the warming oven for you and even put it
all out on the table. All you have to do is say grace. Just
consider this our Christmas present to the both of you. And
little Riley Jacob in a way. Giving his parents a little time off
will be just the ticket."

Mr. Choppy put his hand on Henry's shoulder. "Speakin'
of my godson, tell us the latest. You told us over the phone
you'd be visitin' the hospital around nine-thirty. Everything
still lookin' up on this fine Christmas mornin'?"

There was an undeniable element of relief in Henry's
expression and then in his voice. "Still off the ventilator, I'm
happy to say. And the nurse said he's been real sensitive to
light up until this mornin', but it seems to be wearin' off.
She said he was makin' good progress, all things considered.
And really, that's all Cherish and I wanted for Christmas.
Just his health. Just to have him with us. Couldn't ask for a
greater present than that."

Cherish appeared in the kitchen doorway at that very
moment, looking fresh-scrubbed if a bit tired in a pale blue
housecoat and fuzzy blue slippers. "Merry Christmas, everybody. Please excuse the way I'm dressed, though. I hope
you don't mind, but I didn't see any reason to put on airs.
I've heard of women who try to put on makeup right after
they've been wheeled out of the operatin' room. Well, I know
I'm exaggeratin' a bit, but gettin' all dolled up seems like a
pretty low priority to me right now. I think I'd rather let all
that snow outside do the sparkling. By the way, has it finally
let up? I just poked my head out the door earlier today, but I

haven't ventured any further. Henry keeps sayin' he's gonna make a snowman for us before it melts."

Mr. Choppy returned a very cordial "Merry Christmas to ya!" while Gaylie Girl moved forward and embraced Cherish warmly. "Merry Christmas, and no, I think the snow's done for the day. The sun's even popped out. And don't you worry about your appearance. You look just beautiful, sweetie. You're just as fresh and natural as you can be. And I was just telling Henry, both of you are to relax and let us take over. It's your home, but you'll be the guests and we'll be the hosts."

About a half hour later, the two couples had just started in on the marinated portobellos Gaylie Girl had fixed for appetizers when Cherish brought up the subject of her maternity leave. "I feel awkward about askin' for more time off, but I realize after everything I've been through with Riley Jacob that I really need to be home with him—" She trailed off, putting down her fork and taking a deep breath. It was almost like she was daring herself to say the words. "When he comes home, that is."

Gaylie Girl reached over and gently rubbed Cherish on the arm. "I'm sure he'll be coming home sooner than you think. And when he does, you can be a stay-at-home mom as long as you like. I have lots of work ahead of me as Hale's special projects secretary now. So I have no intention of quitting anytime soon. Oh, here we've been so intent on getting dinner on the table that we forget to share the big news with you. Hale, why don't you tell them?"

Mr. Choppy took a swallow of his sweet tea and explained the gist of The Square Deal to them. "How's that for a great big Christmas present?" he concluded.

Both Henry and Cherish sat in openmouthed amazement, but Henry finally managed to speak. "Six million dollars? Miz Dunbar, you and your family have to be the most generous people I've ever known. We were all wonderin' what would happen to Second Creek and The Square with the terrible fire and all. I guess it really does seem like Christmas after all, huh?"

"A very merry one," Mr. Choppy added. He seemed to be enjoying a private joke as he chuckled to himself a little longer than was necessary. "I was thinkin' about my daddy just now. How he always found a way outta bad times here in Second Creek. It was all built around his complete devotion to our family business—the Piggly Wiggly, of course. He always came through for the community, and no matter what kinda ordeal we had to endure over the years, Second Creek always survived. So in a way you could even call this a very Piggly Wiggly Christmas."

"Sure could," Henry said, his face as bright as the patch of sun now streaming through the dining-room window and falling at the foot of the nearby little Christmas tree.

It was after the dessert of pumpkin pie with whipped cream that Henry and Cherish opened the present that Gaylie Girl and Mr. Choppy had brought them.

"This is just too much," Cherish said, admiring the beautifully wrapped gift after she'd lifted it from its spot on the red Christmas skirt. "I know it sounds like a cliché, but you really didn't have to. Not with everything else you've done. I almost hate to open it, it's so pretty."

Gaylie Girl shot Mr. Choppy a deliberate and mischievous glance. "Isn't it, though? Hale wrapped it himself."

Mr. Choppy let the comment ride with a big, wide-eyed grin, looking exactly like a little boy who'd just received an increase in his allowance.

Cherish finally stopped her admiring and unwrapped it, revealing a handsome, leather-bound photograph album. She had barely gotten the first little gasp out when Gaylie Girl began what seemed for all the world like a carefully rehearsed spiel. "This is Riley Jacob's first album. The first of many to come, I'm sure, though this one should last you for a long time. You'll fill it up proudly with the proof of his growth and health. And then one day you'll turn around and there he'll be—a grown man as big and strapping as his father is right now."

The two women embraced, and Henry offered Mr. Choppy a firm handshake. "I guess there's only one thing we have to say. And that's—would you consider bein' Riley Jacob's godmother, Miz Dunbar?"

Gaylie Girl appeared startled at first but recovered quickly with her usual gracious smile. "Why, I'd be very proud to be, Henry. And it'll be a nice little refresher course for me, since I'm hoping that Petey and Meta will be giving me more grandchildren soon. Got to get back into the habit of spoiling the little ones, you know."

"I'm so glad you said yes, since Henry and I didn't get you a formal present," Cherish pointed out, hanging her head ever so slightly.

But Mr. Choppy was having none of it, stepping up and speaking firmly. "Nonsense. You've given us both the opportunity to be godparents, and that's a gift that'll last all of us for many years to come."

❄

"Are we reasonably on schedule?" Mr. Choppy said, as they drove away from New Vista Acres back toward town. "My watch says almost two-thirty."

"We're doing just fine. Renza said they'd probably be through with their dinner about now, and we could join them for cordials or coffee anytime after that. Strictly open house. So why don't we run home, freshen up, and swing by around three-thirty or so?"

He nodded while keeping his eyes peeled for dangerous puddles. The sun was melting the snow faster now, already relegating the upstart white Christmas to a fading memory. Soon enough, however, he was revisiting the conversation at the Hempsteads.

"Have you actually talked to Petey or Meta about the prospects of grandchildren yet?"

Gaylie Girl seemed caught off guard. "Oh, well, no I haven't. I really don't know if Petey wants to start a family right now. Maybe that was just a Christmas wish on my part. So much seems to be falling into place right now, though. I thought I'd go ahead and wish anyway. Renza seems to think that Meta's going to continue to be very involved in her art gallery as soon as they can get it up and running. When you come right down to it, I'd settle for a happy marriage for them and leave it at that, considering Petey's track record."

"Good thinkin'. But you know, I have a feelin' you won't be disappointed. Anyone with as big a heart as Petey has will eventually want to pass it on to another generation. Maybe this time next year, you and I will be grandparents. That is, if you'll let me remove the 'step' so I can qualify."

"Petey already thinks of you as a father. He certainly respects you. I'm not sure we'll have to qualify anything."

Mr. Choppy let the good feelings sink in as they drove on in contented silence all the way to the city limits. At the last second, instead of making the turn that would take them home to North Bayou Avenue, he headed for The Square.

"I'd like to get a quick look at it now so I can visualize what's to come. We've got a little time to spare, and I don't wanna rush around anyway. Petey told me last night that he and Meta will reconstruct that buildin' exactly the way it was, from top to bottom. Minus the bad wirin', of course. He says Miz Novie has access to all the historical photographs and even some of the old blueprints they keep down at Springtime Tour Headquarters that she's in charge of now."

Mr. Choppy paused with a farsighted expression on his face. "Imagine that. They'll be buildin' it back better than it was. And with the funds y'all are providin' to the others, they'll prob'ly do the same. I've never been a big believer in that blessin'-in-disguise concept, but this fire looks like it's turnin' out to be just that. We did have a few empty, dilapidated stores among the ones that went up in smoke. They won't be missed, but what takes their place could do us up proud."

The car turned into Courthouse Street South, where the hideous view of the charred ruins loomed at the other end, partly and perhaps thankfully obscured by the white walls and terra-cotta slate roof of the imposing courthouse halfway between the two. Mr. Choppy shut off the engine, and they stared at the devastation for a while. There was almost nothing left of the morning snowfall, so the full effect of the ashes, blackened bricks, and beams was in evidence once again.

"I was thinking about Santa Fe just now," Gaylie Girl finally observed. "The way I wanted to bring the feeling I had for it here to Second Creek. But I've come to a surprising realization. My feeling for Second Creek has grown much stronger than anything I ever felt for Santa Fe. It's been a trial by fire, Hale. I mean that literally.

"And when Petey called me up a few days ago and asked me to come out to Evening Shadows to discuss his Square Deal, I was on board in a heartbeat. That has to make me a genuine Second Creeker now, doesn't it?"

He leaned over and gave her an affectionate peck on the check. "I have to believe it does. Nobody who wasn't the genuine article would make the commitment you've made. You've put your money where your mouth is. The way I see it, you'll end up bein' the grandest First Lady Second Creek's ever had. Maybe someday there'll even be a beautiful bronzed statue of Gaylie Girl Dunbar on The Square."

❄

Laurie and Powell's Christmas open house was fully under way when Mr. Choppy and Gaylie Girl finally dropped by around seven that evening. The visit with Renza had largely been a bust, since Petey and Meta had left earlier to return to his suite at Evening Shadows.

"They just can't keep their hands off each other," Renza

had noted, trying her best not to sound judgmental but falling short of the mark. "Of course, I don't begrudge them their fondness for each other. I just think they might be overdoing it."

So it was just Mr. Choppy and Gaylie Girl being entertained by Renza and her tart musings for the better part of an hour in the drawing room of Belford Place. At some point, Gaylie Girl realized one more time that she had better get used to it if Petey and Meta tied the knot as expected. Learning to finesse Renza might not be easy, but it was definitely going to be necessary to keep the peace.

"Well, I suppose we'll see you tonight at Laurie's," Gaylie Girl had said, when it was more than apparent the three of them had run out of things to say. She had even gotten to her feet to force the issue.

Renza was looking up from her spiked eggnog with a hint of betrayal in her face. "You're running off so soon?"

But Gaylie Girl had been certain she was playing at being obtuse and decided to attempt her first finesse.

"Hale and I were thinking about taking a little nap ourselves. I was up half the night cooking for the Hempsteads, you know." And that had done the trick nicely. But not before Gaylie Girl had made a mental note to catch up with Petey and Meta later out at Evening Shadows. After all, they still had presents to exchange.

Things were quite a bit livelier at Laurie's, however, as Mr. Choppy and Gaylie Girl cleared a couple of seats for themselves on one of the sofas and settled in with their drinks amid the other Nitwitts and Powell Hampton.

"You're just in time," Laurie said, absentmindedly

tinkering with the reindeer antlers that she wore atop her head for every Christmas open house. "We've been informed that Myrtis and Euterpe are about to make a momentous announcement." She gestured toward both women, who were sitting next to each other in a far corner of the room, whispering back and forth and otherwise looking thick as thieves.

Finally, Myrtis got to her feet and hoisted her cup of eggnog high in the air. "To the success of my new bed-and-breakfast partnership with Euterpe. We have decided to split the financial responsibilities at Evening Shadows, and Euterpe will permanently occupy my Bloody Mary Suite upstairs. I declare here and now that she is not only grand company but also one helluva floor show at the Steinway to boot!"

The room was immediately abuzz with chatter and cries of "Congratulations!" as the Nitwitts got to their feet and took turns endlessly embracing one another yet again. Somehow Laurie was able to take the floor again and press on. "When did you two decide this? I thought it was against our bylaws to keep secrets as huge as this."

"Oh, we kind of fell into it this past week during the afterglow of one of Myrtis's fabulous dinners," Euterpe explained. "We're going to make it legal and official after the first of the year. And, yes, ladies, I will continue to teach you piano lessons as the Mistress of the Scales. We Nitwitts are nothing if not multitaskers."

"Nothing will really change, you see," Myrtis continued. "We'll still have Sarah with us to keep house and fix all that gourmet food, but we'll split the upkeep and the profits fifty-fifty. And, yes, I'm giving Euterpe a special discount on the Bloody Mary Suite in perpetuity. In return, she'll contribute a special musical program every night we have guests. But we aren't changing the name to Myrtis and Euterpe's or anything like that."

"What about Troy and Simon's?" Renza offered, barely able to keep a straight face.

But Myrtis was more than ready for her. "That sounds like a law firm, and you know it. No, it shall remain Evening Shadows as long as both of us are alive and kickin'."

It was Powell who spoke up next amid the giggles and titters, raising his voice to be heard and changing the subject abruptly. "Laurie, it's almost seven-thirty!"

"Ooh, right," she said, moving quickly to the center of the room. "Everyone, I have a surprise. We've made arrangements with Mrs. Holstrom over at Delta Sunset Village to put in a call on Powell's cell to Wittsie and her daughter, April, and her granddaughter, Meagan. They've been with her all day, and I've already spoken with Mrs. Holstrom about how things have gone. She says Wittsie is having another of her better days, probably because her family is there. But I thought we could all pass the phone around and wish her a Merry Christmas. That way, at least, all the Nitwitts could be together again on this very special occasion."

Powell then went into action dialing up the number. But not before uttering the phrase that he had come to prize more highly than any other over the course of his distinguished lifetime as a ballroom dance instructor extraordinaire: "The Go-to Guy at your service, ladies!"

Laughter swept throughout the room, and then everyone

quieted down, awaiting the call to go through. Finally, Powell said: "Mrs. Holstrom? Yes, it's Powell Hampton calling for Miz Wittsie and her family." There was a pause as Powell held the phone slightly away from his ear. "They're bringing her over now," he told the others. Then: "Hello? . . . oh, yes . . . yes, that's very sweet of you . . . oh, I'm sure they'll appreciate that." There was a further pause, and then Powell put the phone in his lap and proceeded to explain. "This is Wittsie's granddaughter, Mcagan, on the line right now. All of you ladies remember her from our wedding at the Piggly Wiggly, I'm sure. She says she just wants to tell all of you Nitwitt ladies how much she enjoyed being in the wedding with you last year, and she hopes to be just like you when she grows up."

More laughter erupted, along with a "Hello to you, too!" here and there, and then Renza shouted across the room, obviously feeling her Christmas cheer. "Heaven forbid she should grow up to be like us!"

Powell made a shushing noise and wagged a finger. "Renza, she'll hear you!"

Then he picked up the phone again and resumed the conversation. "They all said to tell you hello, and they enjoyed being with you, too." There was another lapse.

"Where's Wittsie?" an impatient Novie wanted to know.

"She's coming," Powell answered. Then he started talking again momentarily. "Miz Wittsie? . . . oh, yes, of course I know who you are . . . right . . . right . . . of course I understand . . . I'll let everybody know." Again he put the phone in his lap and addressed the room. "This is April I'm talking to now, Wittsie's daughter. She says it might be too confusing to put everyone on one after another. It's been a long day, and she thinks her mother is starting to fade. She suggested that one of you Nitwitts come on and speak for all the others. Is that okay with all of you?" He picked up the phone again. "April, can you hold on just a minute? They're deciding who to put on."

Not surprisingly, Renza was the first to speak up. "Well, if that's the way it's got to be, I think it's obvious who should speak for us." She aimed her index finger at Laurie with a smirk. "The one with the mind so sharp, she's got antlers growing out of her scalp. The more things change, the more they stay the same around here."

The others nodded or said, "Of course!" or something similar, and Powell again asked April if she would hold the line.

Laurie took the phone from him and managed a deep breath while collecting her thoughts. There was another short wait and then: "Wittsie? I hear you've been having a Merry Christmas, darlin' . . . it's me, Laurie . . . yes, I'm over here in Second Creek . . . right, I know you're over there at Delta Sunset Village . . . well, I'm here at my little cottage with all the other Nitwitts and my husband, Powell, and Mr. Choppy . . . you remember Mr. Choppy, don't you? . . . that's right . . . the Piggly Wiggly . . . I know we all used to shop there . . . yes, I know it's closed down now."

Laurie momentarily covered the phone and spoke in a stage whisper. "She seems smart as a whip to me tonight. I have no earthly idea what April was talking about. I guess she was just being cautious." Then she resumed.

"Sweetheart, listen. Each of your devoted Nitwitts

wanted to say Merry Christmas to you tonight, but we thought things might get a little too hectic and confusing. So I'm going to say Merry Christmas for all of them . . . what? . . . are you sure? . . . oh, that's funny . . . well, I'll let them all know."

Laurie covered the phone again. "She insists on speaking to all of you. She can't imagine why we don't all want to come to the phone. She even said, 'Cat got their tongues?'"

Renza cackled. "Well, that does it for me. If she can get off a snappy line like that, here I come with my big mouth. Let me speak to her this instant."

Renza quickly rose from her seat, and Laurie handed the phone over without hesitation, knowing better than to start an argument.

"Listen, Wittsie," Renza began, mincing no words. "Merry Christmas and Happy New Year, sweetie. Wish you were here with us. Now, that's two down and five to go by my calculations." She held the phone away from her ear. "See? It's not hard. Which one of you wants to go next?"

In succession Myrtis, Novie, Euterpe, Denver Lee, and Gaylie Girl all stepped up and said their piece. Every "Merry Christmas!" and the various snippets of sentiment that followed were delivered without a hiccup. But just as Powell was about to wind things up, Mr. Choppy smiled and held out his hand. "I'd like to speak to her, too, if you wouldn't mind."

"Of course not," Powell said, handing the phone over. "I'm sure she'd be delighted to hear from you."

Mr. Choppy began speaking with great affection in his voice. "Miz Wittsie, this is Mr. Choppy Dunbar . . . no, that's right, I'm not one of the Nitwitts, but I'm married to one of 'em. You know, that especially counts for somethin' in Second Creek these days. I'm laughin' now because Powell Hampton is right next to me noddin' his head and crackin' a smile . . . that's right, Powell is the one who's married to Laurie . . . yes, they were married at my Piggly Wiggly while it was still open. You were even in the wedding, and you and your little Meagan looked mighty pretty. Anyway, Miz Wittsie, I wanted to wish you a very Piggly Wiggly Christmas tonight because the inside buzz is it's the gold standard of Christmases. You can't do better than that . . . yes, Miz Wittsie, I know you've got your daughter and granddaughter with you tonight . . . I know they love you, we all do . . . well, thank you, ma'am, and I hope God blesses you richly, too . . . good night to you, too."

He handed the phone back to Powell, who quickly finished up with April and then snapped the phone shut. "Mission accomplished," he announced forthrightly, standing up to take a little bow.

Mr. Choppy's heartfelt monologue had a powerful calming effect on everyone in the room, and no one could think of anything to say for a while.

Leave it to Renza, however, to remedy the lull with her customary candidness. "Well, I don't know about the rest of you, but Wittsie sounded all there to me and a whole lot more tonight. Of course, I'm glad she was having one of her best days on a day as important as this. If you're going to shine, it might as well be on Christmas. It's hard to figure out, though. Just when you think Wittsie will fade away, something seems to kick her into another gear. Am I totally off base here?"

"Oh, I completely agree with you," Mr. Choppy said. "I feel strongly that Miz Wittsie is bein' looked after. And I don't just mean by the staff over there at Delta Sunset Village, or by her family."

Renza paused briefly to allow herself a frown but soon pressed on in her inimitable fashion. "By the way, if you don't mind telling me, what exactly did you mean by a very Piggly Wiggly Christmas? Was that supposed to be a little joke of some kind?"

"Anything but, Miz Renza. It was just a little somethin' I verbalized for myself this afternoon as I was thinkin' about the legacy of the Dunbar family in Second Creek. It's a strong one, and it's gonna continue to get even stronger as long as I'm in office with my trusty Gaylie Girl at my side. Oh, and for what it's worth, I believe Miz Wittsie understood exactly what I meant by that, too."

❄

Gaylie Girl could not remember such a pressure-packed Christmas Day in her entire life. Her worries about biting off more than she and Hale could chew had been groundless. They had gone everywhere they were supposed to go, seen everyone they were supposed to see, opened and acknowledged every present they had received, and given out every gift they were supposed to give. In addition to the phone call to Wittsie in the evening, she had found time to call up Amanda and the grandchildren earlier in the day and had wedged in a visit with Petey and Meta out at Evening Shadows to exchange gifts. Now there was nothing left to do but collapse in bed for that fabled long winter's nap so frequently cited as part of Christmas lore.

"We did good today," Gaylie Girl said, sliding down beneath the covers just after eleven o'clock. "It was a lot of work, but this was maybe the best Christmas I've ever had. Oh, I've had more elaborate ones in Chicago, and certainly more expensive ones in places abroad. There was even one spent out in Santa Fe after Petey and Amanda were off on their own for the first time. I didn't have to lift a finger in most of those. People waited on me hand and foot. Not today. I'm feeling a good kind of tired right now, and I like it. Let's do this again next year. Only by then I trust we'll have a healthy godchild to spoil instead of fretting about him around the clock."

Mr. Choppy had just finished fluffing up his pillows and was smiling up at the ceiling with his hands cupped behind his head. He almost looked like a little boy plotting what he wanted to be when he was all grown up. "I like the sound of that. I've spent every single Christmas right here in Second Creek, but I know this one meant the most to me. Not only that, but just a few days ago, I was dreadin' what the New Year would bring. But now I can hardly wait for it to get here so we can get started on The Square Deal."

"You and I are going to make history with it, you know."

"I know. And if we do a really spectacular job, maybe we'll both get statues erected in our honor."

She pointed her finger at the headboard behind them.

"I want mine facing north, so I'll never forget where I came from."

"And I want mine facing south. Because that's where I've always lived, and that's where I'll die."

"Oh, don't talk about that right now, Hale. Just give me a kiss, and we'll see what develops."

"An extra little goodie from Santa, maybe?"

Gaylie Girl played along coyly. "Whatever do you mean, sir?"

Mr. Choppy's laugh was full of mischief, and he added a naughty wink. "Well, it occurred to me the other day that a lady like yourself has just about everything she needs in the way of creature comforts."

"True enough."

"But I also remembered that you couldn't figure out the secret ingredient in Yolie Payne's cream of courage soup when she and the Reverend visited us that time, and she wasn't tellin' either."

Gaylie Girl feigned frustration by pouting her lips. "You know how cooks are."

Mr. Choppy leaned over and retrieved a folded piece of paper from the nightstand, handing it to his wife. "Yes, I do. But sometimes a little friendly persuasion works wonders."

"You didn't . . . I mean, she didn't!" Gaylie Girl exclaimed, unfolding the paper with an expression of utter delight. She scanned the document quickly, taking in a breath of air at the end. "Oh, my goodness! A generous splash or two of cooking sherry! Yolie was right—I never would have guessed. I was so focused in on herbs and spices."

"Can't wait for you to make up a batch. Meanwhile,

there's no reason why we can't keep things spicy," Mr. Choppy added, snuggling up to her and giving her the first of several lingering kisses.

With that, they turned out the lights and put the exclamation point on their very first Piggly Wiggly Christmas together.

ACKNOWLEDGMENTS

Once again, the following cast of characters has made this fourth installment of the Piggly Wiggly series possible: my two state-of-the-art agents, Meg Ruley and Christina Hogrebe of the Jane Rotrosen Agency; my superb editor, Rachel Kahan, of Putnam/Penguin; my personal assistant, William Black, whose Googling skills are exceeded by none; and my large extended Southern family, whose anecdotes and affection have sustained me over the years. May all of you enjoy many more happy holiday seasons!